SHEER DELIGHT

The low-backed bra was strapless. The deep self-supporting cups curved in a leopardskin design over the upper slopes of Suzanne's pouting breasts. Beneath, enclosing the full weight of each big globe, were inserts of semi-transparent tulle.

The long black straps of her suspender belt stretched downwards to the tight-drawn lace tops of her dark silk stockings, framing the tiny briefs – little more than an elaborate G-string – that covered her sex.

'How do you like my scanties, Mr Reporter?' Suzanne asked, glancing at the journalist's bulging crotch. 'Surely they're worth a few column inches . . .'

Sheer Delight

Aaron Amory

Delta

Copyright © 1998 Meyrick Johnston

The right of Meyrick Johnston to be identified as the Author of
the Work has been asserted by him in accordance with
the Copyright, Designs and Patents Act 1988.

First published in 1998
by HEADLINE BOOK PUBLISHING

A HEADLINE DELTA paperback

10 9 8 7 6 5 4 3 2 1

ISBN 0 7472 5839 2

Typeset by Avon Dataset Ltd, Bidford-on-Avon, Warks

Printed and bound in Great Britain by
Mackays of Chatham plc, Chatham, Kent

HEADLINE BOOK PUBLISHING
A division of Hodder Headline PLC
338 Euston Road
London NW1 3BH

Sheer Delight

PART ONE

Tat For Tit

1

Shields was doing his best to fuck an inflatable rubber woman when the phone rang for the first time. Penetration was difficult because he had blown her up too tight and he kept slipping off her sausage limbs before he could get it in.

The phone ringing was in the Sales Manager's office on the far side of the stockroom. Shields cursed, rolled off again, and levered himself to his feet. He hauled up his trousers and without zipping up the fly waddled away between the rows of cellophaned cocktail dresses on rails with his limp tool flapping outside. He banged open the steel and glass door of the office and scooped the handset off the desk.

'Dulok Dresses. The factory and sales departments are both closed at weekends,' he said crossly.

'Oh, shit,' a man's voice said. 'And I wanted to place an urgent order. What time does the place open on Monday?'

'Both departments will be staffed from 8:30 as usual,' Shields said. 'You want to leave a message?' But the caller had already hung up.

Grumbling, Shields returned to his latex blonde. She lay with her legs still spread on the visitors' couch, the black nylon skirt hoisted up to her waist, conical breasts jutting upwards from the naked slopes of her rubber chest. Wide blue eyes stared dispassionately up at Shields from her painted face as he pushed down his pants and climbed onto her again.

Entry was just as difficult, so he pulled a pair of dark nylons from his pocket and drew them up her tapered legs. Maybe the textured material stretched over those inflated thighs would give him a little more purchase and stop the slides? In any case there was plenty of time. Shields was night watchman and it wasn't yet ten o'clock.

This time he found the manoeuvre easier. His penis, trembling slightly and rigid with anticipation, slid easily into the gash between her thighs and the ballooned flesh of her artificial cunt closed tightly over his distended cock-head.

But the blonde wasn't living up to Shields's lascivious fantasy. There was no reaction, no give in her blown-up body as he humped and thrust. The pubic hair was too stiff and wiry, tickling his heated flesh. The vagina, liberally vaselined as it was and surrounded by a horse-shoe inner cushion filled with warm water, wasn't really as convincing as he had hoped. And the latex cheeks of the blonde's arse, between which Shields's balls hung down, were cold to the touch.

In addition to all this, the Dunlopillo sponge-rubber stuffing the seat of the settee combined with the bouncy quality of the inflated model to induce a movement as unfeminine as anything he had ever experienced – and literally off-putting as his tool slipped free again.

He picked up the blonde and laid her stiffly on the stockroom floor. The hard surface, he thought, should at least allow his own weight to compress and expand the air-filled body beneath him as he plunged and withdrew.

Very carefully, he inserted his eager cock and started to see-saw in and out.

The phone was ringing again – a different line this time, in Edward Dulok's private office behind the mezzanine gallery overlooking the stockroom and finishing shop.

Shields yelled his fury into the silence of the deserted building.

He was on duty all night, but he wasn't going to answer the fucking phone this time, even if it was the boss himself calling to check some idiot, unnecessary detail. It was bad enough already that his daydream of seduction by a voluptuous and willing sexpot had been broken twice. Concentrating every lewd thought he could muster on the ploughing in and out of his prick, he renewed his slaving assault on his voiceless partner.

Unfortunately, the start surprised from him by the second phone call had thrust the tab of his zipper hard into the most vulnerable part of the blonde's over-blown crotch.

4

There was a sudden sibilant hiss of escaping air, and Shields was lowered gently until his elbows and knees rested uncomfortably on the concrete floor.

The phone in Edward Dulok's office was still ringing. Cursing more volubly now, Shields dragged himself upright, stuffed his cock back inside his trousers, zipped them up, and threaded his way hastily between the rows of railed dresses. He climbed the stairs to the gallery and snatched the phone from its cradle.

This time it was a wrong number.

Shields wept.

During the time that the night watchman had been occupied between the two telephone calls and his inflated girlfriend, Roger Curnow had secretly entered the Dulok warehouse through a pass door in the tall wooden gates closing the delivery yard at the far end of the building.

The Yale key which unlocked the door had been made by a crooked Soho locksmith from an impression in a bar of soap that Curnow had made the previous night. The genuine key which made that impression had been filched by him twenty-four hours before from the handbag of a busty redhead who was workshop overseer supervising the Dulok production line. The soft soap mould which produced the mortice key opening the door to the building itself was the result of the same hasty pillage.

The opportunity to lift these keys for the ten minutes necessary had cost Roger Curnow two front-row stall seats for Danny Kaye at the London Palladium, a dinner dance at the Mirabelle in Curzon Street, and almost two hours of sexual gymnastics on a chaise-longue in the girl's flat before she finally passed out and left the route to the handbag free.

Curnow would have been happier if the chaise-longue – and indeed the scene enacted upon it – had been shorter. He hadn't expected that the redhead, whose name was Gladys Carter, would be so enthusiastic . . . or so demanding. But, like the Danny Kaye audience at the Palladium, she had cried out for an encore almost as soon as the curtain closed on the first-house performance.

Pillowed on large soft breasts that had only slightly started to sag, Curnow had hoped after their first explosive shafting that exhaustion would in the normal way supervene and he would be free to complete his thieving plan and go home while she slept. But Gladys's practised hands at his cock and balls, kneading, fondling, milking back to hardness the wet shaft, soon squashed that idea as flat as the redhead's pliant belly under Curnow's plunging weight. The first energetic fuck was no more than a curtain raiser, he swiftly understood. She wanted it like that again, hard and deep and expert – but she was eager also to suck and be sucked, to take it behind while kneeling, to be manually brought to orgasm and to swallow lukewarm brandy from Curnow's mouth while he savagely penetrated her quivering cunt.

In the end it was Curnow himself who was exhausted: it was not until after two that he felt able to steal downstairs, let himself out, and prepare what he hoped would be a convincing late-at-the-office and entertaining-an-important-client story for his angry and disbelieving wife.

Still, he had the key impressions he needed.

The outing had been well worthwhile, he reflected as he passed a line of Dulok delivery vans, high-roofed so that long dresses on their rails could be kept off the floor. With the information he hoped to obtain inside the building, he and his partner – rivals to Dulok in the ready-to-wear fashion business – should have a head start in the summer sales campaign, helped by colleagues in the underwear sector who were planning to launch a new, and hopefully sexy, magazine.

He unlocked the warehouse entrance door and slipped inside. Somewhere in the dark distance, he could hear the night watchman swearing. Evidently his partner's plan to use the two different phones had worked out. The watchman wasn't due to make his next round until midnight, but it was best to be super-careful. The boss of a rival firm making a burglarious entrance late at night . . . the results didn't even bear thinking about!

Curnow stole down the length of the machine shop, the electric elements on their benches dully gleaming in the street lighting filtering through grimed panes in the slanting glass roof. He felt his way past the long tables lining the finishing room. The whole length of the stockroom separated him from the part of the warehouse where Shields would be, but he hadn't dared even to bring a pencil flashlight. Instead, he carried a wide roll of heavy-duty brown paper, and a scotch-tape dispenser in his hip pocket.

His target, the office of the production manager, lay between the finishing shop and the stock-room. He eased open the door and slipped inside.

The top half of the steel door framed a window of frosted glass. Inside the large office the only other source of escaping light was a window looking out over an alley behind the warehouse.

Working swiftly in the dim radiance reflected from street lamps outside, Curnow unrolled a huge sheet of brown paper, cut it from the rest of the cylinder with a pair of scissors, and taped it hurriedly over the glass part of the door. As soon as it was in place, he blanked the frosted glass more securely still with a second sheet. He crossed the room and switched on a lamp angled over an electronic typewriter on the central desk.

The office leaped blindingly into three dimensions, a cone of brilliance streaming downward over the desk, filing cabinets, a teleprinter, a photo-copying machine and an inclined draughtsman's table shadowy in the background.

Curnow crossed to the window. A single sheet should be enough to shield him from a deserted alley late at night. He taped the brown paper in place, scrunched up the remainder of the roll and laid it at the foot of the office door to stop light fanning out beneath. Now, at last, he could go ahead with the search he had planned.

Working swiftly and silently, he pulled out the filing drawers on their rollers, flipping through the cardboard folders hanging inside until he located the files that he wanted.

They were all concerned with the underwear side of the Dulok production, mainly orders placed outside for specific deliveries, invoices detailing the delivery of materials from mills and workshops and factories creating artificial fabrics, a certain amount of correspondence with the buyers from higher-class chain stores, and a sheaf of memos from artists and designers suggesting future models for the Dulok range.

Curnow sifted through them rapidly, separating barely a dozen sheets which he photographed under the desk lamp with a miniature Minox camera. Before he replaced them in their folders, he tore a sheet of paper from a desk pad, scanned the material one last time, and jotted down a list of headings with scribbled comments beneath.

The headings included: *Knickers, Open-Crotch Briefs, Strapless Bras, Cami-knicks, Tights, Bodices, Suspender Belts, Girdles, Corsets, Petticoats, Vests* and *'Frivolity' (nipple free) Brassières*. Figures for firm and estimated orders, along with expected production totals, were noted under most of them.

Curnow re-inserted the files, slid shut the drawers, pocketed his camera and notes, and switched off the desk lamp. He dismantled the taped sheets masking the window and door glass, then returned to the warehouse yard and the exit as swiftly and silently as he had come.

When Shields made his round just after midnight and switched on all the lights, there was nothing to show that anyone had been in the production manager's office except an unusually copious bundle of used brown paper crammed into the waste-paper basket. But that would have been removed by the cleaners anyway before any of the Dulok staff came in.

2

David Preckner watched his wife, Sylvia, undress with a mixture of impatience and disapproval.

The impatience was not because he was all that eager to embrace the softly sexy frame of his longtime companion and lover – after all, the children were away: they had all night. The disfavour was not in any way connected with the physical appearance of Sylvia: after twelve years of marriage, Preckner still found that the loose, fleshy body of his wife turned him on.

His negative attitude concentrated solely on the garments she was wearing – or, more, precisely, on those she was stripping off.

A crossover brassière in plain, wired, undecorated satin with wide, padded straps; 40-denier tights which left a red mark where the elasticated top bit into her waist; crotch-hugging, thigh-tight panties in nylon the same peach colour as the bra – were these underclothes really the stuff a man's dreams were made of?

Especially, Preckner thought, when those dreams – and the fantasies they enshrined – centred, as they inevitably did, on the gratification of that part of him that was already lengthening and stiffening even under his critical regard.

But the hard-on, he was aware, was provoked by the emerging curves and rolls and mounds of female flesh, the dark thatch of pubic hair revealed as the tights were peeled down, and not in any way at all by the underclothes which had been sheathing and supporting them. So far as he was concerned, the tights, panties and bra were no more than obstacles to be discarded before Sylvia's voluptuous possibilities became apparent.

Yet they should, David Preckner was convinced, have been

9

a sexy asset to the onset of lust, as subtle and compelling an aspect of an impending fuck as the wet-fingered, milking foreplay which set the pulses racing in anticipation of the scalding penetration that was to follow.

Sylvia was in the bathroom. When she came back into the ornately furnished bedroom, he was holding the offending underclothes in his hands. 'Just look at this . . . this crap!' he said angrily. 'Probably cost you an arm and a leg and it does nothing for you whatever. I mean fuck-all.'

'What's the matter with them, darling?' Sylvia's gravelly voice was soothing. She was scented and pink and glowing beneath a blue polka-dot housecoat in shantung silk.

'Everything's the matter with them,' Preckner said. 'They're zero. They're zilch. Look at this bloody tat!' He held up the brassière. 'It completely covers your tits. Not a hint of the plunge; no sign of the old swelling curve; not the vestige of a clue that there could be nipples at the tip of what the novelists would call those splendid orbs! And what about these?' He flung out a hand towards the tights and slip. 'Can you imagine the gymnastics involved if I was making a pass at you and trying for a grope – even on the back seat of a bloody Daimler!'

Sylvia laughed. Her breasts shook beneath the rough silk of the robe. 'Well, I'm sorry, darling, for the . . . inadequacy . . . of my wardrobe,' she said huskily. 'But I'm afraid there's nothing I can do about it – not tonight anyway. If you like, I could—'

'There's nothing you can do about it, tonight or any night,' her husband fumed. 'Apart from the trashy stores with chromium shopfronts and a *spieler* outside trying to persuade clerks to buy cheapjack transparent nighties for the girl next door, there's nowhere, not a damn place, where you could get sexy underwear that is both classy and well made, and in good taste. Here we are in the so-called swinging sixties – we're the permissive fucking society, for Christ's sake! – and women have never been less feminine, less sexy to look at, less able to . . . to seduce visually. It's all the fault of this unisex rubbish: give the girls the right to act like men, to behave as freely, as daringly as men, fine. But why the hell

10

do we have to make them *appear* as dull as men?'

'Well, I really can't see what I could do—' Sylvia began.

'You don't need to do anything. You're sexy bitch anyway,' Preckner moved towards her. 'It's people like my secretary, Jane, people like Sue I'm thinking of.' Sue Scheiner, the daughter of a Hatton Garden diamond merchant, was married to Sylvia's brother Harry. 'Sue's fat, there's no getting away from it,' Preckner said accusingly. 'She needs something to improve her image.'

'What do you suggest?' Sylvia said. 'You mean because she and Harry are not getting on as well as they might? What do you want for her?'

'I want frills,' Preckner said. 'I want ribbons and bows and ruching and lacing. I want frou-frou. I'd like to see women bulge out of tight-waisted corsets. I'd like to see them pull real silk stockings up tight – fifteen denier of course – and snap them into the clips of a suspender belt.' He grinned. 'And of course, like most enthusiastic males, I'd hope to see the return of what used to be called French knickers, wide open legs edged with filmy lace. Good God, even in the most oppressive mid-Victorian era, when knickers reached below the knee, the legs were tied in place by drawstrings with ribbon bows!'

'So what do you intend to do about it?' Sylvia asked. 'I mean, do you have artistic plans?'

'I intend to supply that long-felt want,' her husband boasted. 'Preckner Gowns are about to dive into the underwear business, in a big way!'

Absently, he drew apart the edges of the shantung robe and gazed at the smooth slopes of flesh thrusting out the lightweight garment. Sylvia's breasts were a joy to him. It was not that they were particularly large. They were certainly full . . . but their special charm for him lay in the soft and rolling *length* their twin pear-shapes occupied on her prominent rib-cage. David, she confided once to her envious sister-in-law, never tired of playing with them: he was always as rapt as a child with an exciting new toy.

'We should have the field wide open,' he said now, thrusting his hands inside the robe and cradling the warm

weight of those breasts in his palms. 'Roger Curnow...
happened... to hear that Dulok's order book for the new
season is exclusively concentrated on the kind of tat you just
stripped off. And their advance orders to the cloth manufacturers are equally staid. With luck we should be in on a
killing here.'

'Given that there's a demand: providing Joe Public and
his wife want to buy,' his wife warned.

'They will.' Preckner was decisive. 'We'll have a new
fashion mag on our side. We'll use the fancy designers whose
ideas Dulok has turned down. And our own range of dresses
will be angled to give a hint – just the tiniest glimpse – of the
frilly delights nestling beneath.' Preckner's hands eased the
shawl collar of the housecoat away from Sylvia's neck. He
pushed the silk garment further back, so that it fell away
from the creamy rounds of his wife's shoulders and slid down
her smoothly columned upper arms.

Sylvia undulated her generous body in a barely perceptible
shrug. The housecoat fell to the floor with a faint swish of
sheer material on flesh, and her breasts rolled free.

Preckner bent his knees. He spread his two hands wide
open, jacking them up so that the weight of each pear-shaped
mound was supported between the splayed forefinger and
thumb of his eager hands. He raised the breasts one by one,
sucking each reddened nipple gently into his mouth to tease
the fleshy bud with a swirl of his tongue. The thick staff of
his cock sprang free of his loins and speared forward,
quivering, between his thighs.

'Come to bed, darling,' Sylvia said. 'It's only two yards
away. You'll slip a disc crouched over like that!'

The bed was king-size, brass-railed to harmonize with the
highly-polished reproduction Georgian dressing-table and
commode in bird's-eye maple. It was covered with a white
bearskin throw and its ivory castors were separated from the
midnight-blue wall-to-wall Axminster by hollowed cedar-
wood protector cups.

Preckner picked up his wife and laid her crosswise on the
white fur cover. Her ample body subsided graciously, satined
flesh on the rich material. She lay on her back with her arms

crossed behind her head, nippled breasts sagging slightly on her rib-cage, the soft swell of belly hammocked between cushioned hips. There was a lazy smile on her face.

For an instant Preckner stood looking at her, the stiffened cock rigid below the hairy plane of his own flat belly. Even after all this time the sight still provoked the familiar tightening of the throat, the thudding of the blood behind his eyes.

One of the things he prized most about his wife was her physical perfectionism, her almost maniacal attention to detail. Revelling in the contrast between her lustrous blonde hair and the dark, dark triangle furring her loins, he reflected that not once in the twelve years that had passed since he first started going out with her, not once had he seen a single sign of darkness at the roots of the tinted golden bell that formed such an admirable setting for her prominent, slightly angular features. In the hollows of her now upraised arms, he had never witnessed the faintest hint of tufts in the natural colour. And even at the end of a busy day the skilfully applied make-up that was good enough to deduct a decade from her forty years remained as perfect as it had been before they had gone out to dine with friends. It seemed almost a shame, he thought, to spoil it now!

So he dropped down on his knees beside the bed.

For David Preckner, privately, this was in a sense a homage to the beauty of his wife, a thankful tribute to the fact that marriage, children and the anxieties of the business world had in no way dimmed the brilliance of the allure she had for him.

For Sylvia it stirred a tiny *frisson* of pleasurable anticipation deep in her belly, for it meant, undeniably, that she was going to get sucked.

The gratification of that anticipation was not long in coming.

Preckner's hands lodged themselves behind her knees. He pushed her legs upwards, folding them back until they were almost doubled, with the thighs spread wide and the knees almost touching her breasts. Then, holding them in that position, he leaned forward and lowered his head to her loins.

For an instant he held his face poised above the darkly matted bush at the base of her belly. A small pulse heaved beneath the skin at the top of the crease reaching towards her right hip, and there was already an irregular twist of pink flesh visible amongst the wiry cluster of pubic hair. The muscles on the inside of Sylvia's clamped thighs were trembling.

Preckner ducked further down, allowing his nose and chin to rest gently against his wife's vaginal cleft. At the same time his tongue lashed out, snaking into the creased flesh gashing her pubic triangle, and his lips closed firmly over cunt. Maddeningly, provocatively, he began to lick.

For minutes he stayed there immobile, knees on the floor, his hands lodged against the backs of Sylvia's folded thighs, only the faint lapping squelch of his busy lips and tongue rivalling the tick of a Victorian clock to break the silence of the big room.

Sylvia remained very still, her frame as motionless as her husband's, savouring the tiny flares of excitement racing outwards from her invaded loins to spread like tongues of fire through the nerves of belly and breasts. Her cupped hands held the big, loose breasts thrust upwards, ready to accept the weight of her lover-husband when he chose to move.

Clamped to the familiar, yielding heat of her pussy, David pushed his tongue between the hotly sliding skin of Sylvia's lustfully trembling labia. It never ceased to amaze him, the complex web of ridges and hollows and curves and quivering buds within that seemingly simple female opening. Nor was he too surfeited with these inner joys to resist a start of surprise each time he experienced the astonishing temperature difference between the slippery warmth of the outer cunt and the burning clasp of practised muscle each time the tip of his tongue or penis tunnelled inside her love canal.

David allowed his tongue to rove. He explored in relentless detail each subtly unfolded depth, swirling the sensitive tip around the unsheathed clitoris as his lips sucked and chewed at the splayed pads of wet flesh pouting amidst Sylvia's drenched pubic triangle.

14

On the bed above him, suddenly audible, her breathing quickened. He heard a choked-off, wordless exclamation as his tongue was engulfed in the searing clasp of her clenching vagina. In front of him, arrowed from beneath his belly like the bowsprit of a man-o'-war, his inflamed and hardened cock was jammed against the bedspread falling to the floor and the under-mattress behind it.

He drew the distended clitoris bud up into his mouth one last time, teasing it lightly between his teeth, then withdrew his head from the blonde's plundered loins.

Releasing her thighs, he clamped his hands to the edge of the mattress and pushed himself up off the carpet. As he eased himself smoothly as an eel between her knees, Sylvia lowered her legs until she could wrap them over his hips, then lock her ankles behind his calves as the whole muscular length of him subsided against her prone, voluptuous body. She caught her breath, feeling hot hands slide beneath her buttocks; the hair on her husband's chest grated against the erect nipples of the breasts held up towards him as he gently lowered his weight.

Pulling her tightly against him, David moved powerfully and adroitly to one side. With a single practised thrust he shifted her from her position across the bed and relocated her diagonally so that both of them now had legs and feet extended on the mattress.

David kneed her thighs open wider. She spread them lewdly apart, raising her legs again to cross them over the small of his back.

Lying against her, he drew his two hands up her flanks, over the fleshy pads of her hips, through the scooped-out hollow of her waist, until his palms received the bulged heaviness of breasts squashed outwards on her rib-cage by the weight of the figure on top of her.

Sylvia's hands were busy too. She had thrust them between her heated belly and the hard, flat plane of the hips and hairy belly pinning her to the bed. Her extended fingers searched for – and at once found – David's heavy, stiffened cock. Cushioned fingertips circled the distended glans, pushing the hard, hot shaft gently down until the seeping tip

15

brushed through the tangle of moist pubic hair to nudge the seamed apex of quivering labia.

The guidance was expert, but it was scarcely necessary. With a slight squirm, a reflex, a steady lunge of the hips, David forced his tool into his wife's eager, ready and skilfully prepared body. Where less than two minutes before his tongue had been splaying wide wet lips and tracing delicate arabesques through complexities of inner flesh, now the rigid, hardened staff of his desire bludgeoned apart the entrance to Sylvia's secret world and slid forcefully as a sword slammed into its scabbard, up into her hot vagina.

Sylvia gasped. Twisting her torso to sense the strong fingers kneading her flattened breasts, she arched her hips up off the mattress to meet David's impaling thrust. Her hands, still trapped between them, stretched down further to cradle the hairy balls slapped against the furrow separating the cheeks of her backside. Her belly heaved up rhythmically to match David's forward lunge, subsided, and then rose once more as he began shafting in and out of her with an easy, controlled rhythm.

Lowering his head, he closed his lips over her open mouth and kissed her hard, the hot tip of his intruding tongue alternating with the pistoned thrusts of the cock spearing up into her belly.

Coupled in this way, they settled into a lazy, compulsive rhythm, each entranced with the flesh of the other as limbs and muscles and nerves and sexual organs combined to form a reciprocating unit that was both flawless in its design and matchless in operation. A director hired to make an educational video illustrating the perfection of a traditional fuck would have had to look no further than the Preckner bedroom on that night if he wished to chart the joys of sex – the controlled excitement remorselessly mounting, mounting until the instincts took over, wildly threshing the locked bodies to the point where the wave broke, sending time and place spinning away into the stars.

It was later – an hour later? ten minutes later? an eternity? – later anyway, after that explosion and implosion of shared ecstasy stimulated by a perfect mutual climax, that

16

Sylvia stirred in her husband's arms and spoke sleepily.

'This sexy underwear campaign you're planning, darling,' she said, 'will it extend also to the creation of irresistible nighties? Will the wives of the world at last have a weapon . . . and husbands finally a means, hitherto lacking, of finding their own women fatally attractive?'

David Preckner was feeding his wife's breasts through his hands, one after the other. 'That ain't, as the song says, necessarily so,' he observed. 'You, honey, for instance, you have no need! You better turn over in fact right now: the sight of these tits is making me horny again already.'

3

David Preckner called Roger Curnow early the next morning. 'Don't bother to come in today, Rodge,' he advised. 'We have to get cracking if Operation Frou-Frou is to be a success – and you can help more out of the office than behind a desk, even if the paperwork at the desk is done by Sexy Sandy!'

'There's a chance for lunch with Dulok's redhead,' Curnow admitted. 'The last time I saw her she told me that Edward had turned down a whole batch of designs submitted by Shirley Sabbath – you know, the slumbrous blonde we met at the Jaeger show.'

'I know Shirley,' David said. 'She was at school with Sylvia. That Islington comprehensive that was closed down. According to Syl, she was a scorcher – moved into the fast lane directly after "O" Levels and has never pulled over since!'

Curnow chuckled. 'I heard,' he said. 'They do say she set fire to her mother.'

'We could almost certainly use the Dulok rejects – or at any rate modify them. You'd better get on to the lady right away.'

'Literally,' Curnow said, 'that would be a pleasure! According to other things they say.'

'And don't forget – you're supposed to "cultivate" what's-her-name, that busty fifty-year-old who'll be doing the make-up for the Frou-Frou magazine.'

'Who could forget her, David? Elemental, a force of nature. The name is Brigitte Dubois. From Paris already!'

'If you can find the time, that is, between the redhead, Sexy Secretary Sandy, Shirley Scorcher and anyone else you happen to be shacked up with at the moment.'

19

'What a dream that would be!'

'How's that again?'

'To find oneself between Sexy Sandy, Speeding Shirley and Gladys the redhead,' Curnow explained. 'That would be a date to fight your way out of!'

'Don't tell me – but you wouldn't mind wading barefoot through the lot of them?'

'Right again: a cigar for the gentleman with the blonde wife.'

'But if anyone could do it,' David Preckner pursued, 'you can, Rodge.'

Curnow smiled but made no reply. Amongst friends, he was admired as an inspired, indeed a renowned, cocksman. It had in fact been rumoured in the Windsor Castle and the Scarsdale and the Coach and Horses that the term 'to roger a girl' had been coined to honour his exploits. But the reason he still had friends was that he never, ever made a pass at the girlfriend of anyone he knew.

'I can just see this new mag,' Preckner was saying. 'If we can persuade Luke to do it the way we want him to. That is to say soft porn – but believably enough a review of underwear actually on sale to keep it off the top shelf at your friendly neighbourhood newsagents.'

Curnow nodded. 'Real silk stockings pulled up tight,' he said enthusiastically. 'Suspender belts with little red bows decorating the elastic just above the clips. Satin camisoles slit up each side. Lacy bras with nipple cutouts – bras that can be unfastened *from the front*!'

'Tiered petticoats with multicoloured flounces!'

'French knickers that are wide-legged in front but reveal a bit of buttock behind!'

'Semi-transparent tops in gauzy organza or voile that are *meant* to show the bra beneath!'

'Skirtless swimsuits cut up high to outline the mons!'

For an instant Preckner was silent. His penchant for the sexual allure of underclothes that revealed the existence of what they were supposed to conceal dated from the early fifties, when the music-business weekly, *Melody Maker*, had published a picture taken by the Soho photographer Al

Ferdman which showed – daringly for the period – a tiny wisp of dark pubic hair escaping from the tight crotch of a bronzed blonde wearing a white one-piece bathing costume. Finally he said ruminatively: 'Corsets, perhaps?'

'Certainly corsets. But not the salmon-pink, two-way-stretch straitjackets . . .'

'No way!'

'. . . that keep fat ladies from overlapping! What we need are sexy corsets, couture corsets.'

'Waspies. Guépières. Tight sheaths that end *below* the tits—'

'And stop high enough to reveal our suspender belts.'

'With whalebone and white lacing, but a minimum of each.'

'In scarlet or midnight blue satin, with a frill of black lace to edge the belly and breasts.'

'Or white kid for the rich, to contrast with a sunburned body.'

'Great idea: unstretchable leather against soft peachbloom skin!'

Preckner laughed. 'Sold!' he said. 'I feel like placing, as they say, my order now. For the mag, I mean. If we can get Luke to share our enthusiasm, that is. Could you find time, between girls, to drop by his office and enthuse whoever's handling his publicity?'

'I'm on my way,' Roger Curnow said.

Luke Hornby was a tall, heavy, untidy man with a mop of greying hair – his wife said that, even when he was wearing evening dress, he looked like an unmade spare bed – but his appearance was belied by a perfectionism and reverence for detail that had characterized his previous work in advertising and as a producer of historical radio dramas for the BBC. Preckner and Curnow had every hope that his entry into the specialized magazine business would be equally successful. Certainly the first detail he had attended to, and arguably the most important, had already paid off for all three of them. He had persuaded a Yorkshire industrialist, who was also the owner of a vineyard in southern France, to underwrite financially the launch of the projected magazine and carry any initial losses for the first few months of its existence. 'Croesus is into underwear!' David Preckner had exclaimed delightedly when Roger Curnow telephoned him with the good news.

Visually, the three of them made an arresting team. Hornby's sometimes wildly extrovert appearance and manner – already a marked contrast to the precision of his work – was proving a fascinating foil, in the eyes of column-ists and TV presenters, to Preckner's precise, contained professionalism and the dark, faintly swarthy, masculinity Curnow owed to his Cornish background. There had already been hints – rumours even of a possible scandal! – of a project uniting them in several Sunday gossip items.

Hornby's office – no connection with the magazine, which as yet had no title – was on the top floor of a drab building in a square off Tottenham Court Road. It was a temporary hideout: there was no lift, the stairs creaked and the windows hadn't been cleaned in years.

When Curnow climbed up and pushed open the door, Hornby was perched behind a littered desk pasting up photos and blocks of text amidst a confusion of typescript sheaves, garish covers torn from existing magazines, press cuttings, Sunday supplements and rolls of teleprinter copy.

'It's a small office,' he said. 'But it's dreary. Don't worry: once the moneybags are untied and cash begins to flow, all will be clean glass and stainless steel with a blonde recep-tionist in a brand new block in the heart of the rag-trade district!' He sighed, loosening the tie from beneath a shirt collar that lacked a button, and leaving a smear of paste on his lapel. 'But I need *material*, Roger. There are dummies and paste-ups all over the room, in several different formats, but I simply cannot interest anyone, obviously, in a pile of soft porn text, however horny, without the buggers can see the bloody product! Once you have the designs, how fast can David dream up a batch of prototypes, pour them over a bunch of sexy models, set up the right kind of studio, and start telling them to say "cheese"?'

'You know David,' Curnow said. 'Fast.'

'Good. It'd better be, too. Because it's not until then that we're in business.'

'Everything will be taken care of,' Curnow assured him. 'Who's going to do your advance publicity and promo?'

'Suzanne Towers. She's a smart girl; she'll work for a retainer and a percentage. And she's something of a pin-up among the Fleet Street boys, which can't be bad.'

Curnow nodded. 'Great. Now let me wise you up on the latest from Wildwood Road.' He gave Hornby an edited account of his telephone call that morning to David Preckner at his Hampstead home.

Later he made his way to the Compasses, a pub near the Soho yard at one side of the Dulok workshops and stockroom. He climbed narrow stairs to a dark, oak-beamed dining-room, bagged a table for two and ordered a bottle of champagne. By the time Gladys Carter, the Dulok overseer, joined him, soon after midday, every seat in the place was taken and the noise from lunching customers and the two crowded bars downstairs was deafening enough to keep any conversation strictly private.

The best the chef could offer was a grilled lamb chop with processed peas and chips – an uneasy and indigestible marriage, Curnow thought wryly, with *demi-sec* champagne – but the voluptuous redhead had no complaints. Anything that was expensive was all right with her. In any case, the five-star West End cuisine was a non-starter: she only had an hour for lunch.

Curnow kept her glass well filled, making an occasional note on a miniature pad as he posed expert questions on stock orders and advance deliveries and the new models selected for catalogue illustration. The real payoff for this confidential material – industrial espionage, Curnow explained to his disbelieving wife – would come that evening. *South Pacific*, this time, at the Dominion, followed by dinner at the Coq d'Or in Stratton Street. But if he already had the information, Preckner's partner reasoned, there was a chance that he might terminate the sexual athletics on the Carter chaise-longue at a reasonable hour and get home a little earlier.

Fortunately Mrs Curnow, who had been born in Hawaii, was a passionate devotee of ikebana, the Japanese flower-arrangement art that was as much spiritual as visual, and her own physical demands on her husband were minimal.

It was equally fortunate, Curnow reflected, eyeing Gladys Carter over the rim of his glass, that there was a sufficiency of sexy girls available to satisfy even a man of his horny enthusiasm.

This one – if only it could have been afternoons instead of late at night! – was a knock-out. His unashamedly lecherous gaze took in the twin mounds with their sharply identified points swelling out the tight green sweater on the far side of the polished table; his memory supplied a lustful reminder of the pliant waist and supple belly below. And a stockinged foot – like many women she had eased off her shoes the moment she sat down – a softly exploring foot, jammed up between his thighs, the arched toes stirring his balls and hardened cock, stirred also his anticipation of the joys his date that night would bring.

Gladys's smile, lower lip full and white teeth gleaming, was one of the most lascivious – and frankly inviting – he had seen in months. She dazzled him with it now, shaking a glossy auburn head as he called a waitress over to order coffee. 'No time, love,' she apologized, glancing at a diamanté cocktail watch on her left wrist. 'It's already three minutes to.'

The pressure on Curnow's crotch eased as she felt for her shoe. She pushed back her chair and stood up, breasts jutting above a slim black skirt. Curnow shifted on the hard wooden seat of his own chair. 'But I reckon, just the same,' Gladys said, 'that I could swallow a fast brandy!'

Curnow nodded at the waitress. 'Two large Rémy Martins,' he said.

The redhead downed the dark, fiery spirit in two satisfied gulps. Winking at Curnow, she said: 'Don't do anything I wouldn't do – just keep it for tonight!'

'Baby, I can't think of anything you wouldn't do,' Curnow said.

She grinned again. Raising a scarlet-nailed hand, she

swung around and sling-hipped her way down the narrow staircase. There wasn't man lunching there who didn't hungrily follow her with his eyes.

Shirley Sabbath lived in a converted mews house not far from South Kensington Underground station. It was an easy, four-stop, ride from Piccadilly, but Roger Curnow took a taxi: the processed peas, borne on a tide of champagne and brandy, were lying heavily on his stomach.

Like most of the bijou properties in the narrow, cobbled lane, the house had recently been restored. Geraniums in wire baskets hung beneath the two windows piercing the ochre facade. Below the open, up-and-over garage door, the white curves of a Jaguar XK140 convertible gleamed. Curnow pressed a bell beside a front door sheathed in hammered copper.

'Push – then come up,' a female voice called from one of the windows above.

Eric Gill woodcuts and an engraving by Buckland Wright enlivened the cramped stairwell, and there was a tall Celadon vase from the Leach pottery at St Ives in a niche just outside the archway leading to the first floor.

There were only two rooms. In the living space over-looking the mews Curnow received an immediate impression of money and of good taste. One wall was hung with grey-and-white-striped paper. The others had been painted pinkish-amber over a textured wood-chip surface. He saw a Danish teak desk, modernistic armchairs of white hide hammocked in chrome frames, an egg-shaped basket seat hanging from the low ceiling on a chain, books in modular units. There were Esfahan rugs on the polished board floor and a huge Mervyn Peake canvas was displayed above the hooded fireplace.

The back room was a studio, with inclined drawing boards, anglepoise lamps, and a wide bed recessed into one wall. Not really the nest of an impecunious young artist struggling to make a living by selling ready-to-wear designs, Curnow thought. Remembering the XK140, the 'contempo-rary' Danish and Italian furnishings, a set of Fornasetti tableware, the copper door – and the Sylvia Preckner connection – he suspected a rich daddy.

The girl emerged from the studio with a paintbrush in one hand and the other extended to greet him. She was beautiful. Returning her firm, dry handshake, Curnow registered blue eyes, a firm chin and chiselled mouth, slender legs in blue jeans. Her blonde hair, entirely straight, cascaded over slender shoulders and down her back in a shining stream, to be cut off entirely square in the small of her back. The paint-spotted white tee-shirt she wore could conceal neither the trimness of her body as a whole nor the superb tilt of the pointed breasts naked beneath it.

'What are you going to have to drink?' she asked.

The voice was cool, well-modulated, with just a trace of huskiness. Curnow put her age at twenty-five – twenty-eight at the absolute maximum. 'Frankly, I'd just love a coffee, strong and black,' he told her thankfully.

Shirley Sabbath drank beer from a silver tankard. After they had exchanged the usual courtesies and he had explained his relationship with the Preckners and why he was there, she took him into the studio and showed him the rejected Dulok designs.

'I was a bit cross really,' she said. 'Of course they hadn't been commissioned; Edward owed me nothing, and you have to expect the occasional rejection. But I'd worked hard on this, and I was convinced – I still am – not only that the ideas were good but they were what the market needed.'

Curnow leafed through the portfolio. The designs were very good indeed. She had a fine line and an unerring sense of style. More than that, they were cut and shaped and decorated – at times daringly revealing – in a variety of ways that were not only enticing but sexually explicit. They were in fact exactly what Preckner was looking for. There was even a white wasp-waist corset with frilled edges and front lacing in black ribbon!

'Marvellous!' Curnow enthused. 'I have to check with David, of course, but I'm ninety-five per cent certain: you've got yourself a job here. And one that could very likely lead to a long-time retainer, with accepted designs paid for pro rata.'

'Well, that's super,' Shirley said. 'Absolutely fab! And now I think you must join me in at least a token drink!'

'With great pleasure,' Curnow said truthfully. Despite the working clothes, she was wearing an insidious, musky perfume that was making him dizzy. He couldn't take his eyes away from the tight curves of her denim-clad backside or the loose shift of those delicate, pointed breasts beneath the thin tee-shirt each time she moved.

There was too – he was convinced of it – a warmth, a certain unmistakable good-to-be-with-you atmosphere projected from her in his direction. An atmosphere increasingly evident – in the cool hand laid on his arm, in the approving glances at his dark, positive features, in the occasional eye contact that was held – as the afternoon wore on.

Excitement at the thought of these subtle indications was already stirring a familiar awareness at the base of his belly when she rose from the egg-shaped wicker chair in which she was idly swinging and said: 'This is lovely, really super. But I'm awfully sorry, I'm afraid I have to throw you out now. I have to get ready for an early dinner. Relations. You know.' She smiled.

And then, as Curnow stumbled confused to his feet, trying to stifle the sudden acute disappointment clawing at his diaphragm, she added: 'But it becomes obvious to me, my friend, that there could be . . . things between us. I mean music together is what we might make! The dinner will be over early and I should be home by nine-thirty. Why don't you drop by for a night-cap sometime – not too long a time – after that?'

Curnow's disappointment became intolerable, unbearable.

'Jesus,' he blurted, 'I'd love to. Honest to God, there's nothing in the whole world I'd like better. But – oh, Christ! Oh, *shit*! – the awful thing is, I have a date tonight already . . .'

'Not to worry,' Shirley said calmly. 'I'm all for adventure. Bring her along too.' Another smile. 'In my book, two's company – but three's a party!'

4

For some time now, Roger Curnow had been experiencing a recurring dream. He'd left a party at a big house on a cliff above the sea, and he had to get back to a boat waiting for him below. Grassland sloped down to the cliff edge, but the face itself and its height above the beach remained invisible. Curnow knew he had scrambled up a twisting path to get to the party, but he didn't know at which part of the cliff edge he had arrived.

The boat was visible in silhouette against the setting sun, nudged in to a sandy spit some way offshore – a long, low dinghy with at least twelve people crowded into it. He would have to hurry if he wasn't to be left behind.

But he was afraid of heights and he wasn't sure of the way down. A boy about ten years old stood on the lip below him. 'I was afraid the first time,' the child said, 'but never mind.' And he lowered himself over the cliff edge.

Warily, Curnow followed . . . to discover that it wasn't a cliff at all but a low bluff. He saw a short grassy path with the calm surface of the sea only a few feet below. The water was crystal clear, pleasantly warm, shoulder-high above a ridged sandy floor. Curnow sank into it fully dressed and began to wade out towards the boat.

At first he had wondered if this waking dream could be a metaphor for death (not as fearful as people expected). But after its third manifestation he became convinced – although he woke from it always with a feeling of peace and well-being – that it mirrored in some way an inconsistency in his own character. It wasn't the typical frustration dream that everyone had – the plane that was going to be missed because of a traffic jam, feet that couldn't be pulled clear of a quagmire, the actor waiting in the wings who had forgotten his lines. Still less was it the throat-catching horror of Curnow's childhood nightmare: the tiger under the bed who continually chased him, no matter how many doors he slammed behind him – which was still there, growling on the far side of the communicating door, when he was high above the earth in an aeroplane.

This dream, Curnow thought, was a simple re-statement of a basic insecurity which lay, paradoxically enough, behind his success socially and commercially, and particularly behind his admired success with women.

Curnow succeeded because he had to; he had to prove *to himself* that he could do it.

The dream – its most recent appearance had in fact been the night before – was in any case very much in his mind when he paid the bill at the Coq d'Or and called for a cab to take him and Gladys Carter to the mews house in Kensington.

If Speeding Shirley had meant what he thought she meant, how in hell was his date going to take it when it came to the crunch?

Admittedly, they were not 'an affair', a regular couple: the redhead was in it because she liked to have money spent on her and because she was prepared to free her sexual enthusiasm in return.

But that didn't mean that she was automatically a pushover for group sex in general and three-somes in particular.

Should he in some way forewarn her? Steer the conversation to a point where he could at least drop a hint? Provide a trailer in fact to whet the appetite for the big feature?

On the whole he thought not.

The redhead might refuse, and then the whole evening would be fucked up: he'd be on to an each-way bet that lost out at both ends.

It might be a help – or it could be a hindrance – that the two girls knew each other. They would have met when Shirley submitted her designs to Dulok. It would depend on what they thought of one another. And he hoped to Christ (Curnow thought in a sudden rush of panic) that he could somehow warn the designer not to reveal that she was now showing those same models to the Preckner company. If Gladys knew that, and mentioned it to Edward Dulok, the entire impact of Preckner's new collection, together with the surprise effect of the magazine launch, could be ruined!

Curnow decided that, so far as sex was concerned, he would play it this time by ear.

He would just say that, if Gladys didn't mind, he had to drop in on a business associate for a drink on the way home. After that it was up to Shirley.

The redhead wasn't to know that Curnow had been briefed in a sense already: the blonde was paying the piper: it would be up to her to call the tune!

In fact the dream, like most of them, and the problems it had suggested, dissolved and vanished the moment Curnow and the redhead climbed the stairs.

Shirley was wearing gold lamé pants with a wild silk, peacock-blue top cut very low between the breasts. Her feet were bare. Her eyes, subtly shaded and lined, were electric. Otherwise she seemed to be wearing no make-up.

That youth, Curnow thought admiringly, and those features, could take it!

Whether her appearance had been designed expressly to seduce – or whether this was just a rich girl's manner of slouching around the house without bothering – was unclear. Whichever, the effect was fairly stunning.

But however hard Curnow tried to orient the conversation away from the dress business – after all, each of them in some way or another was in it – the talk, even after the second bottle of champagne, remained shop.

Shirley didn't waste too much time nevertheless. They still had full glasses when she said: 'It is, after all, pretty stupid when you come to think of it – this so-called profession we ornament.'

'Well, I guess most professions could be called stupid, from one point of view or another,' Curnow began. 'I mean it depends on—'

'From every point of view,' the blonde cut in. 'Take the birds, for instance . . .'

'Darling, you take them,' Gladys said with a slight giggle. 'I'll settle for the males any time!'

'That's exactly what I mean,' Shirley said. 'Peacocks and cockatoos and that extraordinary Australian dancing bird – they all preen and shout and display their most vivid colours, making the most of what they've got, of what nature gave them. Baboons exhibit their great red arses, dolphins leap, guppies ocillate and gophers circle around in a ritual parade.'

'Yes, but all those examples are sex displays, designed by the males to draw the females' attention,' Curnow said. 'It's the old look-at-me syndrome. See how clever, how resplendent, I am, by God!'

'My point precisely. And don't tell me that our lot aren't just as interested, just as crazy to attract the other sex – or the same sex for that matter – as the birds. Yet we alone . . .' She shook her head and drained her glass of champagne. 'We're the sole species, the *only* race, deliberately to cover up the interesting parts and show the rest! We're part of a worldwide, multi-billion-dollar, artificial industry exclusively created to hide what people want to see! Crazy, don't you think?'

'You could say that,' Curnow admitted. 'But it ain't crazy for my money: it's bread and bloody butter to me!'

'Because there's this gigantic demand. A demand, like the birds, to be *different* from the rest. But a demand, because of the absurd taboos we invent, to hide rather than display. Look, for example, at this . . .'

Shirley stood up. Lifting the long blonde cascade of hair with one hand, she dragged up the blue silk top and pulled it over her head. Then, shaking her head to settle the hair again, she sank back into her chair, bare from the waist up.

Bravo, Curnow admired mentally. The pointed breasts, small but shapely, were exquisite.

'Am I any different because you can see my tits?' Shirley demanded. 'Does it make me less intelligent, less – or more – of a good cook, less of a suitable person to marry your son?' She unfastened the belt of the gold trousers, opened the zip, half rose to slide them down and off. She sat completely

32

naked in her chair. 'Does this shock you, outrage you, make you want to leave?'

'Not when you've a bust like that to show, duckie!' Gladys assured her.

'Suppose both of you were nude too,' Shirley pursued. 'Would it *really* make any genuine difference to our social relationship? Would we be any less interesting? Or boring? Or pretty?'

'It would make a difference to me,' Curnow answered. 'A big difference. To be frank, it would turn me on like crazy. It would make me want to fuck.'

Shirley laughed. 'Now you're talking, boy!' she said.

Gladys cleared her throat. 'I don't think we'd need to take a vote on that,' she said.

'Splendid! That's my girl!' The hostess rose to her feet again and walked over to the redhead. She was lithe and springy. The legs, slender below her tight little bottom, were elegantly tapered. The belly below her tiny waist was flat. The pubic hair, almost insolently blonde, was not arranged in a wide triangle: it was no more than a tuft, sprouting from the apex of her outer labia like an arrowhead aimed at her hidden clitoris. The pointed breasts swayed – not bounced but swayed and trembled – as she strode.

She stopped in front of Gladys, who was perched in the hanging wicker chair. 'I always wanted to know . . .' she began. 'Forgive me, but I always wondered just how much of this is you' – she placed long-fingered hands each side of the out-thrust mounds swelling so firmly beneath the redhead's tight white lurex sweater – 'and how much due to . . . artificial . . . help.'

'You want to find out?' Gladys reached behind her to unfasten a rear zipper. She spread her hands wide. 'Be my guest,' she said.

Shirley hooked her fingers under the hem of the sweater. Slowly, she pulled the garment up and over the young woman's smooth auburn head. A deep-cupped, crossover bra in reinforced white satin came into view. Shirley draped the sweater over a chair back and reached her arms behind the redhead's generous back. Unfastening the foundation, she allowed it to fall to Gladys's waist. The full, firm breasts, until then completely hidden, sprang free. There was little difference to Gladys's profiled silhouette.

'Fabulous!' Shirley breathed. 'God, I wish I could have a pair of those . . .'

'With what you have, honey, you should worry!' Gladys said. 'But, seeing as we're like taking inventory here, I should tell you that your man over there has one of the best endowment policies written since Jayne Mansfield went into business!'

'No joking!' Shirley said. 'So come right on over, man.'

Roger, who had been hovering rather uncertainly during this exchange, obediently moved towards the two girls. If he was a trifle taken aback by the suddenness of Shirley's change in direction, any misgivings he had held about the direction of the evening as a whole were now dissipated, dissolved, out the window into the exciting London night. Everything, he knew, was Going To Be All Right!

He came to a halt a yard from the blonde. Their eyes met – hers blue, his brown, all of them surcharged with what a poet of a previous era had termed 'certain certainties'. So they both knew – and if the redhead didn't know by now, she was out of the parade. One thing was certain, though, Curnow reflected: she should at least by now know what to expect!

Shirley reached out two hands, still holding his gaze, and unbuckled the belt of his trousers. Curnow – feeling it was up to him to help somehow – shrugged out of the jacket as she drew down the zip and spread open his fly. There was no problem locating the subject of the redhead's admiring comment: Curnow's hard-on was bellying forward the material of his Y-fronts as tight and as full as the spinnaker of a racing yacht before a following wind.

She yanked the elasticated waistband towards her and then down, so that the rigid cock jerked free.

'Oh, my!' Shirley breathed. 'You're something of a master – or should I say mistress? – of understatement when it comes to physical description, Rita!'

'Gladys.'

'Yes, Gladys. From any experience you might have, would you say that . . . the owner . . . of this weapon was a skilled user of it?'

The redhead laughed. She didn't do it often – she was usually too busy – but Curnow was pleasantly surprised to find that the tone was not strident as he might have expected but soft and honeyed, redolent of comfort and warmth. 'Insofar as my researches go,' she replied, 'and in view of the dimensions involved, I would say that the merchandise is more than adequately used.'

'Splendid. Just as I had hoped.' Curnow felt cool fingers on the distended skin of his cock.

He caught his breath as the skin was pulled forcefully forward, over the stiff core and part of the inflamed glans, then pushed back down to the root in a decisive milking motion that sent thrills flaming through every nerve webbed out from the nucleus of his bared crotch.

Gladys had moved in close. One of her hands dived inside the lowered waistband and closed over Curnow's balls. With a slight moue of satisfaction, she dragged out the hairy, wrinkled sac in which they were sheathed, kneading the soft flesh so that the sensitive glands rolled tantalizingly inside. With their free hands, the two girls – Gladys bare from the waist up, Shirley completely naked – shoved down underpants and trousers so that Curnow, still imprisoned by the fingers manipulating his genitals, could step out of them.

Shirley, without slackening her skimming grip on the hard, darkly throbbing penis, stepped back to stare at the testicles fondled by her companion.

'I don't know if he's anything to do with the Stock Exchange,' she said conversationally, 'but although he's in a sense bare-ish, I'd say bullish was a truer indication so far as tonight's – er – transactions are concerned, wouldn't you?'

'A touch of the stallion, just the same, about the moving parts,' Gladys observed. 'You'll see, my dear.'

'I can't wait,' Shirley said.

'Come to think of it, I'm not sure that I can.' Gladys released Curnow's scrotum, stood aside, and rapidly stripped off her skirt, slip, shoes and tights. Voluptuously nude, she stood by him and whisked away his shirt, necktie and under-vest.

Curnow stood there naked at last with his big cock rigidly blazing.

Shirley and Gladys moved in on him, the redhead behind, the blonde in front. He shivered with delighted anticipation as they pressed themselves against him. Gladys's big, firm breasts pressed into his back like pliant cushions just below the shoulderblades. Her arms wrapped around his waist and the wiry thatch of her pubic hair grazed his buttocks and the split between them. Shirley arched her hips forward, lewdly proffering the pelvic region so that his plank-stiff cock was jammed against the public tuft at the base of her belly. He felt, instinctively thrusting his own pelvis forward to meet her, that the heat from his trapped shaft must be scorching her soft skin. Her breasts, surprisingly cool by contrast, grazed his chest, erect nipples rubbery through the dark mat of hair.

Shirley's breath was a little faster now, her hands – cooler still – linked behind his neck.

Gladys's embracing arms were clenched around his hips, the hands again caressing his balls.

Until now, apart from being there behind his big cock, Curnow had contributed nothing. Let the blonde call the tune, he had thought. Well she had called it pretty well, co-opting Gladys with no trouble at all to make it a duet. So maybe now, he thought, it was about time he too began to sing.

His hands had been stiff by his sides, arms motionless as a soldier at attention. Now he stretched them out, one in front, the other behind, to spread eager fingers over his companions' buttocks and clamp each of them tighter still to his backside and pelvis. His naked body, tremoring now with the acceleration of desire, was ecstatically cushioned, sandwiched between two gently straining landscapes of female flesh. He bent down his head and kissed Shirley on the mouth.

'You know the poem,' she said breathlessly when she could free her tongue from the hot suction of his lips. "Let us praise while we can, the vertical man . . . so soon to become the horizontal one." Well for me the vertical was fine . . . but I reckon it's time we moved on to the second line!'

Displacing Curnow's hand from the crevice separating her buttocks, she freed herself and led him through the archway into the studio at the rear of the tiny house.

Gladys followed on behind, close as a caravan to a Range Rover, unwilling to relinquish her grasp on the balls bunched beneath their partner's wagging erection.

Shirley pressed two buttons set within the arch. At once subdued lighting subtly reorganized the room . . . and Curnow heard the discreet whirr of an electric motor as the double bed moved out from its niche and stood clear of the wall.

'Time for the limerick's last line,' Shirley said. 'Who does what, with which, and to whom?'

'Well, there's two of you and only one of me,' Curnow said at once. 'I know there's safety in numbers, but I also know the larger force ultimately gains over the smaller. So I'm going to take it lying down. You know: when rape is inevitable . . .'

'Christ, that's a bit laboured, isn't it?' Shirley said.

'The best I could do off the top of my head. But at least it's *hard* labour,' Curnow replied with a glance at his cock. 'There are two points of reference here: it's up to you two ladies to decide who has the first go at which.'

'Shall we toss for it?' Shirley suggested.

'No – let him do the tossing!' the redhead said with a giggle. 'You take the weapon, dear. I've had that once already.'

Curnow lay on his back on the bouncy bed. The jokiness was rather forced, he thought. But at least it got them oriented into a sexual situation without too much messing around. And that was what they were all there for, wasn't it?

Without wasting any more time, the two girls climbed onto the bed. Shirley straddled Curnow's hips, kneeling with one slender leg on either side of him. Gladys squatted by his head, with a bare foot planted beside each ear.

The cock, swaying slightly with the passage of the blood

engorging it, lay stiffly above Curnow's darkly furred belly. Shirley stared at its thick, hard shaft, at the purplish, velvety head gleaming in the subdued light, then she stretched out a hand and lifted it gently away.

Curnow shifted his body slightly on the bed. The illumination dimmed as Gladys's heavy, fleshily cushioned hips and pelvis lowered themselves into position above his face. He gazed straight up into the russet thatch foresting her vaginal furrow. Damp pubic hairs grazed the tip of his nose.

For an instant, Shirley held the thick, rigid shaft of Curnow's penis vertical, a thumb and four cool fingers securing the distended staff.

Still kneeling, she raised her pelvis very slightly, canted her hips forward, and positioned herself so that the blonde tuft at the base of her belly was immediately above the glossy head of the prick she held.

Inch by inch she lowered herself, stirring the glans gently into the creased flesh triangled immediately below the tuft.

At once a bead of moisture appeared, spreading over those intimate folds until they glistened with the lubrication of her secret sexual juices.

The labia, until then scarcely visible below the marbled mons between her thighs, flowered open. She lowered herself still further, guiding the throbbing cock with her hand.

Subsiding yet again, Shirley's cunt gaped suddenly wide . . . the shaft slid easily, greasily inside . . . and she grounded abruptly on Curnow's pubic bone, the entire length of his eager cock swallowed in the hot, dark fastness of her belly.

His mouth opened to gasp out an exclamation of joy as he felt, first the super-sensitive tip, then the whole, hard, bursting shaft of his rigid prick engulfed in the burning clasp of her pussy. But the words never materialized because Gladys too had lowered herself and his lips were muffled by the soft weight of a hairy cunt grinding into his face.

Curnow opened his mouth wider, lashing out his tongue as far as it would go, licking fiercely among the moist hairs until he located the complex folds of outer labia already wet

38

and trembling with anticipation. He burrowed the tongue deeply between them, parting the inner lips, lewdly circling the unsheathed clitoris, then tunnelled up into the searing depths of the love canal itself. At the same time the cunt as a whole, more prominent, more pouting than the blonde's, was gobbled and chewed by Curnow's working lips.

Gladys mewed softly with pleasure, gently swivelling her hips, oscillating the lower part of her body from side to side to allow the invading mouth and tongue ever more intimate access to her inner flesh.

Shirley was now rising and falling, using the muscles of belly and thighs to slide hungrily up and down the quivering pole of the cock impaling her. In an easy, dreamlike rhythm, she rode Curnow as impersonally – and expertly – as a horsewoman with invisible stirrups. The distended staff was relentlessly skewered in the sucking clasp of her pussy, in and out, up and down, penetrating and withdrawing as effortlessly as a piston in a thoroughbred machine.

Lying entranced between the slaving cunts of these two young women, his whole body electrified by the thrills scorching through his nerves and pounding the blood in his veins, Curnow was suddenly aware – extraordinary thought! – that he had hardly touched either of them, touched with his hands that was, since the three of them had stripped off their clothes.

So much for Casanova Curnow, the sensual stud!

The loss of opportunity could be quickly remedied nevertheless. There were four breasts bobbing above his supine body, two firm and full, two slender and delicate, as their owners squirmed and writhed with laboured breath and an occasional stifled gasp under the twinned assaults of his cock and tongue. He raised his hands to paw the naked mounds swelling below the girlish chests – close together now, he realized, since they had leaned together and were kissing passionately.

He fondled and felt, and squeezed and pulled, cradling soft weights in his palms, brushing his knuckles against fleshy curves, tweaking erect nipples and fingering the full, skinned slopes as they moved.

Minutes later – his tongue still buried, his cock still milked by the rise and fall of the blonde's hot belly – he was obliged to let his arms fall: they had been chased away by four female hands, each pair salaciously busy with the taut droop of alien, unaccustomed tits!

Curnow bent his left arm, reaching back his open hand until his fingertip homed in on the mat of pubic hair plastered over his slavering mouth. Probing within the hot, wet flesh, he encountered the muscled swirl of his own tongue, then swiftly transferred his touch to the inflamed clitoris trembling from its open sheath. Above him, Gladys groaned deep in her throat with content.

Extending his right arm, Curnow fingered Shirley in the same way, caressing the sinewy bud of flesh at the apex of her cunt, feeling the greased column of his tool vanish and then reappear between those heated lips as she rose and fell. She too was now breathing hard and rather fast.

He was never quite sure how long they stayed like this – after all, two bottles of champagne had already been drunk, and the dinner at the Coq d'Or earlier had not exactly been dry. Plus he had downed a couple of whisky-sours to fortify himself before he collected Gladys.

However . . .

There they were, at some undisclosed interval after the first triangular session on the wide bed. Gladys was on her back this time, lying across the bed with her heels on the floor and her legs spread wide. He himself was kneeling between them – it was a low, divan-type bed – with the tip of his cock wedged into the redhead's cunt, waving it like a magic wand among the soft, creased, unusually prominent folds of her outer labia. If he chose to rise half upright, leaving her still in that position, the stretched-out pose extended that part of her body below the waist so much that the sexual canal reaching up into her heated belly became so long that even his great cock was unable to penetrate far enough to touch the sensitive neck of her womb. If, on the other hand, he came in close, crouching, and shoved her legs up and back until her knees rested on her generous breasts, almost half the lengthy shaft was still outside, even after his most powerful strokes.

It was all the same to Roger Curnow. Tantalizing the tip, or dipping the wick, the whole wick, and nothing but the wick – it was all heady and ecstatic to him: the soft, wet, scalding welcome of excited female bodies had gone completely to his head. There was no before, no after, only the pulse-stirring, mind-blowing reality of now.

Gladys was unable to offer a considered opinion on the three different fucking modes, for something had gone to her head too – equally ecstatic, it was true, but a little less abstract than Curnow's joy.

The blonde was sitting on her chest, the heavy breasts cushioned beneath Shirley's tight little backside, and Gladys's mouth was fully occupied between the splayed lips of the young woman's succulent cunt.

It was some time after that (Curnow thought) that they became disentangled and the hostess went to find a third bottle of chilled champagne. Thank God for munificent daddies, he recalled in a beatific haze! But he couldn't remember precisely how they re-organized themselves after the wine had been opened and poured.

What he did recall, with breathtaking clarity, was the first time he gave head to the blonde.

For him that was the big treat of the evening. Sure, he had fucked her before – somewhere in there! – but the thrill of this, even with that slender frame helplessly spreadeagled beneath his bucking weight, had been slightly dimmed by the fact that his cock was already familiar with her cunt through the riding lesson he had been given. That had been great, even perfect in its way, and they had climaxed together explosively – privately too, since Gladys, exhausted, had been sitting this one out. But it hadn't really been a first.

The mouth was something else.

For some reason they were strung out in a line this time, not bunched together in a daisy-chain with all hands on deck and no orifice unfilled.

Shirley was at the top end of the divan, lying on her back with the blonde cascade fanned out below the bed-head. Gladys was prone at the lower end, her meaty backside balanced on the edge of the mattress and her heels once more grounded (perhaps, because of her generous proportions, she felt more glamorous when she was stretched out?). Between the two beauties, Curnow lay on his face with the redhead's face between his thighs and his cock in her mouth. His hands were clamped beneath Shirley's buttocks, his weight was on his elbows, and his face poised just above that fascinating tuft of hair decorating the base of her belly.

Her genitals – or rather the lack of evidence that they were there – had intrigued him from the moment he first saw her nude. The cunt was no more than a slit, a gash in the smooth flesh no more remarkable than the hairless opening barely visible on the body of a little girl. Even when she was riding him – he had seen, lifting Gladys's loins momentarily off his face – the labia were virtually invisible, even on the out-stroke. Visually, his see-saw tool was simply plugging a hole, close-fit as the finger of the famous boy blocking the dyke.

But this girl – Curnow reflected with an inward grin – was no dyke!

Not bloody likely, as Eliza Doolittle said. She was as hetero, as randy – and as voracious with it – as anyone he had ever met. Not excluding the enthusiastic Gladys Carter.

Settling himself more comfortably between her spread thighs, he clenched both hands over the tense cheeks of Shirley's arse and raised her hips gently off the bed towards his avid mouth.

Butterfly-wing sensations already thrilled upwards from his crotch, where Gladys sucked on him as contentedly as a child with a lolly. Now, as the slender blonde drew up her legs then draped them in a friendly way over his shoulders, the excitement intensified tenfold the instant his tongue, darting out swift as a lizard's, touched the almost hairless skin of her mons.

Those labia might be partly hidden . . . but they were certainly there, and they sure as hell made up for what they lacked visually by an astonishing muscular control.

The protruding tip of Curnow's tongue was literally sucked into the hot and hidden maw of Shirley's pussy!

Wildly as he licked and lapped, frenziedly as he worked his clamped lips and probed with that tongue, he felt himself remorselessly drawn into the blonde girl's inner depths, battered and bludgeoned from crevice to cranny as she dilated and contracted the heaving folds of hot wet flesh.

A character in one of Shakespeare's plays, he remembered dazedly, says of a woman that 'her lips suck forth my soul'. Was the dramatist really thinking about mouths when he wrote that, Curnow wondered, or were his sights perhaps set lower?

This particular talent of Shirley's had not been so evident when it was a cock that filled her vagina – perhaps it was just that she preferred tongues – but now she was literally masturbating him muscularly via the mouth; she was in fact tossing-off his tongue!

Indeed, so insidious was her skill that she did in fact bring him to orgasm as he sucked and was sucked.

Shaken as a rat seized by a terrier, Curnow found himself threshing and shuddering, spurting his white-hot load to Gladys's surprise and gratification, his own amazement, and Shirley's moans of pleasure as her two hands held his head clamped to her loins.

It was only later, after a relaxed, almost nonchalant rear-entry fuck with kneeling Gladys – who was herself at the time orally bewitched by the blonde's educated cunt – that he wondered if perhaps he had been a trifle hasty in his reflections on the dyke.

It had been a splendid evening, a wonderful, marvellous party – but it really was time to go. It was well after three: even the nightclubs at which he was supposedly 'entertaining' an important French buyer would be closing . . .

Curnow showered, dressed, swallowed a final brandy thrust upon him by his hostess, and waited politely for Gladys to get ready to be escorted home.

Except, suddenly, Gladys wasn't going home.

'Darling, it's so late I think I might as well stay,' she said huskily. 'You don't mind, do you? And, after all, nobody's expecting me at my place.'

Curnow stood beneath the arch at the top of the stairs.

He made the right noises. Then, turning for a last look at the back room – and the bed – he saw that the two naked girls were already locked together, hands on tits, hands on cunts.

'A pleasure,' he said. 'Believe me, a real pleasure. Thank you both so much for having me!'

He stole quietly downstairs, let himself out, and went to look for a taxi.

At the end of that week, Gladys Carter was called before Edward Dulok and informed that, regrettably, her 'services were to be dispensed with'. A matter of restructuring, her boss said. 'We have to cut down, streamline the operation, bring down prices to meet foreign competition.' She was given three months' money in lieu of notice and told not to come in on Monday.

What Dulok did not say was that his wife, who knew Curnow by sight, had been dining with a friend at the Coq d'Or the night Curnow was there with Gladys. And consorting with the enemy, particularly if it was *not* foreign, was not an activity he was prepared to tolerate.

Gladys was re-employed immediately, at almost twice the salary, by the Preckner organization.

'She knows the business, she's got plenty of experience, she's good with the girls – and we can, actually, do with an extra hand to supervise the new staff we're taking on for the lingerie,' David Preckner urged, during a meeting with his partner.

Curnow, who had in fact suggested the idea, nodded. 'She knows the business all right,' he agreed. 'She's good with the girls, as you say. And she's certainly an experienced hand herself . . . among other things.'

PART TWO

Raymond Large

5

It was possible, of course, that I was acting like a crazy man, agreeing to finance this new magazine – a review devoted to underwear, at that! – with a promise to underwrite any losses in the first six months after its initial publication. Certainly my accountants considered it 'exceedingly ill-advised'. But what the hell: I could afford it; even if the project turned out to be a dead loss, I wouldn't exactly find myself on the bread-line. I may be a Yorkshireman, but I'm not exactly the Eee-by-goom! type favoured by prime-time television. The mills are certainly in Bradford but I live near Great Bardfield in Essex – a Georgian house with twelve acres – and the vineyard behind my château in southern France is making a bomb.

Frankly, though, neither profit nor loss have anything whatever to do with my decision to back the magazine. My choice, made without the slightest reference to bank statements, without a single market consultation, was based on considerations far more personal, much nearer home.

For me, you see, the project was going to be something of a self indulgence.

You ask how come? Well, to tell the truth, the ultimate aim was for me to spoil myself, to grant myself extra pleasures for which the launch of the magazine would be an important pre-requisite . . . but no more than that. Whether it succeeded or failed was immaterial: it was simply the fact that it existed which could – and I hoped would – open new doors of joy for me.

I am an old man now, but for me age has one unqualified advantage: my private pleasures remain unaffected, however old I become and whatever my state of health.

This is because, especially on the physical side, they

remain objective rather than subjective. I have never been an extrovert: my satisfaction derives not from participating, from being included – but from the classic, academic and analytical stance of the uncommitted outsider. I take my pleasures, vicariously, from a distance.

If you wish to be rude, you can call me a voyeur. And it's true that nothing really turns me on, as they say today, more than the sight of other people, perhaps younger than myself, experiencing the delights of the flesh together, however extreme their tastes may be. My presence, on the other hand, rarely results in embarrassment for those whose acts please me, because I prefer myself to remain unseen. And fortunately I have the means, and usually the opportunity, to confer on myself this supplementary advantage.

I was particularly favoured in this respect by a wretched Frenchwoman named Marthe Richard, who managed just after the war to persuade the new government in France to outlaw the superb licenced brothels for which the capital was renowned worldwide. The loss of these luxuriously equipped and voluptuously staffed establishments was a severe blow to the bon-viveurs and honest libertines of the world, as well as putting a large number of beautiful and talented ladies out of work. But, selfishly, I have to admit that for me personally – and I do really mean personally – the disaster brought rich rewards.

From such famed houses of joy as Madame Kelly's Chabanais in the Rue des Moulins, or No. 14, Rue de Monthyon, I was able – when they were being officially dismantled – to acquire a variety of equipment indispensable to the furtherance of my desires. These included sections of carved panelling with concealed spyholes, glass floors which were opaque from above but transparent from below, and of course the inevitable and always useful two-way mirrors.

There was also, for summer garden-party use, a splendid *camera obscura* whose series of astutely angled reflecting surfaces could furnish an overhead view of group activity to an operator concealed in the tower of a small gazebo or folly built in the copse at the far end of my Essex estate.

So how does this tie up, you may ask, with a project to finance a new fashion magazine?

Opportunity is the one-word answer.

At a time when this unisex nonsense has encouraged women to forget how to dress sexily, Luke Hornby's underwear review – especially if it does concentrate as promised on the new Prekner Gowns collection – should open a good few doors to people like me.

A fashion magazine means photographs. Fashion photographs mean attractive models. Girls who model sexy underwear are grist, as they say, to my visual mill.

But, quite apart from the – shall we say cerebral? – thrills of watching such delectably dressed creatures at first hand, literally in the flesh, my position as financial backer will bring me into contact with even more exciting possibilities.

If I'm picking up the tab, nobody can stop me attending the studios where the photos are posed and taken. I'll be surrounded by half-nude females whose very profession is to display themselves! There may even be fetishist opportunities – I know these avant-grade photographers – to see exteriors, with scantily-clad beauties posed unexpectedly in public . . . against statues, in buses, on a park bench, you know the kind of thing.

Most importantly, apart from these non-sexual visual pleasures, such proximity will give me the opportunity to recruit 'guests' for my private parties, to sound out possible collaborators, to explore perhaps hidden fantasies and desires which have yet to be realized. Maybe even to discover, unexpectedly, fellow enthusiasts.

Being in a sense 'the boss' when the product of an organization relies on the exhibition of the female form undeniably brings with it certain advantages of a private kind . . .

So what if the review is not a success?

Financially, as I have explained, who cares? In the six months I have promised to underwrite, a man of my experience would be a fool if he couldn't make enough fruitful contacts to last well into the foreseeable future. In any case, even without that, the six months in such company itself would be well worth the expense involved.

There is too the consideration that, tax-wise, an occasional loss is no bad thing.

But I think that the magazine will succeed. I am convinced there is a desire for it and for the items it will bring before a glamour-starved public.

The interest, female as well as male, is already there, I am sure. I can even quote you, by way of proof, a couple of current press cuttings.

The first was a filler, what the Fleet Street boys call a 'squib', shoved in at the last moment to make up the space when a gossip column fell short in one of the 'quality' Sundays. It read:

There is news at last that vintage femininity still lives! For those readers who mourn the passing of the traditional, fully-fashioned, seamed silk stocking – teamed customarily with a suspender belt and stiletto heels, I bring good news. Help, I can tell you, is at hand (or foot). Let me introduce you to SHEER, an organization based no further away than Miami, Florida, in the US of A. The company, mail-order specialists, has been formed specially to replenish your lingerie loss (the acronym stands for Seamed Hose Evoke Erotic Reveries). Ten bucks in the form of an international money order will bring you a sample mailing pack complete with black-and-white photos to remind you what you have been missing. For details, write to the following address . . .

It's just an indication, but I think it's significant. The second quote's a bit longer – and perhaps a little more serious. Translated from the French fashion mag that everyone switched-on has to have on their teak coffee table, it was reprinted in the London glossy with the largest circulation.

Socially and psychologically [the Parisian specialist wrote] a love of lingerie is no less 'fetishistic' to an analyst than an interest in rubber clothes or boots and leather: it is just that it's a far more acceptable deviation than a penchant for the whip and chain. Somehow, photos of pretty young women in lingerie are regarded as mildly 'erotic' while the very same nanas wearing a leather shirt are seen as seriously sick. But in the opinion of this writer, all those male huskies who like their magazines festooned with stockings and suspenders are every bit as bent as the boys who seek out spanking ladies in the small-ads.

Which, again in the opinion of this writer, is not so very much.

But it has to be admitted, an interest in black stockings and frilly knickers is but a step-in away from a full-blown French maid fetish, and the difference between a lace basque and a tight-laced restrictive corset is surely only one of degree – or severity.

Today it is widely seen as 'normal' for a man to find cute girls in stockings sexy. But beware, Messieurs: folks will look at you askance if you cry when they take them off!

It is a curious reflection, though, that now we have become a 'permissive society', the forward marches of unisex and tights have united to drive interesting underwear from lingerie departments. Things in fact have got pretty grim for frou-frou fans since stockings vanished from the shops and bras became plain and flesh-coloured. In this libertarian age, the wish to purchase something as saucy as a suspender belt – still less, Heaven help us, an item as reprehensible as an elasticated garter! – inevitably sends the searcher, blushing, to a 'specialist' emporium, usually on the seedier side of town.

Gentlemen, I rest my case. These tip-of-the-iceberg indications, in my respectful opinion, do genuinely suggest that Luke, together with Preckner and Roger Curnow, may indeed be on the right road to filling a gap in the ready-to-wear business which most of the present-day manufacturers ignore the existence of.

Time will tell. In the meantime, in every sense, I shall be watching this space!

6

I knew the blonde was an adventuress the moment I set eyes on her.

Let me qualify the term at once. In the nineteenth century, perhaps even more in the nineteen twenties and nineteen thirties, the word adventuress was strictly pejorative: an adventuress was a woman, usually desirable, with an eye on the main chance, out for all she could get, especially from the husbands of the ladies who used the word so spitefully. She wasn't a whore – or not exactly, though she might use her charms to extract rewards, monetary or otherwise; her morals were questionable socially rather than sexually. She was a woman brave enough to be independent when women weren't, a woman therefore distrusted and disliked by wives, who saw their tidy little marriages – and their bread and butter – threatened.

The term is very rarely used now – perhaps because, in this decade, it could apply to practically every female under fifty – but I use it myself in an entirely different sense. That is to say, more simply. And literally.

For me an adventuress is an independent woman, certainly. But no opprobrium attaches itself to the usage. She is just a person sufficiently adventurous to flout the conventions, to permit herself what would once have been called adventures.

Sexual, of course, in my particular, and private, use of the word.

Shirley Sabbath – and what a name in this context! – fitted the bill exactly.

She had talent too, and – something that intrigued me even more – her freedom of expression was immediately discernible in her work. The first set of designs that Luke showed me were sensational, restrained enough to be sold in high-street shops yet undeniably oriented sexually – in such a way, subtly but unmistakably, that the attention was unfailingly drawn to the physical properties of the wearer. Here were knickers flounced and frilled over the hips to the nth degree – but tightened and smoothed between the thighs in such a way as to emphasize the crotch, outlining the bulge of the mons and even suggesting the split below it. Here were slips cut to plunge like a knife-blade between the cheeks of the backside, lacy underskirts intended to show as if by mistake below the hem of an outer garment, bras smothered in detail that stretched almost from the waist to the armpits – but calmed down over the actual breasts to hint at the dark nipples through a gauzy insert.

She had created a suspender-belt that was not only cinched in at the waist but secured more firmly in place by two elasticated straps passing between the legs – and framing the pussy as exactly as a picture on the wall. There were Directoire culottes that flounced down to lace below the knee, voluminous tiered camisoles that frothed as far as the ankles, semi-transparent Empire-line bodices that pushed the breasts up as high as an eighteenth-century courtesan's.

Those were the completed designs. Among sketches outlining future ideas, Shirley had – with an ironic bow towards current non-fashions – extended the tights upwards into wide shoulder-straps in what was later to become known as a body-stocking.

The most daring design – restricted to the more specialist shops – was a very scanty, flesh-coloured bikini. The particularity of this was that the lower part, little more than a G-string really, was covered on the outside with deep-pile tufted nylon that resembled pubic hair . . . so that the person wearing it looked more naked than when she wasn't!

This 'frivolity' was available in three shades: blonde, brunette or auburn.

The great day, of course, was when the first mock-ups of these designs, in a variety of alternative materials, were unveiled behind the strictly closed doors of the Preckner

Gowns showroom just behind the Waring and Gillow department store.

Shirley, typically enough, had agreed to model the prototype designs heself. After all, if anyone knew how they ought to look – and how they should be shown – she did. And the garments had in any case been built on a tailor's dummy of roughly her size.

There were eight of us waiting with subdued excitement for Shirley to appear – four on behalf of the new magazine, four representing the dress company. We divided that way: Preckner, Curnow, Gladys Carter the new workshop superintendent, and Tom Silver, the advertising executive who handled the Preckner account, on one side of the catwalk; Luke, myself, and two women I hadn't met before on the other. These were Suzanne Towers, who would be doing publicity and promotion for the review, and Brigitte Dubois, the typographer and make-up expert.

Suzanne was short, dark, about thirty, with the sort of eyes that sparkled and a tight, reined-in body that was very shapely. The French woman was as Gallic as a Parisienne restaurateur or brothel keeper caricatured in a TV sitcom. She was big, busty, gravel-voiced with that catch in the throat that's reserved for the French and sandy hair in spectacular disarray. She looked, indeed, like a female version of unmade-bed Luke!

She also looked, in her corduroy trousers and painter's smock, as if she could be a very butch lesbian . . . but in fact, as I found out later, wasn't.

The lighting in the salon was low-key. Loudspeakers in the background discreetly relayed a Beatles record called 'Love Me Do', which had just shot up the Hit Parade. Shirley walked out onto the catwalk wearing frilled French knickers and a front-laced white basque with ivory high-heeled shoes.

She made a very good – and very original – model. She didn't ape the haughty expression and pause-turn-swirl walk of the professional mannequins. Her action was nevertheless ideally suited to a catwalk, for she prowled, she loped like a tiger in a cage, pacing this way and that as if she was impatiently seeking the nearest way out. Her hair was up, so

55

that the shoulders and back-interest of the designs could be appreciated – and every move she made, from the slouched walk to the quirky twist of the pelvis, was expressly adopted to draw attention to – to underline – the overt sexuality of her body and the sensual undertones of the garments complementing it.

In the brief pauses while two girls from the Preckner workshops helped her to change, conversation on either side of the catwalk was animated. It was clear that the designs impressed.

Sometimes, when Shirley halted momentarily before striding back to the dressing-room, she would lower her gaze and catch the eye of one or the other of us, breaking the exhibition-cum-theatre effect to establish a sudden personal relationship with the audience. Her expression then was marvellous: a fascinating marriage between near-jokey complicity and that insolent yes-I-want-you-but-don't-you-dare challenge that seems reserved to slender blondes.

I was fascinated to observe the effect this had on different members of the audience.

Gladys Carter stared at her with shining eyes. Preckner nodded slowly with a half smile: his current dream was coming true. Luke launched a beatific smile in his model's – and possibly his future's – direction. Tom Silver looked abruptly away . . . but I was convinced it was to prevent him actually slavering at the lips!

The two other women showed nothing but a keen professional interest.

It was the slumbrous regard fired at me that naturally interested me most – much more complicity and very little don't-you-dare in this case, it was that intimate we-know-don't-we? variety that told me my original reading of Miss Sabbath had been right. Especially after I had been targeted a second time.

There was champagne and congratulations and heady anticipation all round when the show was over. It was some time before I was able to get Shirley alone, out of earshot of the others. She was ready enough to come: after all, I was the man with the chequebook, wasn't I?

'It's been a great pleasure – a really intense pleasure – watching you this morning,' I enthused, choosing the noun and the participle carefully.

'I know,' she said, looking me straight in the eye. And telling me in fact: I know you.

'I'm sorry this was a one-off, that there won't be a return engagement,' I said.

'I don't see why not,' Shirley said coolly.

Very good, Madam. Message received and understood. I said: 'Perhaps you'd care to come out to my place sometime? Every now and then I like to have a few friends – close friends – around.'

'I wouldn't be surprised,' she said, still holding my gaze.

'It would, again, be a really intense pleasure,' I repeated – knowing that the exact choice of words would convey to her the phrase 'watching you' which I had deliberately left out.

'As long as I can bring my own partner,' Shirley said.

7

An opportunity to test the correctness – or otherwise – of my beliefs about Shirley Sabbath presented itself sooner than I expected. And it happened in such a way that nobody could say it was in any manner engineered by me. I had nothing whatever to do with it.

Which is always the best way for those interested in (forgive the phrase) watching briefs!

It so happened that Brigitte Dubois, the Frenchwoman who was going to design the format of the magazine, was living on a Thames houseboat moored opposite Cheyne Row, in Chelsea.

And it happened that Brigitte was throwing a party – partly for friends in the magazine business, partly for fashion writers and other press relations, and of course partly for members of the team she'd be working with on the new publication.

And naturally enough, along with Preckner, Curnow, Shirley and the others, she invited me: although I had nothing to do with the project editorially, I was, after all, technically the publisher.

The houseboat, like most of those on Chelsea reach, was a converted Rhine barge – a heavy, broad-beamed craft, low in the water, with slanting floors, a huge saloon, and at least half a dozen smaller cabins.

I arrived some time after sunset, parked the Rolls in a side street, and threaded my way through the evening traffic along the riverside to reach the embankment. It was just after high tide: below me the black water swirled silently towards the Pool of London and the sea. On the far side, lights from what remained of the Festival of Britain fun fair shimmered through the dusk beneath the trees in Battersea

Park. I crossed the ridged gangplank to the barge's top deck.

I was only half way across when the strains of music from the south bank, as fractured as the fun fair reflections in the broken water, were drowned in the thump and blare of jazz from the party below. I pushed open the wheelhouse doors and trod down a steep companionway into a maelstrom of chattering, shrieking voices and a surge of densely packed bodies beneath the canopy of cigarette and cigar smoke weaving in the illumination of ship's lanterns placed around the beamed saloon.

There must have been at least fifty people jammed in there, a motley crowd dressed in anything from tuxedos to windcheaters, from blue jeans to cocktail dresses. The music was very loud – some New Orleans' speciality from one of the Dixieland groups, Mr Acker Bilk's, I think – and the conversation equally hectic. Before I was swallowed up I caught sight of Preckner in a dinner jacket, his wife Sylvia in a backless silver sheath, and Suzanne Towers coralled in a corner by three newspapermen waving glasses of champagne.

A barman in a white rollneck with an anchor across the front was dispensing drinks behind a brass and mahogany bar. I shouldered my way through and picked up a brandy and soda. My hostess was a few feet away, talking to Curnow and Miss Sabbath. She was attired – I can think of no other word – in something floor-length apparently made of burgundy hessian, with trimming at the neck, arms and hem of plaited raffia. Or it might have been bleached cord. Her hair was still a mess, but she looked kind of impressive just the same. Shouting a greeting, she raised a big hand and beckoned me over.

Curnow wore a dark suit, Shirley was swamped inside a huge thick-knit sweater that reached almost to her knees. Below this the bottom of a very short skirt was just visible. And then black suede highwayman boots with flaps that turned over above the knee.

'That's very chic, very Bazaar,' I told her after we had made the polite party noises. 'But what a shame – if I may make so bold – to hide such a pretty frame inside so

60

voluminous a canvas!' I allowed my glance to rest on the twin prominences only just disturbing the fall of the heavy sweater. 'Let us at least hope that some of your own . . . fascinating . . . creations are paying tribute to the inner Shirley, even if they remain invisible to the rest of us.'

'You're a dirty old man!' she said, with a grin to show she wasn't being rude. 'The outfit did in fact come from Bazaar, the Knightsbridge branch. As to what I'm wearing beneath it, I'm not telling: I like to keep my vice versa!'

'*Touché*!' I said. 'Although it would be nicer if the touch was physical rather than purely verbal.'

'In my experience,' Shirley said, looking me straight in the eye, 'especially in the case of sophisticated gentlemen, the verbal is very rarely pure.'

But before I could reply, the party swaying around us had surged in a different direction, somebody was calling Brigitte from behind me, and Curnow had taken Shirley's arm and steered her away.

It wasn't until some time – and several brandies – later that I was able to corner our blonde designer again . . . and then it was in a fashion that was much more evident to me than to her. The situation, nevertheless, was not without surprises that had nothing to do with Shirley herself.

Some people had left. There was enough space here and there on the sloping floor for a few couples to dance – modern jazz from Johnny Dankworth this time – but the houseboat was still populated enough for individual comings and goings not to be especially noticed. The party had in any case spilled over ages ago into sections of the barge fore and aft of the saloon and even up on deck.

Not specially noticed, I said. But noticed by me, all right. Because after all that's my thing. Parties in particular, and specifically those continuing into the night, where the drink and the rolling of joints seem inexhaustible, are mines of invaluable information to me. You have no idea – once the inhibitions have been drunk and smoked away – how much people can reveal. In facial expressions, in body language, in covert glances, the movement of a hand, the shifting of a stance – to the keen student of behaviour such clues furnish a precise indication not only of intended or hoped-for activity but also evidence of past experience, present relationships and inner feelings both positive and negative.

They can also lead, if the keen student himself is adroit at vectoring in on concealed frailty, to rewarding and unexpected contacts – both overt and covert.

It was because of this that I was particularly fascinated by the behaviour of Roger Curnow that night, not long before midnight. It was at a moment when the music had stopped, the dancers were immobilized, and there was some journalistic celebration – or anniversary, or presentation – organized by the hostess. At any rate some bespectacled character was making a speech with an arm around the shoulders of another. As the guests surged towards the far end of the salon, where the couple stood behind a riser mike, I saw Curnow – still with a hand on Shirley Sabbath's arm – spin her deftly around and give her a gentle pat on the backside, urging her towards a corridor opening off the nearer end of the big room. Unobtrusively, the blonde, who was standing at the rear of the crowd, stole across the two or three yards separating her from the doorway. She slipped through and was lost to sight down the passageway.

By this time Curnow himself, standing near the companionway leading down from the deck, had melted into that opening and hurried aloft.

Intriguing.

Since I was standing only a few feet away, apparently enthralled by the speech, it was easy enough for me to back off and melt unnoticeably after him.

A cool breeze rattled the stays at the mast of a sailing boat moored in the adjoining berth. A taxi with blazing headlights raced past along the embankment. On the far side of the river, the fairground music had stopped and fewer lights gleamed through the darkness.

Curnow, silhouetted against illumination from the embankment street lighting, was making his way between ventilators and glassed hatchways towards the stern of the barge. I tiptoed after him.

Just forward of the taffrail, an awning sheltered another companionway leading below.

With a hasty glance over his shoulder – I had dodged into the shadow cast by the wheelhouse – he lowered himself to the stairway and disappeared from sight.

Treading very warily now, I followed him again.

The lighting below deck seemed unnaturally bright at first, but I could see when I had crept halfway down that that he was in a long passageway – the stern section of the one Shirley had vanished into. He stood in front of a closed cabin door.

As I watched, he tapped lightly on the panelled wood – with fingertips, not knuckles.

The door opened and he went inside.

It didn't need an Einstein to work out that the person opening it had been Miss Sabbath, S., designer of ready-to-wear undies, architect of flounces and frills.

More intriguing still.

Not because of the fact that they were closeted together, but because of the why.

Curnow, I knew, was married; Shirley, I knew, was not. I also knew she lived alone.

So why should they bother to engineer a secret tryst on a Thames houseboat loaded with dozens of brawling, partying people? If each had the hots for the other that much, why not simply leave early and go back to her place?

I knew the answer, and it verified at once my reading of – and interest in – the young blonde.

Shirley was, as I had thought, an adventuress in my sense of the word. She got her kicks tinkering with fraught situations; lovemaking in improbable places and impossible ways turned her on!

And this – something I had strongly suspected all along – turned *me* on rotten!

I could use Miss Sabbath. In more ways than one. For the moment, though, I would simply content myself with – ahem! – a more visual confirmation, and contemplation, of my subject's physical frailties. I tiptoed to the door, knelt down, and put an eye to the keyhole.

63

The cabin inside was dimly lit. A ship's lantern with a wire guard hung from the beamed ceiling. Beneath it, Shirley stood, bare to the waist, her hands on her slender hips and the pale hair cascading down her naked back. The overhead light, directly above her breasts, cast long, pear-shaped shadows over her smooth belly. Curnow, still fully dressed, must have been squatting or kneeling in front of her: I could see no more than his suited forearms and his hands because of the limited field of vision offered by my keyhole. But the hands, dark-haired where they emerged from starched white shirt cuffs, were indicative.

They were creeping beneath the wide, lace-trimmed legs of the scarlet silk French knickers that were – with the black suede boots – the only garment Shirley now wore.

The lighting, as I said, was dim. But it was bright enough to show clearly the darker patch of moisture over the crotch, where Curnow's busy fingers thrust and probed under the shiny material.

Fascinating.

I shifted on my heels, trying to give myself a wider view of the cabin. My heated brow, the head tilted sideways, was hard against the brass plate covering the lock, the cock trapped inside my trousers uncomfortably hard, when I hear the low voice above and behind me.

'*You'd get a far better view if you'd join me in the cabin next door . . .*'

For a pulse-hammering moment there was dead silence. Then, in the distance, I heard music blaring again from the saloon. Water slapped against the hull of the houseboat as it heaved against the receding tide. Stumbling to my feet, I swung guiltily around.

My hostess, Mademoiselle Dubois, monolithic as the classic earth-mother, stood a yard away. In what remained of the illumination flooding from the lantern over the companionway, I could see that her craggy features were composed into a friendly enough smile.

I gulped. Friendly or not, what the hell was there for me to say?

An old man on his knees, spying through a keyhole? *Quelle*

horreur! But did she know who was in the cabin? She must have realized, obviously, that there was someone. But was she aware of what was going on?

Before I could work that one out, the smile widened and she spoke again.

'Come – why not enjoy yourself and be comfortable at the same time?' She held out a hand. Dumbly, I took it and allowed myself to be led towards the companionway.

The door of the first cabin we passed now stood ajar. She opened it and pushed me inside. The lighting was very dim. The only illumination there was filtered through a porthole from the street lamps on the embankment above. I made out a desk, a chair, built-in lockers with brass fittings which gleamed through the gloom, and a low bunk against the wall separating the cabin from Shirley's.

Brigitte Dubois eased the door shut and moved towards the bunk, the corded hem of the hessian dress rasping against the polished wood floor. She gestured towards the wall. It was heavily panelled, with a carved frieze at the upper level. 'If you stand on the bunk,' she said in a low voice, 'you'll see that the two rams' heads, one at each end of the frieze, conceal small spyholes with a splendid view of next door.'

I stared at her.

'You take the left one; I'll have the right,' she said. She lifted the hem of her dress and climbed stiffly onto the bunk.

'Good Christ,' I croaked, finding my voice at last, 'you're not saying . . . I mean you don't . . . that is to say, you're not telling me that you too actually—?'

'That I like watching? *Mais oui – bien sûr, moi aussi je suis voyeuse.* Certainly I share your – shall we say specialized – tastes. If you look the way I do, it's much easier, and much quicker, than hanging around waiting for some uncouth type to ask you out on a date.'

'You're one of us!' I breathed. 'But, dear lady, my newfound friend, that is the most marvellous, the most wonderful discovery! I can see we shall have . . . a great deal in common.'

'Undoubtedly, *cher Monsieur* – but for the moment confine yourself to what you can see here!' She held out a hand. I took it and climbed up beside her on the bunk.

The spyhole was virtually invisible among the intricacies of the carving. I had to explore with my fingers before I found it – within the open mouth beneath the ram's nose. But it afforded an admirable view of the brightly-lit cabin beyond.

We stood on that bunk, the two of us, faces pressed to the panelling, in silent – but friendly – concentration on the scene. Fom time to time the mattress creaked, as the quickening of our breaths transferred itself to the muscles of thighs, calves and finally heels.

The next cabin was a replica of the one we were in, with the bunk against the far wall.

Shirley stood on it, facing us, the booted legs spread wide. Curnow, minus his jacket now, knelt upright on the edge, facing her crotch. His fingers, hooked into the waistband of the red knickers, were slowly pulling the loose silk sheath down over her shapely hips, revealing the sudden pale tuft of pubic hair speared above a glistening cunt, down over the thighs . . . and then over the suddenly closed black suede as she drew in her legs to step out of the undergarment . . .

The boots, one after the other, draped themselves over Curnow's shoulders. He was supporting her, sitting there with her pussy just below his chin. His hands rose to grasp her hips and his face was lowered into her loins. He began – we supposed: we could only see the back of his head – to slaver and suck.

Shirley's breasts began to shiver. She held them, head tilted back, mouth open, fingering erect nipples with forefingers and thumbs.

After a while Curnow lifted her away and laid her on the bunk. She had one leg on the floor, the other, knee bent, splayed against the wall. He sat on the edge of the mattress, leaning over her – and this time we could see the gaping lips of her cunt, spread wide by his marauding fingers, the dark vault of her inner flesh lapped by his busy tongue. As his lips closed over the clitoral bud, a tremor shook the alabaster swell of Shirley's belly. I heard a slight exclamation, rapidly choked off, from further along the panelling to my right.

Soon after that, Shirley herself sat up and loosened Curnow's necktie. She fingered open – and then off – his white shirt as he played in turn with her breasts. He stood up to let her unbuckle his belt and open his fly. She pushed his dark trousers down to his knees and then slowly dragged white Y-fronts over his muscular hips.

Curnow's cock – thick, dark, purple-headed and heavily veined – sprang free. It was clearly stiff as a plank and hard as ironwood. Still sitting, she lowered her head and took it in her mouth.

When the blonde hair tumbled forward and momentarily hid her face and his thrust-out pelvis, I risked a swift question. 'Does she know she's being watched?' I asked Brigitte.

I heard a soft laugh. 'What do you think?' she whispered. 'Of course she does. That's an essential part of the turn-on for her!'

I nodded. Just as I thought. Just as I had hoped. Shirley would be an invaluable . . . accomplice.

By this time both the lovers had been aroused – maybe for different reasons – to a fever-pitch of desire. Twitching with excitement, shuddering with lewd thrills as their hands roved and probed and stroked and milked, they heaved on the bed with threshing limbs, the girl's head flaying wildly from side to side as Curnow's buttocks clenched and he thrust under her expert manipulations.

Finally they rolled off the bunk and he spread her legs lasciviously wide. She lay on the floor, breasts heaving and hair fanned out, splaying the inflamed lips of her own cunt with both hands. It was then that Curnow literally threw himself on her, plunging his great prick furiously in as her mouth flew open in a stifled scream.

Impaled as securely as a butterfly on a display board, she arched up skewered hips to meet his powerful thrusts. His hands were beneath her backside; hers clawed red weals from his back.

As smoothly as a glass-cased machine in an exhibition, they began to fuck.

I glanced at my fellow voyeur. So far I had resisted the

temptation to suggest that maybe we just might . . . well, perhaps help each other? In one way . . . or another?

But no. Better not. I could see that the hessian had been hoisted waist-high, that both my companion's hands were hidden.

I unzipped my fly and took out my rigid cock. Eyes pressed hard to the hidden spyholes as our subjects heaved and bucked, both of us began to wank.

PART THREE

A Case for the Corset

8

Suzanne Towers was sharing a buffet lunch with David
Preckner and Roger Curnow in a ritzy West End bar called
the Captain's Cabin, at basement level in a side street
between Haymarket and Lower Regent Street. The décor –
panelled walls with fishing nets and portholes – could have
been borrowed from Brigitte Dubois' houseboat in Chelsea,
but the cold counter presided over by a genial giant complete
with white smock and chef's tall headpiece, was strictly West
End. The three plates balanced on their small corner table
were brimming with paper-thin rolls of York Ham, cold cuts
of duck breast and rare beef and an appetizing selection of
fresh salads. Suzanne alone had opted for Scotch salmon
still tepid from the fish kettle, with a Béarnaise sauce and
slices of avocado and cucumber.

They were waiting for the coffee when she raised her glass
of Chablis to each of the men in turn and said: 'Delicious!
Now, talking of sex . . .'

'Were we?' Preckner said. 'Talking of sex, I mean. In any
case I'm always ready for that.'

'In the publicity and promotion business,' Suzanne told
him, 'one has to be ready – indeed eager – to talk about it
any time. Or all the time. What do you think I'm wearing
under this?' She glanced down at the neat, waisted suit in
black barathea which showed off her shape so well.

'You tell us,' Curnow said. 'It's much more exciting that
way.'

'Charcoal tights with a plain uplift bra,' she said. 'But I
have a chance to trail the new mag this evening, and I need
frills and frou-frou. I want the sexiest undies you have, David
dear.'

'From the collection, you mean? But they're only

71

prototypes. They're not for sale yet.'

'To borrow, sweetie, not buy. And I promise I'll undress before anything indecent occurs.'

'Sweetie yourself, I'm not entirely sure I'm with you,' Preckner said genially.

Suzanne reached for the wine bottle. 'Do I have to spell it out for you?' she asked, pouring into the men's glasses and then her own. 'My date tonight is with a columnist – I'm not going to tell you who – and five gets you ten we shall probably end up in bed together. If we do, I shall undoubtedly remove my clothes first. And if the last of these happens to be a particularly sensational set of undies, he's going to notice, isn't he? And he's going to comment – I shall see to that. When he does, I shall treat him to the spiel I'm working on: how there's a great demand for a swing back to more feminine lingerie. And then – surprise, surprise! – I'll feed him a trailer plugging this splendid magazine, angled in that direction, which is about to hit the streets. If that doesn't rate at least four column inches, my name's Marjorie Proops.'

Preckner inclined his head, smiling. 'Smart,' he said. 'Which model do you want?'

'Either the white lace-up basque with the frilled blue panties, or the semi-transparent black number with the slit legs and lace midriff. I'll drop by your showroom later this afternoon to choose the one I look best in.'

'Sold – or rather lent – to the lady with printer's ink on her eyebrows,' Preckner said.

'There's only one thing.' Curnow sounded dubious. 'Suppose he *doesn't* notice? If I was the bloody columnist, I'd be so feverishly eager to get you into that bed that I wouldn't see what you wore, even if it was on fire!'

'Watch it, Curnow,' the girl said. 'One day, if I'm in need, I may want to hold you to that!'

'My pleasure,' Curnow said.

The journalist's name was Aidan Carriage. His column graced the leader page of the *Globe* – the wittiest, most go-ahead, of the quality Sundays. They met in the old Press Club, near the bombed-out husk of the Wren church beside the Reuter newsagency building in Fleet Street.

Suzanne turned every drunken head at the bar when she came in. She was wearing a slinky red velvet cocktail dress which, despite the thickness of the plush velour, looked as much sprayed-on as the thinnest of satins or silks. The dress, knee-length and halter-necked, left her back bare almost to the waist. With its emphasis on sculptured shoulders and smooth, darkly tanned arms, it succeeded in making her trim body both voluptuous and compact. With it she wore high-heeled sling-back sandals in gold kid and a heavy gold chain on her left wrist.

With the black hair falling in soft waves to her shoulders and her wide brown eyes, she looked quite ravishing. Carriage was entranced. 'Fabulous!' he enthused as soon as she had taken off her duster coat. 'Really marvellous. I could eat you!'

'Later,' she said, the laugh warm and friendly without being coarse. 'But first you have to eat food. You promised me dinner, remember.'

'We'll go to the White Tower in Percy Street,' he said. 'With that bronzed skin and those slumbrous eyes, you're a natural for moussaka, shishkebab and the adoration of obsequious Greek waiters!' He shook his head. 'You look sensational.'

'I'm afraid the global effect may be a little tarty,' Suzanne confessed. 'But, brother, you ain't seen nothing yet!'

'I can't wait,' the columnist said.

'You'll have to. At least until after the second brandy,' she told him.

The second brandy was in fact served in Carriage's apartment in St Paul's Church Yard, where the coffee was less good than the thick Turkish brew poured from copper pans in the restaurant, but the chairs were more comfortable.

The seductive brunette lazed in a deep-buttoned leather number with one leg, shoeless, drawn up and just enough thigh showing to reveal that she wore stockings rather than tights. She was cradling the big brandy balloon in both hands, forearms and elbows peach-smooth against the dark, overstuffed arms of the chair.

Carriage stood by the turntable of a hi-fi complex. Ella Fitzgerald was singing 'Miss Otis Regrets' in a low, husky voice. He held the bottle of Carlos Primera in one hand, his glass in the other.

He was a tall man, perhaps marginally on the wrong side of forty, but his dark, handsome face, lined across the forehead and on either side of a mouth always ready to smile, could have been any age. He strode lightly across the room now – most of his moves were elegant, if a trifle studied – and splashed a measure of the dark Spanish brandy into Suzanne's balloon. 'Not exactly doing myself a favour,' he said. 'You told me after the second . . . and here I am, making the damned drink last longer! Still, it allows *me* more time to appreciate and admire the outer charms of sexy Suzy.'

She smiled up at him. 'If I'd known I'd be with such an eager Aidan,' she said, 'maybe I'd have stipulated three! But I have to remember I'm driving home.'

'What do you mean, driving home?' Carriage pretended to be vexed. 'You said later; you definitely promised: after the second brandy. You even tempted me, you said I'd seen nothing—'

'Nothing *yet*! I was stalling; I didn't specify this very night. You'd threatened to eat me, after all.' Suzanne grinned. 'I know we're carnivores . . . but I didn't realize you'd turn out to be as carnal as this.' She raised the glass and drained her brandy.

The columnist reached down a hand, closed strong fingers over her wrist, and pulled her gently to her feet.

They stood close together. She stared boldly into his eyes. A slight smile curved her lips.

'My God, Suzy, I can't keep my hands off you!' Carriage said hoarsely. He reached out both hands – the bottle and glass had already gone – and drew her towards him.

He crushed her lithe body against him, one hand on the cool curve of her bare back, the other clenched over the tight velvet swell of her bottom, urging her hips and pelvis forward, jamming her slender, pliant form against his belly, against the hardness at his loins.

Her breasts, swathed closely in the svelte material, were

squashed against his chest. She was breathing rather fast now, hands resting lightly on his broad shoulders. Carriage lowered his head and kissed her fiercely on the mouth.

Suzanne's whole body tensed, tight as the string on a drawn bow.

Beneath the red velvet, Carriage could feel the compressed mounds of flesh rise and fall. Long fingers slid from his shoulders to cradle the back of his head, his nape.

The kiss lasted a long time. Breath snorted in their nostrils as the two tongues probed, explored, wrestled hotly in the wet caverns of their mouths. By the time they drew apart, both of them were trembling.

Abruptly, the columnist released his grip and spun Suzanne swiftly round so that her back was to him. Reaching both arms around her, he cupped his hands around the breasts swelling out the halter neck, forcing her body hard against his chest, thrusting his hips forward so that his rigid penis ground into the gap between her buttocks.

Suzanne caught her breath as she felt the long, hard outline bore into her soft flesh . . . and her hands flew up to wrap over his, pressing them harder to her breasts.

A moment later she gave another small gasp. Without diminishing the pressure of his loins, Carriage had released a hand to untie the fastening of the halter, allowing the top of the velvet to fall forward over his remaining grip and her own.

To be half dressed only above the waist of the garment was no part of Suzanne's plan. Quickly, she twisted away, thrust the dress down over her hips, and stepped out of it. She turned to face him.

Carriage stared at her. 'Christ!' he said.

The underwear set was impressive – and suggestive – enough.

In fact she had chosen neither of the models she cited to David Preckner. The one she had chosen was even sexier.

The low-backed bra was strapless. The deep, self-supporting cups curved wide strips of material with a leopardskin design over the upper slopes of the breasts, and these were replaced – just above the visible nipples and supporting the full weight of each globe – by inserts of semi-transparent black tulle. The leopardskin, cut in at the waist to make the breasts look fuller, then continued downwards. But only as far as the top of the belly, where it arched steeply to form a high combined suspender belt, leaving the lower belly, complete with the centred navel, bare.

The long black frontal garter-strips of the belt stretched dizzily from hip level to the tight-drawn black lace tops of Suzanne's dark silk stockings. A small diaphanous panel of the tulle united the lowest curves of the breasts and continued as far as the centre of the suspender-belt arch.

The net effect of these three gauzy panels was to emphasize the satin quality of the wearer's skin and at the same time suggest an arrow pointing at the naked belly and the tiny briefs below.

These, little more than an elaborate G-string really, comprised flounces of tulle dipping – below the straps of the suspender-belt – from hips to crotch, where the material just sheathed the pubic hair and mons, leaving a final lozenge of leopardskin to hide the cunt itself.

'Do you like my smalls? Do they impress you?' Suzanne was smiling. The columnist still stared.

'Like?' he said huskily at last. 'That's something of an understatement, sweetie. They are not far short of the utterly sensational!'

'Good. I had a faint suspicion that they might be – unveiled – so I hoped they might please.'

'Not exactly the word I would choose,' Carriage said. 'I've only one regret.'

'Which is?'

'They're so damned pretty that I can't bring myself to rip them off, the way they demand.'

'Ah.'

'Would I be too . . . that is to say, would you mind if I was rude enough, and personal enough, to ask where in hell, these days, one can buy something like that?'

'At the moment you can't. They're designed, and made by friends of mine. But they're hoping to market a whole

76

collection soon. Probably with a new glossy magazine tie-up.'

'This I must see,' Carriage enthused. 'You must tell me about it. If you can, that is.'

'I can give you an inclusive, if you want.'

He smiled. 'That should be worth half a dozen column inches of anyone's piece.'

'Later,' Suzanne said. 'At the moment, the piece that interests me' – a rapid glance at the journalist's bulging crotch – 'is about eight column inches of quite a different sort!'

'That's my girl!' Carriage said. He picked her up and moved her bodily into his bedroom.

But it was in fact not until quite a while later that she allowed him to undress her fully. The columnist, nevertheless, was sufficiently entranced not to insist. Finally, it was she who started to strip him.

There is something particularly intimate – almost conspiratorial – in the feel and sight of a woman unravelling a necktie . . . first the pull on the strand above the knot, to loosen it; then the slow, busy-fingered feeding of the wide end through the knot, pulling it free; and lastly the smooth but unyielding caress of the doubled silk against the collar band as the tie is drawn away.

Suzanne made it almost into an art form that night, manipulating the strip of shiny material as if it was a musical instrument, her delicate fingers sensitive yet relentless. Her removal of the tie, and after it the shirt and string vest, had about them the inevitability, the remorseless progression, of the good fuck – and the climax which each of them knew must follow.

Carriage was too fascinated with the Preckner creation to interfere. His attention was concentrated at first on the black tulle brassière insets and the dark haloes of nipple and areola dimly visible behind, sharpening to a breath-catching thrill as he stretched out eager hands to take the full, warm weight of the breasts in his palms.

It was only when the girl bent her head to suck the hardening buds of his own nipples up through the hairs on his chest that he gazed down past the dark waves of hair to feast his eyes on the lower half of the bra-and-belt combination.

The long, tight lines of the garter straps, and the stretched black lace of the stockings they clipped, extended the pale columns of Suzanne's thighs as far as her padded hips . . . and emphasized in some subtle fashion the vulnerability of the leopardskin mons cushioned tightly between them so far below.

It was then that Carriage abandoned his passive rôle and took a more active part in the scene.

Excited nipples burning and cock thrust hard against the restriction of his trousers, he dropped suddenly to his knees, snaking hands up behind her to clasp the cool globes of her naked bottom. He thrust his lean face forcefully into the diamond of nude flesh between the steeply arched suspender belt and the downward swoop of the flounced briefs, tonguing the navel and belly as he drew her pelvis towards him.

Suzanne gasped, holding Carriage's head against her with both hands, feeling the muscles tremor in the creases at the top of her thighs. On the left-hand side of her neck, just below the jawline, a pulse was racing.

She felt the columnist's hands on her belly now. His fingers were hooked over the dipped waistband of the tulle-and-leopard briefs, knuckles grazing her heated skin. Very slowly, he drew the gauzy flounces down, over the gentle swell of belly, towards that spotted lozenge below the sudden wiry appearance of pubic hair.

He tilted back his head between her hands, staring up at her intense face. She smiled. 'All right,' she said softly. 'But only the slip – and leave the suspenders fastened.'

Within seconds, the briefs were on the floor and her legs were free. Still on his knees, Carriage shoved her towards the low divan that took up the centre of the room. She sat down abruptly as the mattress caught her behind the knees, her stockinged legs spread wide.

He was already between them, his avid gaze homed in on her lewdly displayed genital area. Somehow the matted thatch of black hair and the folds of coral flesh gashing it, obscenely exposed between the pale swell of belly and thighs, seemed doubly, trebly, salacious among the complex of artificial materials tightly webbing the nakedness above and below.

The leopardskin lozenge had been moist when he stripped it away. Now Carriage saw that the fleshy whorls of Suzanne's labia were glistening as her cunt flowered open. He buried his face between her thighs and fastened his mouth to the hot, wet, hungry depths gaping there. She crossed dark legs over his back as his tongue, lasciviously probing, speared up into her.

Later, feeling all at once absurd with his lower half still clothed and his bursting cock trapped, Carriage withdrew from her and rose to his feet, unbuckling his belt. She sat up on the bed and unzipped his fly. The tool she drew out was unusually thin, but very long, hard as a rock, and equipped with an oversize head. Reaching out, she closed her mouth over the pulsating tip.

Softly crooning his joy, he stood there shaking, his head thrown back while her closed lips and burning hands milked his hardness and her tongue swirled over, under and around his aching glans.

But it was only minutes later – each of them keyed up now to a pitch of excitement that kept every nerve in each of their bodies screaming towards their loins – that their mutual lust took over and they were unable to hold themselves in any longer.

Suzanne fell back on the bed with a small cry, drawing up her legs and fingering wide the splayed lips of her cunt with both hands. Carriage threw himself on top of her, plunging the long, stiff shaft of his prick straight between them, powering his way up into the secret clasp of her belly as she arched greedily up to meet his hectic thrusts.

The climax when it came – and it wasn't all that far away – left them both shaking, half laughing, half sobbing with the relief that had lifted them so far above the solid earth.

Some time after that – it was before their second fuck,

when at last she had permitted him to strip her completely – some time after that Carriage looked out through the open window at the moonlit bulk of the great dome of St Paul's. He was holding Suzanne's naked breasts in his hands. Shaking his head, he laughed softly to himself.

'What is it?' she murmured sleepily.

'Just a thought,' he said. 'If Sir Christopher Wren had seen these . . . that bloody cathedral would sure as hell have been designed with *two* towers!'

9

Tom Silver wasn't sure exactly why he had made the pass at Gladys. Sure, she was voluptuous, she looked sexy, her auburn hair somehow suggested the private area between her curvy thighs. Most importantly, for him at any rate, she was *there*.

And so was he. But nobody else was.

Just the same, was it really smart, so boldly to try and make the workshop supervisor of his latest client – and on first acquaintance at that?

Tom was the youngest account executive at the high-powered Winston-Rogers advertising agency, and Preckner Gowns was his first important client. From what he had seen of the product he was to push – the sort of lingerie you would normally find on under-the-shelf magazines in a Soho sex shop – finding editorial cooperation should be a doddle. And picture display on the fashion pages should be even easier – providing he didn't use up all the more outrageous models to illustrate the advertising campaign he was drafting.

Gladys Carter had arrived at the studio where the first photo session was to be organized with a hamper of Shirley Sabbath's creations soon after midday. Silver was already there – a tall, lean, dark man with a fringe of beard that did not, as he hoped, make him look older but only emphasized his youth. It was when he was helping her carry in the load from the taxi that he became aware of the not entirely subdued sensuality that emanated from her as insidiously as perfume behind a feminine ear or music from a distant room. It was raining heavily and she wore a silver rubberized showerproof, tightly belted at the waist, that subtly indicated with every move she made the warm and fleshy masses shifting beneath it. Tom, at the time, was very deeply into flesh.

It was with eager eyes, therefore, that he approved the tight green sweater with its outlined breasts and nipples, the generous backside in its equally tight black skirt, when she took off the raincoat and shook the drops from its shining surface.

It was when they were hanging up the underclothes on rails, in the dressing room the model girls were to use later that afternoon, that the first move was made – accidentally, it seemed to him. Gladys turned unexpectedly away from the rail, reaching for the hamper, which stood on a table behind them. As she swung around, one heavy, sweatered breast brushed hard against his upper arm. It could have been coincidental, of course, but it sent unmistakable thrills coursing through Tom's body. 'Oh, sorry!' he blurted automatically.

'Don't be,' Gladys said. She smiled, laying a hand on his arm. 'Not bruised, I hope?'

'By that?' He blushed, glancing at the sweater. 'You must be joking!'

'I never joke when it's a question of contact,' Gladys said.

It was not until later, when they were back in the studio, that the next move was made.

The way Tom had arranged it, the décor he had used looked more like a set for a TV sitcom than a photographer's eyrie. Gladys saw filled bookshelves, a dining table with staid chairs, an open roll-top desk littered with papers, worn easy chairs. In a separate corner, the counter, cupboards and sinks of a modern kitchen were suggested.

'That's right,' he said when she remarked on the set dressing. 'No velvet drapes, no satin cushions strewn, no romantic flats in the background for this session. In sets like that, lingerie like this looks, well, normal. More daring than usual perhaps, but expected. I want to emphasize the fact that this collection is *extra*-ordinary, *ab*normal and totally *un*expected – by showing the garments in conventional, rather dull, surroundings. Contrast is the name of the game.'

'It's an idea,' Gladys admitted. 'No exteriors?'

He grinned. 'Only when the contrast is more marked still. No shots with mannequins under Etruscan arches in front of classical columns, beneath colonnades. We hope to get a standing-room-only London bus, with every female passenger dressed in nothing but our underclothes. And the sexiest model about to drop off the step at a crowded fare stage in Park Lane.'

'Is that the most daring number?'

'Not really. That one calls for us to be as daring as the girls – if we get away with it.'

'For instance?'

'It's outside Buck House. You know the way the sentries stand there, all gorgeous in their scarlet coats and busbies? And you know the way, every few minutes, they stamp their feet, turn about, and march a few paces away, then turn, stamp again, and return to their sentry-boxes? Well, we aim to stop a car in front of the gates with two girls and a photographer inside – deep focus so that the Palace shows up. As soon as the two soldiers march, we decant the models, each in one of our scantiest outfits, have them fall in step behind, as close as they can get, march a few paces . . . then smile please, click! – and we're away as fast as we can make it. An imperial collection, see!'

'Won't the soldiers object – chase the girls away, put them in handcuffs or something?'

'Tourists are always being photographed beside them – when they're still, at attention. They're not allowed to react, to make the least sign that they notice. I guess it's the same when they're on the move.'

'Well, bully for you,' Gladys said. 'I hope you do get away with it – and no Monopoly!'

'No . . . monopoly?'

' "Go to jail",' she quoted from the famous board game. ' "Go straight to jail. Do not pass *GO* on the way; do not collect money"!'

'Oh, *Monopoly*!' He laughed. And then, staring at her face and looking suddenly away: 'The hell with bloody underwear. You have the sexiest, most sensual, lower lip I ever saw in my life!'

Gladys smiled. She hadn't really been angling for the advertising man; just keeping her hand in, playing the game in her usual manner, a matter of course. But she had a strong conviction that, whatever the situation, the young should always be encouraged. 'I know,' she said calmly. 'Or so they tell me. You want a taste?'

'A taste? I want a feast!' said Tom, all at once brash and bold. He moved towards her. How old was she? Thirty at least. Maybe thirty-five. But this was an experience in no way to be missed . . .

She stood there, still smiling.

She waited, perfectly relaxed, hands by her sides, feet apart, firmly encased breasts thrusting out the green wool in a fashion that had Tom's senses suddenly reeling.

The stance stretched the skirt over her generous hips, underlining the two horizontal creases framing the curve at the lower part of her belly.

Tom swallowed. He was not normally timid or slow to make an advance with girls of his age, but this was different; this – he knew it at once – was experience. He was facing an Older Woman. The hesitation which froze him momentarily was a less a lack of positive desire than the fear that his own inexperience might render him gauche or clumsy in her eyes.

The eyes regarded him in a quizzical, near-challenging way.

Her mouth was partly open, that full lower lip moist and glistening. But she remained immobile, patiently anticipating . . . whatever was going to happen. Clearly the next move was up to him.

He drew a deep breath. Okay, challenge accepted. Silver the scalp-hunter, the Don Juan of SW6, was in the saddle! He moved hastily forward.

The moment before he touched her, Gladys tilted her auburn head slightly back, offering him the lower lip still widened in that inviting smile.

He lowered his head and closed his own lips over it, sucking the nubile crimson flesh into his mouth. A warm exhalation fanned his cheek. He realized she had been holding her breath.

Now her relaxation was tangible as well as visible. The whole complex weight of her body subsided, almost drooped, against him. There was a knee between his thighs. Her breasts, on which he had instinctively homed when he moved in, rested heavily in his hands.

She twisted her head, the knowing mouth sliding, so that the kiss was all at once mutual – lips working, tongues penetrating in the hot, wet fusion cramming them together. The game was under way now. And Gladys was an expert and enthusiastic player.

The young advertising man could feel his heart hammering against the softly cushioned flesh plastered to his chest. There was pressure too – subtle but distinct – at the base of his belly.

His cock, which oddly enough he had been unaware of until now, manifested itself suddenly, strongly, down there. An infinitesimal gyration of the womanly hips clamped to him rolled the hard and aching shaft across the sensitive swell above his pubic hair.

He was breathing hard now, excitedly aware of that too. Pulses in his two wrists beat against the bulged weight of the breasts he held.

Once more, dizzily, as if he was watching someone else, Tom registered the difference. Several of the young girls he had made were equally enthusiastic as this mature redhead. But the expert and practised behaviour of – what was her name? Gladys? – even before she had made any overt moves herself, confirmed his impression: there was a dimension here, difficult to define but unchallengeable, which put the back-seat gropings of adolescents firmly in their place.

Firmly in the wings, that was. Waiting for the prompter's cue. But Tom – arguably for the first time in his embryonic sex life – was centre-stage. And the spotlights were on maximum power!

Intoxicated by the heady thrill of sensual awareness – stimulated perhaps by the idea that he had finally been accepted into the adult league – he allowed his instincts to take over.

Deftly, decisively, he hauled the hem of the green sweater

up . . . up over the warm skin of a pliant waist, above the stiff thrust of diaphragm and ribs, over the heaving bust.

The redhead's breasts, sheathed tightly in see-through lace, fell like ripe fruit into his hands.

'Magnificent!' he breathed. 'They really are superb . . . quite the most marvellous—'

'Yes,' she interrupted lazily, rubbing the whole length of her body gently against him like a cat. 'But it seems to me that you, yourself, could well have something here to be proud of!' The knee between his legs moved upwards, pressing his thighs apart, nudging his balls – and after them his rigid cock – harder against the swell of his belly.

'So they tell me,' he mimicked, suddenly daring, boldly adult. 'You want a taste?'

Gladys laughed aloud. 'Did somebody mention a feast?' she jested. 'The studio's booked for two o'clock. Maybe it's time we – er – dressed for dinner?'

Her hands were at his waist. He felt his belt unbuckled, the strap pulled through. Suddenly the air of the studio was cool against his heated skin.

And there were cool fingers wrapped around his cock, pulling it free of shirt-tails and under-pants, out through an unzipped fly, into the open air.

And into view.

'My goodness!' Gladys said.

Silver's youthful penis was both long and thick. The distended flesh, webbed with purplish veins, was dark in colour, crowned by a pulsating, velvety head, and iron-hard. Her fingers tightened around the rigid shaft. 'I wasn't wrong,' Gladys said. 'That's a really handy . . . instrument . . . you have there, my boy! I imagine you're skilled enough in its use?'

'We endeavour to give satisfaction, ma'am,' Tom said, echoing Jeeves from P.G. Wodehouse.

'With what you have,' she said, 'that should be an automatic ten out of ten.' She reached for the hairy sac of his balls, and pulled them out too. 'The set as a whole is faultless – efficiency and design in the same smart package!' The hand grasping the cock was engaged now in a skimming,

86

feather-light caress, stroking the stretched skin up and down the tool's hardened core.

Tom caught his breath, exulting in the heady thrills searing through his nerves. If there was one technique he had learned on the rear seats of Ford Zephyrs, razor-edge Triumph saloons and even secondhand Buicks, it was how to unfasten brassières deftly, swiftly, with a single hand. With one hand still on the warm swell of lace against him, he removed the other and snaked an arm around the busty redhead to avail himself of this expertise.

The cups of the bra loosened, but did not fall away. Below the strap there was a vertical zipper. He undid that too.

The wanking hand, which had imperceptibly, insidiously accelerated its to and fro caress, suddenly halted. With a final squeeze of the shaft it was withdrawn.

Getting out of a tight skirt, especially for a generously built person, particularly if the undressing is in the hands of someone else, can never really be an elegant, still less a sexy, manoeuvre. To avoid the clumsiness and drop in sexual tension this could provoke, Gladys had pulled suddenly away. With her back abruptly turned, she got rid of the skirt in one rapid and practised movement. Swinging back, she stood before him in underwear and stockings only.

Tom could see now why the move with the brassière had not been an entire success. Below it, the black lace, zippered behind, continued to form a *guépière* or wasp-waist – and this itself, cut high to hip level, plunged down further still with diminishing width, to cover the pubic area and disappear from sight between the legs. The creation was in fact a one-piece garment – basically a modern modification of the oldfashioned cami-knicks in peach-coloured satin or silk.

Its design enabled the suspender-belt to be dispensed with, but long, detachable garter strips fell from just below the waist to the centre of the thighs, where clips, each embellished with a small red rose, hauled up dark stockings topped with the same black lace as the foundation.

The sombre, flower-patterned black lace hugging, plastered to, the creamy flesh of the full-breasted, hourglass-shaped redhead formed a picture that was seductive in the extreme.

Silver, the genitals still lewdly speared from his plundered fly, stared bemused, mouth half open and eyes shining.

'Extra!' he breathed. 'Stunning; I mean really fab!' And then, gallantly: 'The undies are pretty good too.'

'You're a nice boy,' Gladys said. 'Flattery is never wasted: remember that.'

Tom was still gazing at her. He felt much more mannish than boyish, just then – but what the hell: she was The Older Woman; if she wanted to play maternal, that was a game he didn't mind joining in. There were always things you could learn!

'It's out of the catalogue, one of . . . ours?' he said. 'The lingerie, I mean?'

She nodded. 'There are others that are sexier, more frou-frou, plushier,' she said. 'But this is the model I prefer. For me.'

'Hard for me to believe there could be anything sexier,' Tom said, fondling his cock.

She acknowledged the compliment with a half smile. 'Whatever happens,' she continued, 'you don't ever actually have to get out of the damned thing. Whatever happens.'

He glanced involuntarily at the tightly sheathed crotch.

'If one's feeling amorous,' Gladys explained, 'the bra top – as you found out – can be undone separately. But even little girls have to pee sometimes, and that – along with other . . . necessities . . . has also been taken care of.' One of her hands – nails green as the discarded sweater, he noticed – darted down below her belly. Unseen among the whorled pattern of the lace, the crotch too was split by a zipper.

Her fingers and thumb moved.

The garment's genital strip gaped open. Framed by its dark edges, pink flesh and wiry hair thrust themselves suddenly, obscenely, into view.

Standing there with her feet apart, the bra cups now held up to cover her breasts, pussy hairs and moist folds of labia exposed between white thighs and black lace, Gladys was just about the most lascivious sight Tom Silver had ever seen.

He had always found the contrast between shapely, tender limbs, sensitive skin and that hairy genital gash emblematic of the carnal, animal quality of female lust that was normally hidden. And for him, therefore, all the more productive of lecherous thoughts.

But now, this time, the hot, wet maw splayed between slender, scented flesh and the clasp of tightly fashioned man-made material, this was something else!

Silver had never felt such an overwhelming thrill of naked desire, such a compulsion to touch, to hold, to plunge and penetrate. He started forward.

Gladys was already on the move. The cups falling away now from her bare and bobbing breasts, she was hurrying towards the photographer's set at the far end of the big studio. 'Come on,' she called over her shoulder, suddenly bossy. 'It's ten past one already, and we have to be decent well before two!'

'If I say I can't wait,' he panted, hastening behind, 'it's no more than the bloody truth!'

Gladys was crossing the set. 'Mercifully,' she said, 'you thought of adding this old sofa to your contrast décor – the floor's probably dusty and the table would be too hard!'

The sofa was worn. But it was long, and there were no arms attached at either end of the back rail. She lay on it with one darkly sheathed leg touching the floor, arms crossed behind her head, and the big breasts thrust palely up above the black lace.

Tom was struggling to get out of his trousers. 'No, no. Stay dressed,' Gladys called. 'I like a spot of contrast myself. You in a suit and me in a split-crotch foundation – don't they call that the spice of life?'

'It's certainly variety!' Tom agreed. He grinned, completely at ease now with this lazy, sexy, voluptuous enthusiast. 'Give us a bit more time too.'

'How's that again?'

'It won't take us so long – to "make ourselves decent before two",' he quipped.

'Then why waste time now?' Gladys rejoined. 'Come on:

bring that super toy over. I want to feel it inside me – right in, right up – this very minute!'

Holding it carefully in one hand, he brought it over.

She was lying fully back now, both knees drawn up with the legs lewdly spread. Between the tilted slopes of her thighs, her hands lay flat on the lower curve of her belly, the forefingers holding the edges of the crotch zip – and the secret flesh obscenely exposed – open wide.

Tom had one knee on the edge of the sofa. Holding the hard, throbbing length of his big cock at the ready, he supported himself with the other hand on the cushioned rail and lowered himself fast. He plunged . . . deep down between doubled-up calves and tight-drawn stockings, down past the flesh of canted thighs, aiming the cock-head at the lacy gusset so invitingly split.

Gladys squirmed her hips on the surface of the stuffed sofa to position her cunt in line with the advancing shaft. The moment the velvety tip touched the moistly glistening folds pouting through the splayed crotch of her foundation, she arched up to meet Tom's thrust. Craning her head, chin on chest, she watched the veined and rigid staff progressively vanish beyond her raised mons. The hard, hot length glided into her, forcing apart her secret flesh, wedging itself wetly into her belly until she was skewered by the entire pulsating shaft, right up to the hairy base.

'God!' she moaned. 'Ooh, *Christ* . . . that's so goood! Give it to me, lover: let me have it all, every exciting inch!'

Tom was in a daze of sensual joy. Sunk in the heady ecstasy of warm woman scent, he gasped aloud as the super-sensitive nerves of his aching cock were swallowed, engulfed in the burning, softly sliding heat of clasping muscles and dilated inner flesh.

Dipping deep, withdrawing until only the pulsing, acorned tip remained inside, then plunging hotly again, he shafted his cock powerfully in and out of her as she thrust and subsided in time with his pistoned strokes.

His hands clenched on the resilient meat of her bare breasts; she kept hers trapped between their heaving bellies, exulting in the feel of the greased cock ploughing into her pussy, fingering the shaft and balls speared from the open front of his trousers.

Clasped together on the long sofa, Tom's weight partly supported on his elbows, they settled into a long, almost lazy, rocking rhythm, a perfect example of the classic fuck. No point, with time so restricted, messing about with changes in position: why try to improve on perfection? Even the oral approach was forgotten in the electric thrill of their splendidly matched coupling. Gladys's mouth was open; his hot lips clamped over hers; their tongues wrestled. It was enough.

Unlike many young – and older – men, Tom was lucky. Or maybe just skilled. He had schooled himself to the point where he could control his impulses, restrain the genital reflex and continue fucking on and on . . . right to the moment when at last he was seized by the relentless orgasmic surge from which there is no return, no stop-button left to press. But that could be a long time coming!

For a timeless era, there was no sound in the empty studio but the rustle of garments on the hard sofa, an occasional creak, the labouring of breath and a wordless obbligato of groans and croons interspersed with stifled exclamations of joy and half-voiced endearments. The minute hand of the clock on the studio wall jerked down toward the half-hour at the lowest part of the face, started remorselessly to climb the third quadrant. The wheels of passing traffic hissed greasily on the rain-wet street outside. Somewhere above guttering gurgled and dripped.

The moment when it came was inevitable. It had announced itself. They were expecting it. Their lovemaking had attained that point, that zenith of sated lust and fulfilled desire, when anything else is unthinkable, inconceivable. They welcomed the breaking of the wave with ecstasy.

It swamped them both at the same instant. Tom reared his upper half with a shout of joy as his great cock jerked convulsively in its hot clasp of flesh and he spurted the proof of his release far up into the redhead's trembling belly. Gladys's whole body was tremored, shaken and finally contorted with delight as she sobbed and threshed beneath him.

By the time the small cries and murmurs of satisfaction had died away and the breathing had returned almost to normal, the hands of the clock stood at ten minutes before two.

'You should take out a patent for this, you know,' Gladys said, stuffing Tom's limp, heavy penis back inside his trousers. 'You could commercialize it, sell replicas in sex shops all over!'

Tom shook his head. 'It's only a prototype,' he said. 'I'd need a lot more fieldwork, laboratory testing, continued experience, before it was ready for public use.' He smiled. 'If you agreed, of course.'

Gladys patted the wet shaft. 'Try me,' she said.

'Love to, love to. But tell me . . . how can you . . . I mean, aren't you married or something?'

'Of course I'm married,' Gladys said. 'You don't think I can pick up someone like you every day of the week? Variety's fine but there has to be permanence too.'

'Yes, but I mean how—?'

'My husband's First Officer on a cross-channel ferry. By the time he gets down to Dover, makes two return trips a day, and drives back to London . . . well, it leaves me fairly free,' Gladys said.

'Perhaps he has another wife in Calais?'

'Yes, I saw *The Captain's Paradise* too. Alec Guinness, wasn't it? If he has . . . good luck!'

She moved away from him. There was a sound of car engines and slamming doors outside.

The team arrived in two taxis and Raymond Large's Rolls-Royce – Preckner, Curnow, Luke, Shirley, the wardrobe mistress, the photographer and Silver's art director from the advertising agency, along with four stunning model girls.

'I like the set,' the art director said to Tom. 'The décor, all that crappy furniture, the kitchen. Good idea.'

'Glad you approve,' Tom said.

'You must have worked like a bloody slave, though.

Getting up at screech, I suppose, and hurrying through the downpour before it was light?'

'Not really,' said Tom, who had in fact dressed the set the previous day. 'What makes you think I was in such a hurry?'

'You forgot to do up your flies, old boy,' the director said.

10

The studio was suddenly very crowded. On set the photographer was experimenting with the lighting. His camera, an oldfashioned Rolleiflex, was mounted on a tall tripod just behind the sofa. 'Much the best, much the quickest way to arrive at a good composition,' he told David Preckner, 'when you can look straight down at the viewfinder, actual neg size, instead of manhandling an SLR 35-mil up to eye level.'

Preckner smiled. 'I'll take your word for it,' he said.

The art director was hunched over a desk at the far end of the room, studying dummies of the new magazine with Luke Hornby. Curnow was discussing work schedules with Gladys; Shirley Sabbath and the elderly Raymond Large, smiling, looked as if they were exchanging secrets – and from the dressing-room, where the wardrobe mistress was checking the fit on her four models, came an excited burble of female chatter, punctuated by an occasional shriek of laughter.

The only absentee from the team was Brigitte Dubois, the French typographer and make-up specialist. 'Why waste her time?' the art director said with a shrug when Tom Silver pointed this out. 'She can't do a bloody thing about page design until she's seen my pictures.'

The four girls had been very carefully chosen – no question of simply ordering a mixed quartet from an agency. 'Among other qualities,' the photographer confided to Curnow, 'each of them is, or can be – shall we say accessible? – given the fact that one's cards are played right.'

Each of them was an underwear specialist – slightly shorter, a little fuller in the figure than the hipless, phthisic beanpoles employed to show the high-fashion dress collections in London, Paris and Rome. 'Two different worlds,' Laura, the greying wardrobe mistress, told Silver. 'No dress designer would touch a girl who'd shown or been photographed for undies. Oh, my *dear*! How utterly, utterly down-market can one *be*!' She mimicked a precious, falsetto accent. 'These girls, on the other hand, model things that women actually wear. They're far enough removed from the ethereal high-fashion mannequins for clients to be able to identify. You know – ladies who *need* bras and foundations and knickers, people who can say: "Oh, that's pretty! I could see myself in that." '

Silver smiled. 'One can see where your own sympathies lie!'

'Naturally. I have a weight problem – as you can see,' Laura said.

Preckner's models had been chosen to show as wide a selection as possible of the new range. They were all approximately the same height, weight and shape, but there the similarity ended. One was a cropped-hair blonde, one a shoulder-length brunette, the third a redhead with long, straight hair to the jawline and a boyish side parting. The fourth girl was the most exotic – a beautiful brown-skinned Jamaican with fine, almost oriental, features and black hair falling nearly to her waist.

Each of them fell into the 36–24–36 size category. 'One up on the customary bust measurement,' Curnow said. 'But what the hell – the collection's supposed to be ultra-feminine and sexy with it, no?'

The models were called, respectively, Eve, Zita, Marie and Sandrine.

They were to be photographed singly, collectively, and in trios and pairs – each of them to be showing a different confection from Shirley's drawing board in every shot.

The first picture was a group pose – and the designs were so impressive that the girls' initial appearance provoked a spontaneous spatter of applause, over which Luke's deep voice could be heard murmuring: '*Very* smart! A real delight for the eye, my dear.'

Zita, the brunette, had been poured into a hip- and waist-hugging two-piece with stockings. Like Gladys's choice, this combined a lengthened bra with a suspender belt. But the bra had wide straps and a single back zipper, and the belt part arched straight into the actual suspenders, leaving the crotch to be covered by a separate brief like the lower half of a skimpy bikini. The impact of the ensemble, sexy enough in shape, derived nevertheless from the material used: lace again in a design of flowers and leaves, but in a vivid, electric, royal blue appliquéd to Shirley's favourite semi-transparent black tulle. The blue covered the self-supporting, wired bra and a central panel as far as the belt arch as well as the tight crotch triangle; the rest of the torso was sheathed by the tulle, which also formed the panty waistband and flounced above the bared backside.

Eve's cropped, almost boyish head, had been used as a contrast – a near-masculine contrast – to the glamorous, sensual and super-feminine transparency of a pale mauve negligée that was draped over a fleshy body nude except for a showgirl-style *cache-sexe* or G-string. The garment – Shirley's tongue-in-cheek sideswipe at the current unisex vogue – had a scooped-out, frilled neck-line, fastened just above the visible breasts with a cinnamon-coloured bow, and an open front falling to mid-thigh length. Short, full sleeves, heavily ruched, half hid the upper arms – and all the edges, sleeves included, were lace-trimmed with inserts of the same ribbon threaded through.

The tops of Eve's pale mauve stockings were decorated with the same lace, the same ribbon.

Sandrine's outfit – another two-fingered gesture in the unisex direction – was at the same time feminine, ultra-sexy and yet almost virginal! Basically it was also ultra-simple, being no more than a classic, loose, man-style pyjama suit. Like the oldfashioned, long-trousered, wrist-cuffed originals, it was even in striped material. But it was here that the designer's imagination played its seductive part. Stripes, yes – but same-colour stripes, alternating the opaque with the translucent. White on white, that was the effect. But solid white changing every couple of inches to see-through white – specifically chosen to highlight the dark voluptuousness of Sandrine's fleshy body partially revealed: it was this that raised the design to star status and again evoked a round of applause from the fashion specialists grouped in the studio.

Redheaded Marie, the last to appear, looked perhaps the most like a pin-up. Described at its most simple, the garment was a white basque, lace-edged, combined with a suspender belt and white stockings. But this did little to convey the physical allure of the under-garment – or indeed of its effect on the nubile redhead who wore it.

Shirley Sabbath, who had designed it, was standing with a clipboard, scribbling furiously. She was drafting a jokey description of her creation which would be passed on to Suzanne Towers . . . and was destined, eventually, to appear in Aidan Carriage's column with an introduction on the lines of 'a woman friend in the fashion business tells me'. What Shirley actually wrote was:

What is a basque? my younger readers may well ask. Their grannies say, A kind of corset. Oh, horrors! The *Oxford Dictionary* reveals: a close-fitting bodice extending from the shoulders to the waist, often with a short continuation below that level. Shades of mum and unmarried aunts again!

The Preckner basque is a corset insofar as it has laces behind, but there, apart from the fact that it trims the waist, the resemblance ends. No whaleboned stays or girdered uplift to crane sagging busts back up to reality here! No agonizing, breath-stifling vice cramping chest and waist! The only vice involved is likely to fire the enthusiasm of the gentlemen fortunate enough to set eyes on the foundation.

For Designer Shirley Sabbath's confection is certainly a sight for eyes sore with too much unisex uniformity. It's a real voyeur's delight! Especially when you see the white lace triangle teamed with it which covers only minimally in front but leaves the (excuse me!) buttocks behind virtually bare.

Fellers, there are only 272 shopping days left to Christmas. If you want to do yourself – and herself – a favour, line up and buy now!

Shirley looked up and studied the model Marie again. She was standing with her back to the designer, weight on one hip, head bent, a wing of dark red hair hiding her lean, aquiline features. Shirley shook her own head. 'Dear God,' she murmured to herself, 'sometimes I think Mrs Sabbath's favourite daughter really is on the road to sartorial success!'

The lacing on the basque was a detail – 'back interest', no more – closing the bodice no more firmly than press-studs or a zip fastener, but it emphasized the model's small waist as acutely as if the bodice had been pulled as savagely tight as a turn-of-the-century dresser could haul. The front – string-width shoulder straps and full, wired cups – was entirely in white lace, form-fitting as far as the hips to follow the dictionary definition. At this point the lace was ruffled, curling around to join thin lace panels reinforced to take the lacing at the back. The rest of the back was plain, tight white. So were the suspender straps stretching from the bottom of the basque to the near-transparent white stockings. These, with their opaque tops and startling white seams, were drawn up almost crotch-high. Framed bottom and top by these and the basque, and on either side by the rear suspender straps, the full, round, fleshy globes of Marie's buttocks were indeed almost indecently exposed. And the separation between them, once more exaggerating their tautly divided bulk, was confirmed by the wisp of white lace keeping the G-string in place, which emerged from the cleft to fan upwards and lock onto the lowest part of the basque.

Sensing Shirley's concentration, the model turned around, jerking her head to flip the lock of hair out of her eyes. Smiling, the voice low and almost raucous, she drawled: 'Not bad, eh? Playing Pygmalion, are we? The best thing is – it's even comfortable to wear!'

'Without you,' Shirley said, 'it's just a bundle of white tat hanging on a rail. So bravo, baby – and thanks!'

Across the bottom of her page, she scrawled: *Suzy – Although it's my own damned design, I simply, somehow, can't do justice to this one in words. I'll attach a pic and leave you and*

Aidan to work out whatever you think would turn on the raunchy reader – and his lady – best!

The photographer, Donald Warne-Johns, and the art director were briefing the models on the layout for the first shot. 'Forget that you're wearing glamour undies,' the photographer said. 'Or rather imagine that you're in fact fully dressed over them. You're four housewives meeting for tea in a suburban pad. I want two of you in chairs by the low table, a third, standing with a cakestand, and the last – Marie, you look the least likely to be making tea! – standing with a kettle in the kitchen corner.'

Warne-Johns retired to the tripod, shaded the horizontal, masked viewfinder with one hand, and watched the four girls take up their positions. From time to time he called out further directions. He was a tall, moustached man with the beginning of a bald patch at the back of his head and an oddly military bearing. Shirley looked at him with interest. A scalp-hunter, she had been told, the original macho stud, with a mouse wife and a foul temper if he didn't make at least half a dozen new conquests every month. Interesting, she thought wickedly, if his pride could be engineered to be the one that came before the fall!

'No, no: forget the bloody camera,' he was calling. 'Keep talking, moving; find something to gossip about. Tell jokes. You're four well-dressed, respectable ladies – we're the uncouth perverts who strip away mentally the outer garments and lust after what we imagine to be beneath!'

Eve giggled, running long hands through her cropped blonde hair. 'I had this yankee date,' she said to Zita. 'He told me this was the archie – the archetype, is it? – anyway the most typical example of American humour. There's this guy talking to a foreign tourist, and the tourist says he just got back from Iowa. And the American says, Oh, *we* pronounce it Ohio! You think this is funny?'

Zita had in fact laughed. 'It's a question of geographic stereotypes,' she said. 'In-group stuff contrasting corn-belt hicks with industrialized— oh, forget it, love.'

'Great!' Warne-Johns shouted. 'Just what I need. Now start moving around, okay?'

Legs and breasts and arms and bottoms, crammed into lace, seething in ruffles, shadowed by tulle, animated the set. The photographer shouted again, clicking and winding.

Raymond Large, eyes fixed unerringly on the four half-dressed girls, had drawn the art director aside. 'Pete Sampler,' the crew-cut, stocky professional said. 'Pete Try-anything-once Sampler. Sometimes it helps, having a name that fits. What can I do for you, squire?'

'I was wondering,' Large said carefully, 'if you were available – in a private capacity of course, but for a given fee – to arrange this kind of . . . display . . . for individual, personal clients?'

'You mean you want me to fix you up with a live show?' Sampler asked directly. 'Anything's possible, of course, but—'

'No, no.' Large coughed. 'Nothing like that. More of a – er – pageant, shall we say. A charade if you like. At my house in the country.'

'You want to see in real life what today's session only makes you dream about? That it?'

'Something like that,' Large said.

'You're knocking on the right door,' Sampler told him.

11

Donald Warne-Johns was an unusual person. Some would say odd, others went further and used the term mixed-up. Whatever the description, it was true that his life was a mess of contradictions and inconsistencies. 'And that's the least, the very least you can say,' his mousy librarian wife confided one day to her best friend.

Sexually, to take one example, he had carefully fostered his reputation as a lad, a scalp-hunter, the number one stud of his generation. And while it was true that he would make a heavy pass at anything female that moved, whispered confidences among those so favoured – often accompanied by giggles – perpetuated a myth that was equally strong. The sequel, it was said, rarely attained the level suggested by the original scenario. Few of the Warne-Johns' 'conquests', in fact, progressed beyond the categories of the flash, the grope or the slap-and-tickle. Penetration was seldom, if ever, effected.

Donald, if ever he heard them, rose easily above such calumnies. One of the reasons he made so many passes, in so many different fields, was to spread the load, as it were, and dilute the damage. In any case, he was only interested in maintaining the Casanova reputation among his fellow men – and here the brash assurance of the initial approaches was evident for all to see. If anything deleterious did filter through to subsequent boyfriends, it could easily be put down to envy or the spite of woman rejected.

The truth, though, was that Donald Warne-Johns, the delight of the dolly-girls, was really only happy and at ease with fat ladies, when it was *they* who dragged *him* into bed, and then told him what to do.

Such hang-ups, including the quest for the maternal and

the need for a macho image to make up for basic insecurity, are typical of the male in search of a mother-figure. And it was true that much of the Warne-Johns character derived in part from the early marital split-up of his parents, and the web of deceit and falsehood spun around the family by his mother after the divorce.

The received theory was that the Johns part of the name was due to a distant connection with a well-known writer, Captain W. E. Johns, author of boys' stories featuring the air aces of World War One and creator of the folk-hero Biggles. The story was totally untrue. Donald's father's name was Johnstone, and his mother had arrogated only the first half of this, revengefully, after he had left her for a chorus girl in Bradford. The Warne and the hyphen had been added after a brief romance on the rebound with a miner in Wales.

The lady's economical use of the truth had been visited also on the son – whose stories, from the earliest age, had equalled, if not surpassed, the aerial exploits described by the gallant Captain.

The expensive public school whose old-boys' tie Donald wore had no record of his name – of either or any of them – in its archives. Similarly his military career, rather than a commission in the Brigade of Guards, had involved nothing more glamorous that the double stripe of a conscript corporal in the Records department of the East Lancashire Regiment when it was quartered in Richmond.

Neither of these unpalatable verities, however, impeached Donald's colourful descriptions of schoolboy rags, prefectorial beatings or rugger victories over Harrow. Or, for that matter, the self-deprecatory modesty of such throwaways as: 'Buck House duty, old boy? Piece of bloody cake. Only thing I ever learned there was how to roll a decent umbrella!'

It was this childish insistence on make-believe in his adult behaviour – social rather than sexual – that led certain of his more perspicacious, less easily impressed contemporaries to regard him – not to put too fine a point on it, old chap – as a bit of an oddball.

Sometimes however the truth, or an indication of it,

manifested itself in subtle ways – perhaps only by implication – in a fashion of which the man himself was totally unaware. Typical of this was his habit of whistling under his breath while he concentrated on a difficult photo session.

Irritating for some, infuriating often for a model having to hold her position, the give-away here was the choice of tunes thrown up by his unconscious – and their true provenance.

The one manifesting itself most frequently was an infant jingle learned at his council school at the age of seven and never forgotten. There were words, too, to this scabrous ditty. But, perhaps fortunately for his sitters, Donald confined himself when working to the simple melody.

The words, which he could still recall (provided Ma wasn't listening), went:

> Down in the woods where the nuts are brown,
> Petticoats up and knickers down!
>> You like bottom and I like top:
>> See if my key will fit your lock!

Hang-ups, neuroses and sexual peccadilloes apart, Donald Warne-Johns had in fact made himself – after a course paid for with his army demob gratuity – into an extremely good photographer. Rather than static studio portraits, he was exceptionally talented – perhaps because of his own vivid imagination! – at catching his subjects apparently unawares, yet at the same time in a pose or with an expression defining the character, the aura of the sitter, with a truthfulness sought in vain by the classic stills' photographer.

Perhaps nature always insists on the swing of the pendulum: that untruths must eventually be balanced – or annulled or superseded or expiated – by truths. Whatever, it was this flair for capturing 'real' people on film – and contrasting them, in extravagant underclothes, with an unreal situation – that had persuaded Preckner and Curnow to employ him exclusively for their new advertising campaign. And of course the new magazine.

There was an extra studio session two days after the original one. A small number of Shirley Sabbath's creations demanded a tall, very slim model rather than the fuller figure of the classic lingerie type. And to emphasize the distinctiveness of this minority ('Every woman in the bloody country with tits and a bum's got to find something for her in this collection,' David Preckner insisted) the pictures of this girl would be solo, neither she nor the garments ever to be displayed with any of the others.

The name of this fifth girl was Diana. She was indeed tall: none of your standard-five-foot-two caper but a fairly graceful five-nine or ten, Warne-Johns noted as she came in. She was wearing black jeans and a floppy sweater with one of those huge rollnecks scooped out almost to shoulder width that were popular that year. But the woolly wasn't so floppy that it hid the suggestion of full, firm breasts.

Warne-Johns registered the remaining components, passing in and out of the dressing-room with the studied indifference affected by randy photographers lusting after their models. The girl stripped and shrugged herself into the first lingerie set as nonchalantly as any of the models whose bodies were their bread-and-butter. It was all part of the job. If she noticed that the photographer had passed through three separate times to fetch rolls of film, and twice to look for halogen lamps already in place and alight on the set, she made no comment. Perhaps she was used to randy picture-snatchers.

The final rundown obtained by Donald Warne-Johns stacked up: very long, very shapely legs; slender hands, feet and waist; good breasts but narrowish shoulders. The girl was in fact so slim that – apart from the breasts – her figure was almost boyish. 'Sorry, love,' she apologized, the one time she intercepted his glance. 'There's meat on the bum, even if it's a bit tight – but zero out of ten for the hips. Not much more than a hinge really, in my case.'

'Not to worry,' Donald assured her. 'It's the undies that'll show.' He paused, then added: 'This time anyway.'

If he had been a passport officer, Warne-Johns might have added, in the space marked *Physical particularities or distinguishing marks:* Hair dark but pubis tawny, almost sandy, both colours natural.

And if there had been room enough on the form he could also have noted that this near-ginger pussy appeared also to be unusual in the fact that the hairs were silky rather than wiry.

The set this time was so classic as to be virtually a cliché: heavy drapes in royal blue velvet looped across the background, with the plaster bust of a Roman emperor on a white column in one corner. The dozen designs Shirley and her employers had selected showed none of the crotch-tight bared-breast sexual allusiveness of the original collection. They were loose, flowing, lacy cascades – sometimes tiered, often beribboned, always soft – a visual froth that did no more than imply the femininity it so successfully hid. They were the sort of things that could comfortably be worn with roomy tops and flared skirts, or teamed with voluminous, floor-length evening gowns. The concept of this sub-collection had been suggested to the designer by the Victorian conviction that if a woman is totally clothed, from head to foot and neck to wrist, then the glimpse of a single ankle can be almost unbearably exciting and sexy.

Diana was a good subject, intelligent enouth to interpret Donald's terse instructions – 'Half turn, chin on shoulder' . . . 'Sink to the floor: a curtsey to the Empress' . . . 'Hand on hip; saucy eye!' – almost before the words left his mouth. They worked hard for two and a half hours, still using the Rolleiflex, during which he shot five rolls of 2¼ × 2¼ high-speed film, then snapped shut the viewfinder mask and said: 'Okay, sweetie. End of story. Well done. We've got everything they could possibly want!'

He began to dismantle the tripod, dimming the harsh lights with a rheostat.

Diana stopped, half turning on her way to the dressing-room. 'I have to go to the loo,' she said. 'Directions, please?'

'Through the little office at the back of reception,' he said without looking up.

When she came back a few minutes later and began to change, she called over the dressing-room's partition wall: 'That's something I always wondered: *why* do we call it the loo? Where does the word come from? What does it *mean?*'

He was unwinding the velvet from its battens. 'What was that again, sweetie?'

'Why do we call it the loo?'

'That's an easy one,' he replied. 'Basically, it's the same trick as rhyming slang.'

'Rhyming *slang*? How come?'

'The Cockney variety. You know – a kind of double-talk, to hide what you're really saying from those not in the know. So instead of using the real word, you use something that rhymes with it; instead of saying "hat", you say "tit-for-tat"; instead of "hair" you use "Barnet Fair". Then, to make it more difficult, the word of the second phrase that actually rhymes is dropped. So before you go out on a date, you must comb your barnet, hoping it's not mussed up when you put on your titfor.'

'What's that got to do with the loo?'

'Same sort of story. Every schoolboy knows that the verb "to crap" comes from the master plumber Thomas Crapper, who invented the flushing lavatory. Most kids know that the official term for that was Water Closet, or WC. What they don't know is that the Victorian gentility was so firmly entrenched that to use this term was unthinkable. And as for toilet – good gracious, no! So they had to find a euphemism – something that made it clear what you meant, but avoided actually saying it aloud. The word they chose, which included the key-word "water", was the name of the battle, the one where we finally beat Napoleon.'

'Oh, God! Of course – Waterloo!'

'Exactly. And, as in rhyming slang, one part was eventually omitted . . . leaving us the abbreviation "Loo".'

'Well, thanks – you learn something every day!' Diana said

Warne-Johns cleared his throat. 'Going back to Mr Crapper and the kids,' he called, 'there's a rhyme current at the time which every schoolboy knew – and probably still does, if he's young enough not to know about fucking before he's three. I reckon it's possible, because the rhyme was considered "naughty" at the time, that this too may have some connection with your question.'

'How intriguing,' Diana said. 'Dare you repeat the rhyme?'

'Not in mixed company, old thing,' the photographer said cheerfully. 'But we're not mixed-up people, are we? I mean, all artists together, and this is the swinging bloody sixties, after all. So if you insist . . .'

'I can't wait!' Diana said.

Donald's voice had been approaching the dressing-room during this last exchange. Now, in a curiously immature register, he began to declaim:

'There was a bonnie Scotsman at the Battle of Waterloo.
The wind blew up his petticoats, and showed his Toodle-oo.'

Abruptly, with startling effect, Warne-Johns appeared in the dressing-room doorway as he recited the end of the second line, his unzipped fly splayed wide open and his rigid, empurpled penis held towards Diana in a trembling hand as he completed the stanza:

'His Toodle-oo was dirty; he showed it to the Queen.
The Queen gave him sixpence, to get it jolly well clean!'

Diana had been pulling on a pair of black tights when he erupted into the room. She stood half bent forward, arrested, her mouth open and her eyes wide with astonishment. At last she said huskily: 'Put that away, Donald! For Christ's sake, what the hell d'you think you're doing? Put it away at once!'

Pleadingly, he held the massive, throbbing shaft speared in her direction.

'In any case,' she snapped, deciding to compete on his own terms, 'I don't have any small change, so you'll have to clean the bloody thing yourself!'

'The Queen, of course,' he said conversationally, 'would have been Victoria, and not our—'

'*Put it AWAY*! Or I shall have to—'

'Have to what? Call the constabulary? Have a question raised in Parliament?'

'I'll call a pro I know and have you beaten: six for

impudence and six for insubordination.'

'Oh, please! Sweetie, do give me her telephone number,' he quavered.

Diana turned away with a sigh of exasperation. She had been expecting something ever since that slightly menacing 'Not this time anyway'. But nothing like this! She continued the pulling up of her tights. Elasticated panties fitted snugly over them. She pulled the last lingerie top over her head and reached for her own bra.

Warne-Johns had walked unconcernedly up behind her, his cock still wagging from his open fly. Now, close enough to sense the heat of her body, he wrapped his arms around her waist.

Diana tried, smothering an exclamation of anger, to twist away. But the arms were strong and tightly clamped. The whole hard length of his tall, lean body was jammed against her back; she could feel the stiffer, almost springy column of his lewdly exposed prick grinding into the cleft between her narrow buttocks. 'Donald, *please* . . .!' she gasped between set teeth. 'We're supposed to be grown-up, damn it. Do stop behaving like an overgrown schoolboy yourself.'

'It's always the same,' he whispered, the breath hot against her ear. 'We work half the bloody day, we bust our gut composing super pictures – but the best, the most interesting, parts are always hidden.'

'Donald . . .'

'You've been showing yourself off all morning, tempting me with your lovely body. Surely the least you can do is let me see the rest. After all, I'm making you sexy for everyone else!'

Diana struggled unavailingly to wrench away the arms imprisoning her waist. Warne-Johns was a strong man: his deprecating tales of military exploits were plausible. Intrusive fingers glided beneath the elastic waistband of her panties, lifted the gauzy upper part of her tights away from the flesh of her belly.

For an instant Diana went limp, unclenching tensed muscles to lie a deadweight in the photographer's bear-like hug. She didn't know what to do. The situation was ridiculous, but she didn't know what she *could* do. Shout for help? The studio was booked until three o'clock, so who would be listening?

Abuse him? Threaten proceedings? Try to humiliate him (You call that a cock? Why, I've seen better than that in a teenagers' gymnasium!)? Useless. Judging from his reaction when he was threatened with a beating, he was a bit of a maso; to be devalued, menaced with eventual punishment, would probably excite him still futher.

She caught her breath. Fingers of the hand obscenely exploring her lower belly were trailing through the silky fringe of her pubic hair. Warne-Johns's cock was boring into her arse. The invading fingers had reached the top of her cunt, spreading apart the rubbery lips, sinking hard into the hot inner flesh, irritating the clitoris.

Imperceptibly, she began restoring the tonus of her muscles, tensing a little here, relaxing there, slightly stiffening the back and thighs.

Christ, she was wet, she was sliding! Butterfly tremors flickered outwards from her savaged loins: totally against her conscious will, the chemistry of her body was responding automatically to the lascivious, unwanted manipulations of the ape in whose grasp she was trapped.

'That's my girl!' Warne-Johns breathed in her ear. 'I knew you wanted it all the time.'

Diana made her decision. 'Have a go!' She urged in a choked voice. 'While you're at it, make yourself at home. Be my guest. Come on in, the water's fine!'

'Yes! Oh, *yes*!' he breathed, fingers working, the tights hard against the back of his hand.

It was then, as excitement unavoidably loosened the vice of the clamping arm, that the model girl acted. Twisting violently to face him, she squirmed free of the raping hands, let herself go totally limp once more, and dropped through his encircling grasp to the floor.

In a moment, she had swivelled away, risen to her feet from all-fours, and backed swiftly to the rail of undergarments against the dressing-room wall.

He stood facing her, trousers absurdly dropped to the

111

knee by the violence of her exit, cock speared through Y-fronts and the disarranged tails of his shirt. 'All right,' Diana said, 'if that's what you've got – let's see what you can do with it. Show me, if you're so keen to start.'

She walked towards him with one hand outstretched. Anything to keep that heavy body off her – but she thought it wise to risk the danger of another hug initially: attack is the best method of defence, and all that.

She stopped in front of him – he hadn't moved – and took the thing in her hand.

Within the rigid core, she could feel the pulsing blood throb against her fingertips. The glans, outsize for the girth of the shaft, was glistening. It was shaped a little like an oldfashioned fireman's helmet. Closing her hand over it, she pulled the skin up towards the head, trying a few experimental strokes.

The photographer's breath hissed between clenched teeth. His eyes were staring and his lips stretched wide in an expression that was half smile, half rictus. Although clearly exulting in the see-saw thrill flaming through his loins, he doubled up slightly, withdrawing from her grasp. 'N-n-no!' he panted. 'It's very . . . I mean it's super and it's most kind . . . that is to say – well, I can manage, thank you.'

'You can . . . manage?'

'It's the sight, you see, the image,' he blurted out. 'It's my profession, after all, the image. But I never get to see . . . what I want to . . .' His words trailed away into silence.

'What exactly *do* you want, for God's sake, Donald?' She had relinquished the hardened cock. The immediate danger of enforced intimacy seemed to be over. Now, in spite of herself, she found herself intrigued.

'You!' he choked. 'To see . . . don't you understand? To watch you do it. To yourself, I mean, privately.'

'You mean you want to see me wank, to masturbate, in front of you? Is that it?'

Warne-Johns' long-drawn-out 'Yes!' was like the sigh of an expiring man.

Diana shrugged. What the hell: anything to get this stupid situation wrapped up! And at least she wasn't going to get pawed around and fucked by someone she didn't particularly like. She moved over to a desk, stripped off tights and panties, and sat on the desk top with her legs drawn up and her bare heels perched on the edge. Mutual masturbation was in no way her thing, but she could easily enough fake something to turn on this . . . this bloody deviant, this kink! His own hand was on his cock now. His eyes were staring. With a conspiratorial grin, she slowly splayed her knees.

He could see the whole sex catalogue now – bare breasts drooped over the constricted chest, belly creased by her doubled-up pose, pubic hair spiked between the canted-up thighs . . . and between them the pouting labia. She leaned forward against her knees, wrapped both arms around them, and used her hands to draw the lips of her cunt even further apart.

Warne-Johns was already at work, skimming practised fingers up and down the hardened staff, jacking himself off with his eyes on the model's crotch.

Diana made a show of giving herself a thrill, three fingers stuffed into the vagina, the other hand apparently working her clitoris frenziedly. She rocked her body from side to side, uttering small crooning noises as she slaved away.

The photographer increased his speed. His hand flashed up and down his crimsoned cock as hard, as relentlessly, as a reciprocating beam engine or the operating shaft of an oil well. His pants were around his ankles; his free hand kneaded and fondled his balls, pulling them away from his body as he milked himself dry; harsh, gasping cries croaked in his throat.

Diana judged her faked orgasm to a nicety. She clutched her cunt fiercely with both hands, forcing them hard against her loins. Her whole body shuddered, straightened, convulsed, then bent double again. Her heels drummed on the edge of the desk. And, head flailing from side to side, she let fly a series of tortured moans that would have been a credit to a hard-core Danish movie queen.

At once Warne-Johns' head tilted violently back and he shouted aloud. His hands blurred, pumping the swollen cock. His hips heaved, started forward, then froze as the shaft jerked wildly, spewing a fountain of spurted white high into the air while he groaned and shook.

When the last squirted drops had fallen glutinously to the floor, he dropped to his knees, leaned his head over them for an instant, then rose shakily to his feet. Turning away without looking at her, he pulled up his trousers and pants and strode away towards the washroom.

Diana took care to be fully dressed before he came back.

He was smiling. 'Odd, isn't it,' he said cheerily, 'I mean that rhyming slang thing about the Battle of Waterloo?'

Diana stared at him. 'Very,' she said. He was speaking as if nothing whatever had happened since the subject first arose, as if the entire distasteful scene had been wiped from his mind, obliterated, clean as a sponged slate.

'But the oddest thing of all,' he continued blandly, 'is that our Victorians cut off half the word to stand for the jolly old toilet . . . and, what do you know, the bloody French cut off and used the *other* half for precisely the same reason: in parts of France today, it's still referred to as *le water*! Funny old world, isn't it?'

'Hilarious,' Diana said.

'Mind you, they had lost the battle,' Warne-Johns said. He began to pack up his gear.

Diana wasn't to realize the oddest thing of all about that morning until ten years later.

Hurrying to her next appointment, she was running down the studio steps on the lookout for a taxi when she almost cannoned into a goodlooking young man coming up. 'Oops! – Oh, gosh, sorry,' he exclaimed. 'You must be Diana. I've come to jabber with Donald about your pix.' He held out his hand. 'Tom Silver. I'm handling the advertising campaign for David Preckner.'

She took the hand, smiling. Her smile was warm. A real man, a normal one, at last! 'I shall enjoy working with you, Tom,' she said. And meant it.

What neither of them was to know was that, at the end of the decade in question, they would be holding hands again, but in a rather different context – in front of the registrar uniting them as man and wife during their marriage in Chelsea Town Hall.

Or that, almost another ten years after that*, Mrs Diana Silver would have become a leading activist in a very hush-hush secret society of wealthy London lesbians.

Funny old world, isn't it?

*See *Male Order* by Aaron Amory, also available in Delta.

PART FOUR

Edward Dulok

12

I don't really know why I should have decided that I wanted
the blonde. It was a spur of the moment thing anyway – but
suddenly it was absolutely imperative: I had to see her nude,
I wanted to touch her, to feel the smoothness of her skin,
the weight of her breasts in my hands. She was all softness
and warmth, and I needed that comfort against me, around
me. You get the general picture: the girl attracted me and I
wanted to fuck her.

It was in Old Quebec Street, just behind the cinema in
Marble Arch. One of those flashy drinkeries that were
springing up all over the West End to persuade tourists that,
yes, they really were in swinging London, the land of Carnaby
Street, the Beatles and joints for all, the haven of promiscuity
where the girls said yes before you even asked. It called itself
a club but wasn't. That is to say you didn't have to be a
member to get served. There were no cards, no subscription
list, no rules – except that they reserved the right to chuck
out anyone they didn't take to. The drinks of course were
three times dearer than those at the ritziest pubs.

Inside, the place was about par for the course – a long,
narrow room with panelled walls, a long, narrow mahogany
bar along one of the walls, oak tables with wheelback chairs,
low-key bracket lighting diffused by crimson Tiffany shades.

It was called the Paradise Club, can you imagine!

The tables were all occupied: Americans, a red-faced
northerner with a pewter tankard of beer, four Japanese
whose bodies were webbed with the straps of cameras, light
meters, fieldglasses.

The blonde was on a stool at the far end of the bar.
Shoulder-length hair, make-up, good legs, crossed, with one
high heel hooked over the cross-bar of the stool. She was

smoking a cigarette in a long black holder.

Commercials at the end of the bar nearest the entrance were chortling, heads together, at dirty stories. The barmaid was Australian, cheeky, a sweater-girl with big ones. She was assisted by a white-jacketed bruiser who looked as if – many, many years ago – he might have been knocked out in the first round by Gene Tunney. Maybe he was pressed into service if there was a client the management didn't take to.

I hesitated in the entrance, blinking my eyes to accustom myself to the gloom after the bright afternoon sunshine outside. The only vacant stool was between the last of the commercials and the girl. Afterwards, of course, I realized that it was probably part of the décor: there would always be an empty stool next to her. Until the entrance of the right kind of punter.

What the hell. Maybe the commercials were considered too rough a trade. There were three of them anyway.

I slid my charcoal pinstripe onto the seat of the stool.

A ranging glance. Lots of blue eye shadow, false lashes, a good mouth – heavily carmined, as the novelists say – and a powder-blue angora sweater, threaded with silver, with a vee-neck just deep enough to reveal the inner slopes of lightly tanned breasts. Pretty good, eh? I nodded politely, half smiled.

The ranging glance had been intercepted. It didn't take the most sophisticated of radars to read the score.

The blonde was leaning one bare elbow on the bar counter. The hand of that arm was supporting the long holder between the teeth of that red mouth. She removed the stem of the holder for long enough to nod and return the smile – a three-quarters model this time.

The barmaid's superstructure was confronting me. 'What'll it be, sport?' she asked.

'Scotch,' I said. 'Black Label. A large one, with ice.'

She turned away and reached for a bottle on a glass shelf – not one of those upended in the dispenser cradles. You have to know about these things if you don't want to be conned.

I swivelled to face the girl – the full treatment this time:

smile, interested expression, eyes (I hoped) twinkling with intentions both good and evil. 'I don't suppose,' I began, deliberately shy, let 'em think they've hooked a good one, 'I mean to say, would you be interested . . . could I possibly offer you a drink . . . I mean like a refill?' I indicated the shallow, longstemmed glass in front of her.

'Well, that's very kained of you.' The accent conservative club genteel. 'I thought you were never going to ask!' A well-judged, deprecatory downward look. 'The only thing is, I'm afreed I'm on champagne cocktails.'

'Aha,' I said, signalling same-again to the barmaid, 'an expensive girl, then?'

'Not when you know how much I have to give!' The full smile this time. Radiant.

'Then, in the fullness of time, you'd better have at least two,' I said.

'A pleasure,' she said. 'What's your name, Jack?'

'Edward, actually. Edward Dulok. I'm in the dress business.'

I was afraid she might say she was in the un-dress business, but she resisted the temptation. 'Maureen,' she said. And then, carelessly: 'I live just around the corner: I have a permanent suite at the Cumberland.'

'Very nice too,' I said, my eyes indicating that the subject of my approval was less the hotel next door than the structure revealed by her plunging neckline.

If we kept the dialogue going at this level, we could get picked up by a talent scout for Ealing Studios and made members of the Screenwriters Club in Greenery Street.

I'd noticed that her champagne cocktail had been fabricated with a fluid that did genuinely come out of an unopened champagne bottle. What with that, the proper whisky, and Maureen's smile, I was prepared to settle, tonight anyway, for the club we were actually at.

Why not? My wife, Elvira, was off to the Metropole Hotel in Brighton for a dirty weekend with a girlfriend. Our marriage anyway was of the type known as 'modern': Elvira would in time be regaled with a blow by blow account of the evening, dialogue included. I had nothing else to do.

Maureen uncrossed her legs.

To me the insidious swish of tightly-drawn silk over silky thighs sounded loud as the scream of a telephone calling me to work. 'What say we have a spot of dinner,' I proposed, 'first.'

We did that. Afterwards it was the Cumberland. In the crowded foyer, thronged with tourists, bellboys, early diners, and residents milling around the display cases and newspaper kiosk, she took my arm and said in a low voice. 'I'm in 573. We'll go up separately. Take a lift to the sixth floor and walk down one: one never knows where the bloody house detectives are in this place.'

The 'permanent suite' was in fact a perfectly ordinary small bedroom with a bathroom and loo. If it really was permanent, I guessed the house detectives, singular or plural, would be in receipt of a regular stipend to ensure that they were always on the wrong floor at the right time. Heavy traffic to the sixth, inevitably descending on foot to the fifth, would scarcely pass unnoticed, even in a popular hotel as busy as this. Still, I supposed it added an extra thrill, romantic gilt on the sexual gingerbread, if the punter was made to feel conspiratorial, putting one over on the men in suits.

The walls of the room were cream, the carpet sage green, fitted. The one window looked out on an air shaft, white tiled, striped with as many vertical black stackpipes as a port scene by Bernard Buffet. Beneath the window was a desk-dressingtable, faced by an upright chair.

Maureen sat on the narrow bed – a television set on a bracket projected over it – and smiled. 'Well, darling, what do you like?' she asked.

'Oh, thanks – I guess I'll just stay on Scotch, I think.' I wasn't really paying attention: she genuinely was quite beautiful.

She looked momentarily disconcerted. 'Oh . . . I – er – that isn't exactly what I meant. But of course, of course,' she added hastily. 'Soda, ginger ale, or on the rocks?'

I told her. The breasts so closely moulded by the angora looked full – slightly oversize even – but firm and admirably shaped. Below the tight, rather short black skirt, her legs were as splendid as they had been when I first saw them in the Paradise Club.

There was a minibar at the foot of the bed. When she opened the door, I saw that the tiny fridge was crammed with one each of Scotch, Gordon's and Remy Martin, several tins of mineral water, and about a dozen half-bottles of champagne. 'In that case I'll stay on mine too,' she said.

I nodded. Better than paying a higher rent, I thought.

She fixed the drinks, sat back on the bed. I took the chair.

'Cheers!' she said, raising her glass. 'Now I'll ask you again: what would you like? And don't dare answer Scotch on the rocks!'

'You said in the bar that you had a hell of a lot to offer,' I said. 'I could see that there. I can see it even more clearly here. What I want is you.'

Not one of my best efforts, admittedly. But how would you answer a question like that, in circumstances such as these?

'Yes,' she said. 'Okay. But I mean like in detail. What are you into?'

Between the entrance door and the bathroom, the wall housed the doors of three built-in cupboards. Two of these were sliding, the third could be opened. Maureen opened and slid. The open door, lined with a full-length mirror on the inside, revealed shelves and drawers packed with clothes. Both the other cupboards were jammed tight with specialist gear hanging from rails: jeans and jackets and topcoats and corsets in leather; dresses and catsuits in different coloured rubber; long gowns and breeches in shiny vinyl. Ranged at the back I could see high-heeled boots, and attached inside the doors a couple of riding crops and straps suspended from a tie rack.

'Choose,' Maureen said.

To be honest, I'd no idea that she might be a specialist, a dominatrice catering for the whips and chains gang. 'What I'm into,' I told her, 'is women. Tonight the one I want is you. End of shopping list – unless you'd like to leave the door with the mirror open, then at least I can have two of you!'

123

She was staring at me. 'No kidding! You're actually a straight! Well, how about that!'

'I'll put it another way,' I said. 'If it's not too unutterably boring – and if it doesn't ruin your image of men as a race – I want to fuck you. I want to ram my prick into your lovely body and fuck until we both come together and die of joy!'

The blonde laughed. 'Well, that's very naice,' she said. 'I guess, after all, it takes all sorts! Anyway, darling, I'm reely flattered.' She began pulling the blue angora over her pale head.

The bra was a snap-front crossover with padded shoulder-straps. Plain white with a wisp of lace edging the arched upper part of the cups. Size C, I guessed. She didn't really need it – or them – I judged when she shrugged out of the garment. I was watching pretty carefully too. I'd paid for my seat after all.

But I found myself, nevertheless, in an odd position. I mean, I wasn't in the habit of paying for it. And that was no macho boast. In the swinging sixties who needed to? I wasn't into the kinky scene or turned on by black leather. Elvira and I had a pretty free relationship – you could almost call it swinging – but at the same time I'd always thought that the mechanical kind of sex, where you slaked your need the way you took a drink of beer on a hot day, was particularly un-rewarding. If fucking had any value, it had to be a transaction between two persons, not a matter reduced to the delicate friction of two skins. Which was why, I thought, most pros made so few attempts to tempt their clients to come back for more: they knew bloody well that what they gave wasn't much cop. If it was just a thirst-quenching job, why bother? Why not just take yourself in hand and masturbate in front of sexy pictures? It was cheaper, and – as the man in the story said – you meet a better class of person.

Yet, despite all this, here I was in a hotel room with a B-girl. Someone I should have known, must have known right from the beginning, was on the game. Someone who by definition didn't interest me.

How come?

Answer: she interested me like hell. Explanation: it was just one of those things.

She unfastened and unzipped the skirt, stepping out of it rather elegantly. She wore gunmetal stockings, pulled up by a panty-girdle with attached suspenders. The stockings were silk.

'*Very* seductive,' I said. 'You don't see that much any more! It's all tights these days.'

'Hell's own difficult to get,' Maureen said. 'I had to con these out of a friend coming from America.' She lay on the bed and spread her legs. 'You want me to keep these on?'

'Yes,' I said. 'I think I do.' She unfastened the crotch gusset and started work on the girdle.

When she was naked except for the stockings and high-heeled black shoes, she said: 'Your turn to undress now. If you want, there are hangers behind the door in the bathroom.'

'I want all right,' I said. 'Among other things, I want to get as close as *humanly* possible to you. And that means no clothes.'

'You are funny,' she said. 'You say such naice things!'

When I came out of the bathroom, naked – with the most splendid hard-on I'd had for at least three days – she had changed position. She was sprawled rather stylishly with her back against the wall, one stockinged leg drawn up, head in hand and weight supported by that elbow. Rather like Goya's famous nude duchess. Only a little more available.

Intelligent, though. If the punter bothered to undress, it meant that he expected more than a hasty snack, handed to him on a plate. So zero points for lying on the back with the legs apart.

Maybe I was being offered the Blue-Plate Special because this was a client she did want to keep? Or could it just be that I was funny – my sense of humour appealed to blondes?

Perhaps, in the fullness of time, I'd find out. Meanwhile – other things first. I sat on the bed.

We could hear three different television channels from nearby rooms. Someone was playing loud rock 'n' roll music on a radio. The clatter of dustbins being stacked by kitchen

125

staff at the foot of the air shaft was punctuated by the bray of an ambulance or fire engine, presumably on the other side of the park. Oh, yes: and there was a furious man-and-wife shout-up in 575. Otherwise, a cloistered calm reigned in our little love nest.

At least the television wasn't on.

Maureen smiled lazily, the blonde head still resting on her hand. She reached out her free hand. Long, rednailed fingers wrapped slowly around the throbbing proof of my lust for her.

The whole of my body tensed. The most important parts were already stiff.

'You're naice,' she drawled. 'You sit well. Not too much hair on the chest. Goodish muscles. And this' – a small, intimate squeeze of the cock – 'looks promising. I think I may be going to like you.'

'If that turns out to be true,' I said, 'you can be absolutely certain that it will be mutual.' I reached out my own hands, both of them, towards her breasts. Both of them. 'But, joking apart,' I said, 'you really are stunning; I mean totally gorgeous!'

'Who's joking?' Maureen asked.

It was one of those sessions that just happened to start right – everything in the right place, at the right time, in the right way – one of those rare experiences in which you know, from the moment the light turns green, that success is inevitable, it's written, impossible to play a bad move. Better still, that it's going to go on right, continue right, and stay right, right to the bloody end!

A blueprint you didn't even dream up yourself, a plan neither you nor your partner had organized, which nevertheless turned out to be perfect, despite – or because of – such differences as there might be in the matter of sex, taste, opinion, physical attributes, intelligence, or plain sensual preference. A one hundred percent, dyed-in-the-wool, state of the art, zero fault bullseye, in fact. Compatibility is the word on the bottom line. Or successful chemistry if there's room.

To put it another way, a good fuck.

It had started with the breasts. There was something about the way, in that duchess pose, they hung slightly down from the chest – hung horizontally, not vertically – that not only emphasized their firmness, fullness, resilience and the fact that they were not dropped in the ordinary way, but also brought to mind with aching intensity the tactile ecstasy of the whole taut-soft, caressing magic of the female form.

As soon as I felt their warmth and weight in my hands, the moment I heard the soft, almost inaudible, catch of her breath, I knew.

I think she did too – instinctively if not with her conscious mind – for from that instant on, everything we did, each move, every touch, any succession of strokes and squeezes, seemed almost pre-ordained: we were actors pulling out all stops ordered by the director in a scenario we hadn't written ourselves. Or that's the way it seemed to me.

Probably for Maureen too, for at one point she breathed: 'Baby, this is lovely!'

At that moment we were still elongated on the bed. Kind of face to face, each of us now resting on an elbow, the eyeball contact quizzical, challenging, conspiratorial. What have we *here*, chum – and how are we going to play it?

The answers to those questions were already under consideration by our free hands.

She had never let go of my cock. The thumb and first finger encircled the base in a vice-like grip; the other three fingers curled down and under to cradle the balls in their hairy sac. With this particular hold, a simple swivelling motion of the wrist – right to left, left to right, up and down and back – gently pistoned the lower half of the shaft and at the same time hoisted, released and kneaded the balls. The secret of it was that the grip on the cock was tight, very tight, but the movements were all feather-light.

The butterfly nerves were already tremoring, fanning out across my belly like flickers of summer lightning.

If my tool had ever felt harder, more bursting with pride and desire, I couldn't remember when the hell it was!

My own hand, palm flat on the blonde's dark public

thatch, was contenting itself – just temporarily, you understand – with a gentle, insidious pressure, softly rotating the thin layer of flesh over and against the pubic bone, at the same time drawing upwards the skin at the very top of the thighs and (hopefully) the extreme fringes of the labia concertina-ed between them. Expertly done, this circular caress – once it had widened and deepened and the pressure increased – could coax up the inner labia to friction and excite the clitoris itself.

I think I managed to make it myself, this time, because as my breath quickened I was aware of tiny tremblings and suppressed starts agitating the beautiful body beside me. Maureen's mouth was held open; hot breath played over my neck and chest.

I couldn't, of course, hope genuinely to stimulate, excite and finally drive crazy a professional: why should my cock, my body and person, turn her on more than those of any other punter? But I liked to think that at least I could offer her some kind of pleasure while she attended to my needs.

After a while – her breathing had deepened a little – she rolled more onto her back and, without letting go of my cock, lay flat out and snaked the freed arm beneath my waist.

A palm pressed hard against the base of my spine, urging me closer. The hand knifed between my buttocks, forefinger exploring. She shifted again, releasing the balls and using the whole of that hand to milk my stiffened prick, fist clenched over the throbbing shaft to squeeze moisture from the compressed glans. At the same time my circling hand cupped over her pussy as a whole and the forefinger sank, was positively sucked, into the warm, wet crevice between the lips of her cunt.

The finger trapped in the heat between my buttocks had found my arsehole. I caught my breath as the tip wormed its way suddenly in, penetrating the clamped sphincter, probing the passage beyond.

I lay skewered on Maureen's bed, buggered by her raping finger behind, tossed off by her lewdly pumping hand in front.

I'd lowered my own head to the pillows now, releasing

that hand to dabble and claw and cradle in the fleshy weight of the blonde's nippled breasts.

My heart was trying to jump out of my chest. Just as I was about to pull her beneath me and roll over on top, Maureen moved swiftly herself. She freed my prick from her masturbatory grasp, sat up, doubled herself forward, then stretched out flat on her face in the opposite direction. At the level of my hips, she raised her head and closed softly cushioned lips hotly over the head of my inflamed cock.

I gasped. Every nerve I had seared down to the inflamed staff, quivering under the sluiced assault of that sucking mouth.

Her knees were beside my head. My hands were free. I levered them beneath her hips and lifted her, still sucking, across me. Her legs parted and I lowered her wet pussy onto my face.

Wiry hairs tickled my nose and chin; moist folds of flesh settled over my mouth. I opened my lips and speared my tongue into the streaming, scorching depths of her cunt.

The hips above me shook. I could feel small shocks shuddering through the belly clamped to my chest. A stifled exclamation choked through the gobbling noises at my loins.

She was leaning on both elbows now, both hands at the genitals serviced by her slavering mouth, one fondling the cradled balls, the other riding thumb and fingers wildly up and down the base of my plank-stiff cock. I forced my hands between our heaving bodies to clutch the tautly swelling weight of her trapped breasts. My knees jerked up to clamp the ribs below her shoulders.

For what seemed a long time we lay there coupled together. My lips sucked in and pushed out the sliding wetness of Maureen's cushioned inner and outer labia. Between them the tip of my tongue charted the ridged and hollowed recesses of the burning inner flesh beyond, lapped the sinewy bud of the unsheathed clitoris pulsating there. My cock, a world away, manipulated with agonizing ecstasy by those expert fingers, was being sucked, always up and ever deeper, into the seemingly depthless cavern of Maureen's mouth. With each tight, clamped withdrawal, with every heartstopping plunge of that working mouth and tongue, I could sense the approach, remorseless, inevitable, of that high plateau of sensitivity from which the only escape is the jump into the abyss.

We were in fact dangerously near the climax which neither of us, at that time, really wanted, and I could sense the tension mounting as relentlessly as the mercury in a thermometer, when the spell was broken by the absurd.

Loud and suddenly piercing from the adjoining room, the shout-up we had heard before burst into venomous life.

A man's voice, hoarse with rage: *'I didn't bring you all the way to bleeding London to waste my bloody time fucking in and out of perishing museums!'*

'You only brought me to London for one thing – one fucking thing, as you say – and that's to stuff your stinking prick into my hole!' The woman, of course. Young? Certainly furious.

'Just because you got tits – a sight too big at that – and a cunt between your bloody legs, you think you're God's gift to bloody mankind. Why don't you fucking shut up and simply open them? That's all they're good for anyway. That and tramping around flaming bloody museums.'

'Shut up yourself, bastard. That's all you are good for, Alan: fucking; shooting off your stupid prick and shooting off your mouth. You're crude, mate, you're uncouth. You don't—'

'Shut your fucking mouth, bitch! Crude, is it? Well let me tell you something, little . . .'

But the pearl of wisdom about to be confided to the little – er – lady was lost to mankind for ever. Her gentleman's words were abruptly cut off by the slamming of a door – the bathroom, the entrance? – and died away into silence.

For Maureen and myself, after such an interruption, there was only one possible result: we both collapsed in our respective positions, helpless with laughter.

'Well, you and me,' I gasped when I had found my breath, 'at least we know what we're here for!'

'And not in no fucking museum, neither,' Maureen quoted in a masculine tone.

For some reason, she was now standing up on the bed. I was still on my back. She had planted a foot on either side of my hips – the high heels had gone – and bestrode me like an Amazon: dark stockings, black bush and secretly gaping cunt below pale belly and breasts in as fascinating a package as I had seen in a long time.

Looking down at me with the blonde hair falling over her face, she grinned. 'I like you,' she said suddenly. 'You're fun.'

The Kensington accent had disappeared since we got – shall we say? – together.

'Sometimes, you know,' she confided, 'it gets bloody boring, standin' beside the bed here and bein' a bitch goddess! And the punters, the really kinky ones, don't half want value for money! You stand here, giving some feller a whippin', tellin' him he's got to be punished because he's a naughty little boy or a dirty old lecher, handin' out the thrills, stacked up with the gear. But does he ever think that *you* might be uncomfortable too? Does he hell!'

The blonde hair swished from side to side. 'The boots are too tight,' she said. 'The bloody corset's laced up so hard it's givin' you indigestion. If you're into rubber, it sticks to you all over and I don't really get turned on by the smell. And as for the pain in me beatin' arm if it's a two-hour session . . . !' She shook her head again.

Conspiratorial smile. 'It's a hard life!' I agreed.

'In that case,' Maureen said, staring down at my rigid cock, 'you can be of some help. Most of my men, I tell 'em, "Get down on your knees!" You, my friend, seein' as you're in that state, you can get *up* on your knees and give my pussy a bit more tongue before we continue!'

'It will be a pleasure,' I said.

It was, too. I knelt up between those slender, darkly tapered legs and closed my palms over the tight little cheeks of her backside, drawing her hips towards me. At the same time, my right hand kept moving, fingers edging into the heated crevice separating her buttocks. The middle finger sank further still, finding hair, moist flesh.

I pushed abruptly, burying it up to the knuckle in the warm, tight clasp of her anus.

Maureen uttered a small sound. And then – as the pressure jerked her pelvis against my face and my tongue laced once more into her cunt: 'Ooooh! . . . Baby, I like! Just keep on in there; don't stop . . . or at any rate not until I tell you . . .'

We remained in that pose, her body tensed, muscles on the insides of her thighs trembling against my cheeks, her hands on the back of my head, while I slaved away at her genitals.

The wiry hair covering her mons ground against the bridge of my nose. The secretions that were witness to our mutual lust streamed down my chin. From time to time the lower part of her body was moved by tiny, involuntary starts or quivers as my tongue burrowed into or lapped over an extra-sensitive surface within the hot, wet, succulent embrace of her inner flesh. But mostly we remained statuesque, only the hidden interiors aflame with the fury of our desire.

Finally, she lifted a stockinged leg and draped it over my left shoulder. I reacted at once to the cue, doubling the pressure of my hands on her buttocks, lifting her clean off the mattress so that she could swing the silken swell of the other thigh over my right shoulder. She was sitting on my shoulders in what you might call a 'piggy-front', heels clamped to my waist, my tongue still buried in her cunt.

Straining to keep that position, I tensed my abdominal muscles, leaned forward, and laid her gently down on her back on the bed. She was releasing small cooing cries of pleasure.

The hands holding my head against her heaving loins were lifting it away, away and up, urging my face through the damply matted pubic hair to the pale, cool sweep of her belly.

Again I obeyed the implicit imperative. I eased my body up between her suddenly splayed thighs, up and over and along the scented undulations of flesh until I could lower myself onto her, head to head. And of course hip to hip.

My throbbing, plank-stiff tool lay against the hot, wet pout of her cunt.

Maureen reached down hands to guide me in, but it wasn't necessary. I flexed my hips, back and forth. I swivelled them very slightly. I pushed. And my hard cock slid into her as easily, as greasily, as warm and moist and squeezily as . . . well, as it does in the way of a perfect fuck.

At another time, in another place, with a different partner, the boisterous interruption from the next room could have broken the spell and ruined everything. The sense of inevitability, of pre-ordained triumph, could have been laid waste. But not this time.

I had been right, I knew I was right, and I was still right. It was indeed, in its way, a perfect fuck. It was silk, it was satin, it was honey and flowers. Clasped each to the other in fleshy bliss, we moved swiftly and expertly into that sliding, coupled rhythm, that gently reciprocating, suddenly accelerating, all at once blindingly explosive rhythm that lifts the two partners high as the stars into the ecstatic sky, equally excited, equally shaken . . . and then, if they are lucky and they really did get it *exactly* right, leaves them equally sated and identically thrilled on the shore as the great wave recedes.

Maureen and I were lucky – as I knew we would be – and we did get it exactly right, that splendid evening at the Cumberland Hotel in London in the swinging sixties.

'You know something, dear?' she said dreamily as we lazed on the bed some time later. 'We were kissing – I mean mouth to mouth – we were actually kissing a lot in there!'

I sipped my champagne – we were both on it now – and looked at her quizzically. 'And so?'

She stripped off the one stocking she still wore. 'We don't,' she said, 'usually. We girls don't normally kiss, or allow ourselves to be kissed, by clients.'

And then, perhaps because I looked surprised: 'Because it seems, you see . . . well, a bit too kind of *intimate* . . .'

13

Being married to a woman who is bisexual has its advantages. And by bisexual I don't mean a dyke who occasionally beds a man for marriage, money or even kicks; still less a hetero sexpot suffering bad vibes a shade too often from the opposite sex, who runs home to mother from time to time in search of warmth and comfort and sensitivity. I mean a girl who is genuinely and equally capable of being turned on by either sex: your actual, original Let-'em-all-come.

Elvira was one of those. My face didn't decorate the other side of the coin: I'm strictly hetero. But it worked out well for both of us. For my wife, it meant that she wasn't bored because she had nobody but me: she could put it about wherever and whenever she felt like it – guys too, occasionally, if the mood took her – without the risk of aggro from a jealous hubby. And it left me independent enough to play the field any time that *I* felt the desire to spice my life with variety.

This wasn't all that often – Maureen was a one-off, an exception – because the formula left each of us always with an interest in the other. And the desire, too, to *be* of interest to the other. We didn't take one another, as they say, for granted. Each of us turned on the other.

We worked, in fact, at our marriage. After seven years we were still working, in every sense of the term . . . but so was the marriage.

One reason of course was that the whole thing had been discussed and agreed before the actual nuptials. That's an essential: no nasty shocks, no hysterical scenes, no jealousy or recriminations. The other – the only other – reason was that we only had one rule.

The rule was binding and absolute: sexually, we did tell tales.

Each of us promised faithfully – and it was a way of being faithful too – that each and every extra-marital adventure would be revealed to the other, omitting no detail, however slight! This was the key to our success. No secrets.

No secrets, so no stressful cover-ups, no lies to tell, no un-wishful thinking (Isn't she/he seeing just a bit too much of him/her? There's *something going on*! Don't say he/she's going to leave me!) And of course, as I say, a total absence of jealousy. I was free to take advantage of the Maureens. My wife fascinated me. If Elvira felt like female sex, or met some sudden first-sight passion, she could switch over to all-systems-go without worrying. With the result that, if she fancied the male, it was usually – though not inevitably – me.

Such an approach of course – and this is one of the joys of the relationship – stimulates a very extra, extremely special complicity uniting the couple. It's the most exclusive club in the world: the one restricted to only two members.

I thoroughly recommend the system . . . if you're in a position to make use of it.

Oddly enough, I was contemplating the use of it myself on my way home from the Cumberland after I left blonde Maureen. A use altogether out of the ordinary, for us at any rate, and one that was in a sense perhaps more selfish than usual – though the goal was professional rather than personal.

For once I was going to *use* Elvira – if she would agree.

It dated back several weeks, and the problem involved my competitor, Preckner Gowns. Or at least I suspected it did.

I remember the day of my first doubts very clearly. I'd arrived at the factory very early to organize sales and promotional material for a Welsh buyer I was having lunch with. It was so early that Shields, the night-watchman, was still on duty. I remember seeing him in his cubby-hole, messing about with, of all things, a bicycle puncture repair outfit – one of those flat tins with sand-paper strips, stick-on patches and rubber solution in a tube. I don't know what he was trying to repair, but it certainly wasn't the inner tube of a bicycle tyre. He had shoved it away – a bit guiltily, I thought – crammed it into a desk drawer before I could see. But what stuck in my mind rather more than the matter of Shields's nocturnal pastimes was the affair of the phone calls.

There had been two of them, the night-watchman told me, one in the Sales Manager's office, the other in mine. A little before ten o'clock at night. The first had been someone who said he had an urgent order to place – yet hung up without leaving a message, although Shields had offered to take one. The other, ringing, Shields said, for a hell of a long time – long enough for him to hurry through the workshops, past the stockroom and upstairs to my private office – the other had claimed to be a wrong number.

Odd.

Odder still was the supposed purpose of the first call. Who the hell phones a *factory* to place an order, however urgent, at ten o'clock in the evening? On a weekend at that? And without leaving a message? Don't tell me that any retailer in his right mind would do that!

That call was a phoney if ever I heard of one.

The second was pretty suspect too. Why let it ring so long if the caller was unsure of the number? And he hadn't, Shields said, been the least put out when his 'mistake' was pointed out.

It was perhaps because of this trivial mystery that I was particularly attentive when I got to my office – or perhaps it was what I found there that made me remember so clearly the phone calls.

I had almost completed my promotion portfolio when I realized that a folder I needed would be in the production manager's office. I went down to fetch it. The folder wasn't in the file where it should have been.

It was there when the manager and I left together after the staff had gone home the previous evening.

I found it quickly enough. In the adjacent file. It had been replaced in *Linen Tea-Gowns* when it should have been in *Lingerie*.

The operative word was 'replaced'. Since the day before, someone had taken that folder out, then put it back in the wrong file.

So who? And why?

I began a detailed examination of the manager's desk, filing cabinets, cupboards. I could find nothing out of place, nothing missing, nothing wrong.

Then I happened to notice – I was standing in the middle of the room, staring at nothing – I noticed something reflecting outside light at the top of the glass pane in the office door. I walked over to investigate.

A tiny strip of transparent sticky tape. A ragged edge as if the tape had been torn quickly away.

I found two more – thin slivers where the tape had torn – at the edges of the office window.

I called the cleaners, who had arrived before me.

The windows had been washed the Friday morning, I was told. The fragments of tape had definitely not been there then. If they had, the water would have washed them away anyway.

No, the chief cleaning woman told me: there had been nothing special, nothing unusual about the office when she came in at six.

Except the unusual amount of brown wrapping paper crumpled up and rammed into the metal waste box beneath the desk. Large sheets, torn but apparently unused.

And, yes, there had indeed been traces of sticky tape along the edge here and there. Difficult to get rid of sometimes, as it stuck to the gloves.

I went back to my office. I didn't need to call 221B, Baker Street, to make the necessary deductions.

While Shields's attention was distracted by the fake phone calls, someone had broken into the building, masked the windows of the production office, switched on the lights, and gone through our files. Then, making only the one mistake replacing documents, they had left unseen, taking nothing with them.

And the only clue I had was that there must have been at least two persons involved: the caller and the burglar.

The purpose of this planned raid, although it sounded melodramatic and even pretentious?

What it was fashionable now to call industrial espionage!

In the *rag-trade*? Industrial *espionage*? Do me a favour, mate!

So what other explanation could there be? Someone wanted to know what we were up to.

It was some days later that at least one penny dropped. Elvira happened to see our workroom supervisor dining – very expensively – with David Preckner's partner, Curnow.

I fired the woman at once, of course: you can't have an employee who knows everything there is to know about your business hobnobbing with the partner of a close competitor. Naturally I didn't give the real reason. If there *was* anything going on between them, I didn't want to let on that I knew. So it was the old restructuring routine, money in lieu and a false smile accompanying the final handshake.

It was later that I wondered whether – apart from an obvious carnal interest – there might have been in some way a business connection uniting that unexpected twosome.

So what conceivable manner . . .?

Of course: the break-in! The only other unanswered question in the last few months.

Could it have been engineered by people employed by the Preckner organization? Possibly with inside information supplied by the supervisor?

That was a suspicion which grew in my mind. It became a near-certainty when I learned through the rag-trade grapevine that the woman had immediately been re-employed by Preckner.

But, again, why? What for? There can only be two reasons why a ready-to-wear manufacturer would want advance information on a rival's forthcoming collection: because there was a line he wanted to copy, and if possible market first; or because he was planning something totally different and wanted to make sure that there really were no parallels between his range and his competitor's.

So which could it be?

It was too late for an in-house investigation now: I should have checked while the woman was still on the payroll. But there was nevertheless one way that might, that just might, be fruitful. It involved – I'll admit it again – a slightly suspect use of my own wife.

I should say here that Elvira and I didn't tempt – neither of us *suggested* possible outside partners who might interest the other. That, in a sense, would be bypassing The Rule. In any case, there would be no point in my encouraging her to make it with another guy or girl. That would be my choice rather than hers. And choice was the whole point of the relationship – individual choice by one or the other, because of a sudden fugitive desire, or for that matter an irresistible urge – the details to be shared between us later. I'm not by nature a voyeur, so there would in any case be nothing extra for me in a setup involving the other half with someone I produced out of a hat.

Unless of course it was going to help the business.

So wasn't that the case here?

Elvira, you see, had a real genius for turning people on. Male or female, young or old, if she fancied them, she had them grovelling in no time!

It was that characteristic I proposed – if, as I say, she agreed – to make use of here.

Because I had long suspected that Gladys Carter, the sacked supervisor, was something of an each-way bet. She was a very well stacked young woman, with lots of flesh in all the right places, and a smile that was . . . well, if not a come-on, at least welcoming. Also I was pretty certain I had noticed, passing through the workroom one or twice, the odd lecherous glance at one or two of the girls.

If Elvira could seduce her, then get to work with her magic wiles . . . well, who knew what pearls of intelligence we might not come up with!

The opportunity came when my wife returned from her dirty weekend in Brighton. I had listened, with the usual interest and excitement, to a graphic recital of the bedtime gymnastics. But Joyce, she told me, voracious and demanding though she was, had reached a point where she was in danger of demanding too much, in the wrong way. And a clinging vine, even a faithful one – especially a faithful one – was the last thing Elvira wanted. The only permanent relationship she had was with me.

A perfect moment to tempt her – for once! – with a taste of something new!

We were sitting, as usual, in the television room. The secret Marilyn videotape – special import from the US of A – was animating the screen. I had done the Maureen recital, Elvira had finished with Joyce – and, also as usual, we had turned each other on to the point where we were both horny as hell. That was why, ritually, our confessions games were always played naked.

Elvira wears her dark hair very short: shallow waves in almost a thirties fashion. Unless, of course, she's into the wig collection. She's tallish, with good breasts, very slightly dropped now, and the most nubile, voluptuous, cushiony, bloody well *female* hips and belly you ever saw. Or felt, if luck was on your side.

It was on mine now. Or more specifically on my knees. The fleshy, sexy deadweight of my wife's bottom and upper thighs lay heavily in my lap as I sprawled in an armchair. Her pliant hip pressed against my belly. I had one arm around her and a breast in my hand. The fingers of the other teased her pubic hair.

And near, oh very near, only centimetres away, my iron hard cock speared up between her parted thighs, throbbing only a literal hairsbreadth away from the glistening lips of her cunt.

I'd gone into the industrial espionage bit to make her laugh. Her soft belly tremored under my caress; the breast rose and fell in my palm. She squeezed her thighs together, trapping the rigid column of my prick. 'You're leading up to something, aren't you?' she asked. 'I know your approach lanes, my love. It has to be sexy, doesn't it? So tell me: a new conquest?'

She shifted her position slightly, squirming her pelvis so that she could bring down one hand to press the velvet cock-head in against the hot, wet, partly open lips of her pussy.

I caught my breath. I very nearly dropped it, at that!

The sliding quiver of that moistly welcoming inner flesh,

trembling against the supersensitive zone immediately below the distended tip of the glans, was relaying a catalogue of thrills I didn't know existed, a web of excitement searing up from my cock to set fire to the whole area of my loins. 'A conquest, yes,' I admitted huskily, when the breath came back. 'But for you and not for me – if this particular tryst could interest you, that is.'

Cool fingers pressed the burning cock-head in and out, in and out of that electric labial embrace. 'Intriguing,' Elmira said. 'A new line for you – for us? The details, please – at once!'

I gave her such details as there were, mainly my own deductions from the data available. I filled her in on the guesswork, if you like. Then, wording it carefully, I outlined the way in which I figured she might help. If she wanted to.

Elvira laughed. 'You mean the busty redhead, darling?' she enquired. 'Big-tits with the friendly belly beneath? Why it would be a pleasure!'

And after that, moving suddenly: 'To seal the bargain, though, you must get on your knees in front of this chair and give me head . . . so that you can have – dare I say it? – a foretaste of *my* pleasure to come!'

14

Maybe, I thought, walking from the showroom to Piccadilly Circus, maybe industrial espionage wasn't so farfetched a concept after all – not in world where everyone seemed to have gone mad and nobody noticed anything unless it was wildly exaggerated!

I felt strangely out of place – admittedly I was in Carnaby Street – the one alien, the extra-terrestrial from the flying saucer, marooned in the Martian wilderness that was the London of the sixties.

Carnaby Street was a dingy thoroughfare behind Regent Street, until recently the haunt of cheap, pavement-bashing prostitutes farmed out by a Soho gang run by the Maltese Messina Brothers. A street of furtive comings and goings, of doors closing quietly and unspoken threats of razor-slashing.

Now it was technicolour gone crazy, a loud, blaring, thumping carnival of bad taste and poor design – the year's fashion show that wasn't. It was crowded with longhaired young men wearing winkle-picker shoes and union-jack tee-shirts, pert girls whose available cunts were only just hidden between the tops of tall boots and the hems of short, short, skintight leather skirts. Hideous pop music thumped, twanged and yelled deafeningly from the with-it shops – some of which displayed their wares on revolves like those on a pre-war stage, all of which were crammed with day-glo colours, photo blow-ups and tableaux of leather-suited plaster mannequins manacled together around cork palm trees or pyramids of musical instruments.

What the fuck was I, a manufacturer of pretty dresses for women without much money, doing in a world where the activities of fashionable hairdressers, guitarists and photographers vied with the drug habits of dissolute playboys for front-page space in the serious newspapers?

Dante, I thought, would have loved Carnaby Street. There was a crumb of comfort, however, as I turned into Beak Street: the last store of all was relaying this week's arrival in the Top Ten. It was by the Beatles. And it was called 'She Loves You'. That made me feel better; it made me think of Elvira.

If I was faced with industrial espionage, maybe she could do a Janet Bond and come up with a few answers and the big unmasking scene. Sean Connery, after all, had once been a Carnaby Street model!

I lunched with a chain-store buyer at the Café Royal. At three o'clock I emerged into a sundrenched Regent Street and bought an armful of that day's scandal-and-scare from the newspaper seller under the colonnade at the Piccadilly Circus end. A dry wind scattering bus tickets, empty cigarette packets and scraps of paper along the hot sidewalk flapped the full-size *Daily Mirror* poster hanging below the stacked journals and magazines. In the biggest of bold red capitals, the paper demanded: WHAT THE HELL IS GOING ON IN THIS COUNTRY?

Back in the office I leafed through my purchases to see if I could find an answer to the editorial question.

No answers; just a catalogue.

Stephen Ward, the society osteopath linked to the call-girl scandal which had provoked the resignation of War Minister John Profumo, had been arrested for 'living on immoral earnings'. The leading article in the left-wing *New Statesman* was headlined 'Are Virgins Obsolete?' The *Daily Herald* chimed in with 'Are We Going Sex Crazy?' The school magazine for an expensive snob boarding establishment for girls posed: 'Is Chastity Outmoded?' and a special edition of *Encounter* wrapped it up with 'Suicide of a Nation?'

Just questions at home then. In Scotland, behind closed doors, the Duke of Argyll was suing his wife for divorce and leaks from the courtroom hinted at unlimited sexual scandals, involving innumerable eminent people, being cited as evidence. A cyclone in East Pakistan killed more than 20,000. President Kennedy, who had outfaced Khrushchev over the Cuban missile crisis, was wildly cheered by more than a million Germans in West Berlin. The Queen of England had been booed in the street by supporters of the Campaign For Nuclear Disarmament on the Aldermaston March. A British government spokesman had admitted that Kim Philby, the foreign correspondent who had vanished in the Middle East earlier that year, had been the 'third man' in the Burgess-Maclean spy saga. In Parliament, a private member's bill allowing hereditary peers to disclaim their titles was passed. More than a thousand Yugoslavians were killed in an earthquake at Skoplje. Editorial columns in *The Times* and the *Scotsman* commented on a further sharp deterioration in relations between the Communist regimes of Russia and China. The percentage of Buddhist monks committing suicide by fire in South Vietnam was rising steeply. So were the recorded profits of United Distillers and other giants in the drinks and tobacco industries.

'Christ!' I said aloud in my empty office. 'What time's the next space shuttle to return me to bloody Mars?'

I shoved the whole lot, dailies, evenings, magazines and reviews, into the waste bin under my desk – a twin of the one in the production manager's office which had housed the industrial espionage evidence.

Someone was tapping at the office door. It was the production manager himself. 'Miss Elton-Shaw is here to see you,' he announced. 'For the interview.'

Ah. The applicant for the work supervisor's position left vacant when I fired Gladys Carter.

I sighed. 'Show her in,' I said.

I flipped through the CV before the woman appeared. Christian name Agatha. Age thirty-two. Graduate of the Combined London Schools of High-grade Personnel Management (CLSHPM). Satisfactory references from M&S, the John Lewis group, a Plymouth rainwear specialist and – handwritten – a trouser-maker in the East End who was (I happened to know) the supplier in secret to some of the capital's ritziest private tailors. 'O' Levels, 'A' levels, and all that. And Cheltenham Ladies' College, of all upmarket schools! At least the interview should be different.

It was.

Miss Agatha Elton-Shaw did not, for a start, look the kind of lady who would be at home presiding eagle-eyed over two or three score nine-to-five seamstresses aged anything from eighteen to fifty-five.

Eagle-eyed maybe. A kind of lady certainly. But more the jolly-hockey-sticks type with green wellies, a barbour and Adrian's Range Rover at point-to-point weekends.

You get the general idea? The visuals did nothing to spoil the picture.

She was tall, undeniably athletic, yet with a clumsiness that was almost gauche in certain of her movements. She wore no make-up, her fair hair was drawn tightly back into a bun, and her blue eyes were a little prominent. There were cheekbones and a good jawline in her lean face, though the first thing you noticed about it was the oversize front teeth which rested on the lower lip and were never entirely hidden, even when she wasn't smiling.

Smiling, I saw at once, was a device she used a lot. Perhaps to account for the horse teeth. I also saw (high marks for initiative) that she was wearing a Dulok dress – one of our summer specials: printed cotton, red, blue and yellow flowers, with a white linen collar and cuffs on the short sleeves. The dress revealed long legs, nothing much at bust level, and respectable hips. And of course there was the plummy voice.

I asked my usual lead question. Why was she applying for this particular job?

'Oh, well . . . Gosh! . . . for several reasons,' she replied. 'First, to be honest, I want to stay in London. Secondly, I'm mad about clothes: to be in the dress business still excites me. Then, well, it's the *supervisory* bit. I mean, I've always got on jolly well with my girls, and one does, after all, prefer a *responsible* position, rather than being bossed around all the time, doesn't one?'

'One does,' I admitted dryly. Her answers, I thought, were about par for the course – and the proprietorial 'my girls' could indicate the right kind of officer approach.

There were more questions, technical ones, designed to check her knowledge of and experience with the manufacturing – as opposed to the personnel – side of the trade. And then, I have no idea why I chose this particular one, I picked up a reference letter. It was, as it happened, the last job she had had. 'Why did you leave Otterware?' I asked.

'The rainwear specialist?' She smiled. 'Actually, they left me.'

'Meaning?'

'Business was expanding too fast. They needed new premises. The place they found was in Huddersfield. And, I mean . . . well, one can accept the south-west at a pinch, but to live and work in the industrial north' – a ladylike shudder – 'is simply not on, is it?'

'I suppose not,' I said.

'Apart from which, there's the cricket.'

'The . . . cricket?'

'Can't let the team down in mid-season, can one?'

'You mean – you *play* cricket?'

'Of course,' Miss Elton-Shaw told me. 'My people live in Surrey. I keep wicket for the village eleven.'

'I don't understand about the expanding business,' I said, more because I could think of no suitable reply than because I was really interested. 'I mean, I know it rains a lot in Devonshire, but this is a particularly dry summer and I would have thought—'

'Oh, it's not the actual macs,' she interrupted. 'The waders and proofed skirts and fishermen's jackets and suchlike. It's the huge boom in private orders, the made-to-measure, the specialized equipment that's made the move necessary.'

'Specialized *equipment*?' I echoed.

'You know.' Another toothy smile. 'Own-design private orders made up, customers' ideas worked out, mail order. And of course the spread of the SM subculture.'

'Call me stupid, but I'm afraid I don't know.' I picked up the reference again. 'Otterware? I'm afraid I'm not familiar with the brand, but . . .?' I let the sentence die.

Agatha Elton-Shaw had been sitting in the visitor's swivel chair. Now she thrust her tall figure upright and paced up and down in front of my desk. 'The company started in the north of Scotland,' she announced. 'Rain every day! The two types who founded it had a workforce of four. They used only Wigan and the lighter weight Indiana – thin canvassy material rubberized on the outside – for their outerwear. You know: the classic shiny black mackintosh. Then they found that there were a lot of people, not primarily interested in keeping dry, who would pay good money for rubberized rainwear, especially if it was black. The kinky sex brigade, not to put too fine a point on it. So they expanded and migrated south. Pretty soon they were into the specialist stuff: more than half the output was mackintosh jeans, shirts, underwear, helmets, you name it. Plus the more specifically kinky private orders – sheets, pillow cases, even strait-jackets at times!'

'What you call the . . . SM subculture?'

Agatha – by now I felt I knew her well enough for the Christian name – stopped in mid-stride. She nodded. 'Sex parties, dominant females, boots and chains, private dungeons. You know this wildly popular television series, *The Avengers* – that's black leather, but it's all part of the sixties scene.' She shook her head. 'Sometimes, when I hear the term swinging used, I think it means swinging from the jolly old chandelier!'

'It takes all sorts,' I encouraged, hoping for more.

More is what I got.

'To return to Otterware,' Agatha said, 'what really boosted them was the arrival of latex and what's called natural rubber on the scene. After all, mackintosh is quite stiff: there's only so much you can do with it in the matter of cut and fit. But latex' – a big shrug – 'it can be welded or moulded rather than stitched or machined; it fits like a second skin! We started off with two new lines: the Skinsilk range – mainly rubber catsuits for skiers and other water sports – and the heavier gauge sheet latex or vinyl for the Closefit outerwear series. But frankly it's the big new market for "private" restriction equipment – punishment helmets, face masks, gags, rubber corsets, mistress dresses, hospital nurse gear in white – this is the branch of the business that's spelled out Huddersfield.'

I was thinking of Maureen's two cupboards. 'After that, you may find it dull here,' I ventured.

'Like love,' Agatha said, 'interest is where you find it.'

She sat down in the chair again. Seeing her immobile, I was aware during a moment's reflection of something I had increasingly noticed while she was in motion.

Despite the awkwardness of her posture, the at times coltish lack of elegance in her use of arms, legs and torso, there was about her in some way an extraordinary aura of concealed dynamism, a sense of suppressed or latent energy awaiting only the right stimulus to trigger it into action. She reminded me a little of a greyhound waiting for the trap to open.

Maybe, padded up, the entry of the bowler's fast ball into her gloved hands gave her the required lift? I thought unkindly. And there, for the first time, I seriously misjudged Miss Elton-Shaw and her view on life.

I realized this a bit later the same evening. The staff had gone home; the production and sales teams were at a trade paper shinding at the Troc; Shields, the night-watchman, wasn't due in until eight, when it was almost dark. I had virtually decided to offer Agatha the job – no other candidate who was remotely suitable had appeared anyway – and I was showing her around the place: workshops, stockroom, loading bay, packaging plant, the small office that would be hers. At one point we stopped in Shields' cubby-hole and, goodness knows why – memories of the break-in night perhaps? – I absent-mindedly pulled open the drawer of his little wooden desk. Blue eyes glared up at me and vivid red lips wolfishly grimaced.

'Christ!' I exclaimed. 'That's awful. I mean I didn't intend to . . .'

'What is it?' my new supervisor asked.

Wordlessly, remembering the incident of the puncture outfit, I pulled the limp head and shoulders of the neatly folded inflatable lady into view.

'I didn't mean to pry,' I said guiltily. 'Poor old Shields!'

'As you observed,' Agatha said, 'it takes all sorts.' She

tested the slackly grinning mask with a finger and thumb. 'At least she's not plastic!'

I rearranged the rubber woman as well as I could and closed the drawer. We were on our way back upstairs to seal our bargain with a drink in my office when Agatha said: 'The interesting thing about your watchman is . . . whether he blows up that woman because he can't find a real one to go to bed with him, or whether he uses her because he's so much into rubber that he can't make love without it.'

'Search me,' I said. 'I wouldn't know. Anyway, I'm afraid I'm not myself into what you call the SM subculture.'

Agatha was sipping a large Scotch-on-the-rocks from the cocktail cabinet behind my desk. 'Everyone's into it,' she said, looking at me over the rim of her glass, 'in one way or another. Or capable of being led into it. In every sexual coupling there's this division – the top and the bottom, the boss and the slave. And the boss doesn't necessarily have to be male.' She gave me the smile. 'To say nothing of plain human curiosity.'

'True enough,' I conceded. 'But it doesn't go as far as the inflication of pain, or submission and restriction physically, of the whole—'

'Look at the *Kama-Sutra*,' she cut in. 'At all the Arab and oriental sex practices, at the Japanese Geisha tradition, even at some of the northern European indoor winter games! From love bites to an occasional slap on the bum or the implied bondage of wrestling and bear hugs. It's all there.' She drained her glass. I refilled it. I splashed more whisky into my own. I drank.

'Bondage,' Agatha said, 'is no more than an exteriorization of an emotional situation that exists already: the leader and the led. The distinction between SM and an energetic tussle on the sofa or the double bed is artificial, illusory. It's no more than a matter of degree.'

I smiled. 'You may be right,' I said loftily. 'In theory. But I'm afraid this is one direction in which I, for one, would find it totally impossible to be – as you say – led.'

'You want to bet?' Agatha said.

150

I'm not entirely sure how it happened. Perhaps the third whisky was stronger. And there was certainly an element of the school-kid 'I dare you!' challenge in there somewhere. Maybe the obstinate *demand* to be proved right is stronger in all of us than we care to admit. Maybe it's just that I have to – always have to – have the last word in any argument, can never, ever be in the wrong. Whatever the basic reason, there was this crazy urge that evening which led me into the situation before I realized that Agatha's obstinate demand to be proved right was at least as strong – and at least as obsessive – as my own!

I say an urge that led me . . . but in fact it was I who was doing the leading. At first anyway.

And I had said, angrily: 'All right, then. If you're so certain: prove it!'

In other words I was accepting her bet.

So there I was, fully dressed, lying back in the visitor's chair with my arms bound to my sides with my own belt, my wrists tied together behind my back with my necktie, and my ankles secured with the same-material belt of the Dulok dress that Agatha was wearing!

She wasn't wearing it now. She had left me helpless there for a few minutes while she took the big shoulder bag she carried into the executive loo on the first floor. When she came back she looked rather different.

For a start, the bun had been unwound and the drawn-back hair shaken loose. It was shoulder-length or more, kind of a golden blonde and very glossy. And, framed by this softness, her lean features acquired a hawkish, almost predatory look.

Instead of the flowered dress, she was attired – I think that's the jargon word – in a very narrow, knee-length skirt in black kid glove-leather, a skin-tight vee-neck blouse in red latex, and elbow-length black rubber gloves. The blouse had loose three-quarter sleeves and was plastered to her angular body closely enough to show that she wore no bra, and that she was almost flat-chested but with extra-large nipples, outlined by the shiny material.

She was, I have to say, an arresting sight. Not sexy, or not for me, but certainly impressive.

So what now?

(I should explain here that the ill-tempered, slightly tipsy and increasingly heated discussion which had resulted in this situation had been conducted nevertheless with icy politeness. It was implicitly understood that this was a difference of opinion on a single subject, an academic question debated by two independent adults, which had nothing whatever to do with the fact that we happened – outside the debate – to have an employer-employee relationship. I had offered her the job; she had accepted; the job – whatever occurred – remained hers. The bet I had accepted? That in a simple SM situation, which I agreed to accept, she would be unable to turn me on.)

With a woman who wasn't my type physically, and after an impersonal discussion that was totally objective, this was just about the least likely basis for a sexual 'transaction' that it was possible to imagine! Craftily, remembering how many promising dates had been killed stone dead by 'frank' discussions of sexual tastes, I had deliberately steered things onto this level.

I did my best to keep them there now. In as normal a way as I could in my position, I made no comment whatsoever on Agatha's fetishistic appearance, and simply asked: 'Are you specifically interested then, in a personal way, in the SM thing? Or is it just a generalized—?'

'I'm interested in everything,' she cut in brusquely. 'I like to know the way people work. It's part of my job in any case.'

'Yes, of course. To supervise, you have to be able to order, to command. But surely not to the psychological extent of examining their . . . private . . . impulses?'

That was a mistake. She seized on the point. 'My CLSHPM diploma included a year's philosophy and two years' psychology,' she said. 'It's the private impulses which lie at the root of public behaviour. One cannot hope to exert authority over people if one doesn't understand how they tick. If one is controlling a workshop full of twenty or thirty women, it's not enough to be aware of them individually: one has to learn also how that multiple individual, the mob, works.'

True enough. She was probably very good at it too: she had the right schoolmistressy approach. But this time I made no reply. I wasn't going to field every ball.

She was working her hands more tightly into the fingers of the rubber gloves.

'For the moment, however, Mr Dulok' – a tight little smile – 'we shall forget the crowd and concentrate on the individual. Since you have challenged me and accepted my wager, we shall proceed to examine the fashion in which you tick.' Smile. 'I intend to find out how *you* work!'

She strode across and stood by the chair. The gloved hands, I noticed, were very long, very thin, with powerful fingers.

My bound legs were stretched out in front of me, heels on the floor, as I half lay in the chair. She swung one summer shoe over them and stood straddled above my knees, looking down at me with those black rubber hands on her hips. The leather skirt was stretched very tight by her parted legs, with horizontal knife creases between the thighs. I couldn't see up it – I don't think I was supposed to – and the material gave no indication of the structure of belly and mons slung between her cushiony hips.

I was struck suddenly, soberly, by the utter ridiculousness of the situation. Here I was in my own office, already late for dinner, pinioned with my own belt and necktie, staring stupidly up at a rangy county-type female I'd only just met – and just employed, moreover – who was dressed like a window model from a Carnaby Street store!

How crazy could you get?

Crazier, I found out. She had leaned down, bending from the waist, her face expressionless, and placed black hands on the front of my trousers.

The belt had already gone. I'd had the suit some time: the fly was buttoned, not zipped.

Coolly, she undid the buttons, one by one. There were six.

She opened the fly, laying back the edges on my belly in two neat triangles. I felt cool fingers reach for my shirt-tails, draw them aside, stow them, swiftly rolled, above the waistband of my Y-fronts. Then, more forceful suddenly, the underpants jerked quickly down, over the belly, past the genitals, until they were lodged tightly against the trouser crotch.

The black gloves lifted my balls, exposing them like eggs in a bird's nest at the lowest point of the splayed-fly triangle.

Then, gently enough, the flaccid tube of my cock was pulled out and up, and laid limply along the part of my belly that was bared.

I lay there transfixed by that expressionless stare – gazing back with as much of an I-dare-you defiance as I could manage. Eventually she moved away, rummaged in her shoulder bag, found a cigarette, lit it from my desk lighter, and sat down in my chair.

She sat there without moving, without speaking, studying my lewdly bared genitals as she smoked, until the cigarette was finished and she stubbed it out in the ashtray.

I matched her silence for silence. Motionless. Staring at the ceiling. The situation, once the basic absurdity had been accepted, was intriguing perhaps – but certainly not sexy as far as I was concerned. If it was a question of who reacted first, I reckoned I could outstare her at that.

Abruptly, she pushed back the chair and rose to her feet. She walked back to me and, still without saying anything, she bent down and seized me by the shoulders, hauling me into a sitting position. I knew she was athletic but the next ploy took me entirely by surprise. Agatha lifted me bodily from the chair, spun my fettered body around, then grabbed me by the upper arms and lowered me, none too delicately, to the floor.

I lay on my back, staring now at a different part of the ceiling, wondering – once my initial gasp of astonishment was spent – what reaction I should permit myself, whether or not this time the conversation should be resumed. But before any decision had recommended itself she had leapt over me, dragged the leather skirt almost as far as the top of her thighs, and sat down on my prone body.

Her weight subsided on the upper part of my belly, driving the breath momenterily from my lungs as she settled herself astride, facing my feet with her knees drawn up to straddle my hips and my exposed genitals below and immediately in front of her.

Okay, I thought: no eyeball contact. Does this indicate inhibition, embarrassment? So what does she hope to do? Squeeze my balls to make me scream? Slap my cock harder and harder until I agree to suck her pussy? Take off her pants – if she wears any – and ride me like a jockey?

Not much chance in any of those cases if she hadn't got a hard-on to play with.

I was all right there in any case: JT was still as limp as a feather bed.

But I had forgotten one thing, delving much deeper than necessary in the armoury of the dominatrice: the simplest, most direct, attack is usually the best.

No embarrassment, no inhibition, just the most practical stance. I heard her voice, calm, matter-of-fact: 'I wouldn't want there to be any question here that this situation could be viewed in any way as some kind of ploy to engineer myself into your job, a persuasion to soften you up. You had in any case offered me the job before it started. Nor would I like to think that you would in any way use it to engineer me *out* of the job.'

'No problem,' I made myself say. 'The job is yours whatever.' Not that I needed 'softening up': I was good and soft already, and I intended to stay that way.

'This has nothing to do with your life or my life or the job or the company or anything,' Agatha said. 'And I should emphasize here that the gear I'm wearing has not been put on in an attempt to influence you: I'm wearing it for me, not because I'm especially into this kind of thing but because it confirms me – it's an exteriorization, like the bondage – in the rôle I'm playing for these few minutes. I'll say it again: this is a private wager between two individuals, and it has nothing whatever to do with anything outside its own terms.'

'Okay, okay,' I said, wondering whether she wouldn't have

been better advised to take two years' philosophy and skip the second psychology year.

'So now,' she said, squatting on my hips with her back to me, the haw-haw voice as cool as ever, 'I'm going to pick up your cock and toss you off – that's what we used to say in school, isn't it? I can't bear the term wank. It's crude.'

I felt the dampish pressure of shiny rubber against the skin of my tool. She lifted it away from my belly, latex-gloved fingers and thumb holding the soft shaft at right-angles to my loins.

'I'm going to toss you off,' Agatha repeated, 'quite deliberately and forcefully, until you come. I shall go on milking your prick until I bring you to orgasm and you're squirting your spunk between my rubber-gloved fingers.' She uttered a small, vindictive laugh. 'And there's nothing, nothing whatever, you can do about it!'

Oh, yeah? I thought. Make me come when I don't even have a hard-on. In a pig's arse you will!

Tightly tied like that and under her not inconsiderable weight, it was true that there was nothing I could do in the way of escape. To struggle would merely make me look ridiculous. All right: more ridiculous still. But whether or not I came, there was certainly something I could do there . . .

'To make you come will be no problem,' my captor continued remorselessly. 'A piece of cake, you might say. But for the purposes of this wager . . . to win my bet and prove that you *can* indeed be led, even mildly, into the realms of SM, I have to make sure, absolutely certain, that you *enjoy* your orgasm, that it gives you as much pleasure as a standard – er – fuck.'

'You'll be lucky!' I said rather rudely.

'We shall see,' Agatha said.

She began manipulating my cock. Skilfully, it must be admitted, the force tempered with a certain lightness of touch, a featherlight sensitivity of the fingertips evident even through the latex sheathing her hand.

She was using the other one now, pulling my balls away from my body and holding them fondle-tight as the working

156

hand pulled the loose skin of the limp cock forward and up, squeezed over the retracted glans, then hard down, down again with the base of the shaft gripped hard by an encircling finger and thumb.

This was going to have no effect, must on no account have any effect whatsoever, on me. I lay gritting my teeth, thinking furiously of basting and bodices, of gussets and girdles, of felling hands and shoulder pads and Chinese buttonholers. Of cabbages and kings, if you like.

Agatha was crooning wordlessly to herself as she worked. I hoped she was having a good time. Cerainly the expert pull-and-push rhythm with which she was pumping me seemed at least to be giving her something. Too bad it wasn't going to do anything for me! All that wasted energy . . .

I was reminded of a favourite P.G. Wodehouse quote: like Aunt Dahlia with Jeeves, Agatha was staring down at me like a bear about to receive a bun.

I heard her catch her breath. Much lower down the scale I also heard a tiny insidious squelch. The black rubber glove skimmed more swiftly, more surely, up and down my shaft. Shit, I thought angrily, a bead of moisture must have appeared at the tip of my cock-head . . . and the inadvertent secretion was lubricating the pistoned stroke that was now reacting on the nerves of my loins.

I tried not to shift my position, but an involuntary tremor pulsed through my belly, and for a tenth of a second my hips arched off the floor. She was wanking faster, harder . . . and – *Christ!* – I actually was beginning to get hard, dammit! Absolutely against my will, I could feel the stiffening core swell against the outer skin. Try as I would to forget it, to obliterate it, to multiply numbers in my head, I had to concede: I was back in the music business, I had that old feeling!

As my tool lengthened and inexorably stiffened, Amanda's breath quickened. So, too, did the rapidity of her masturbatory strokes. After all, she had something to grab hold of now.

One-two-three-four, one-two-three-four – the measured rhythm pistoning above my unwilling loins became harder, accelerated faster as the shaft became totally rigid. I felt as though she was pulling out the whole of my guts through the cock-head.

No longer totally under my own control, my chest began to heave. The little crooning noises increased in volume as Amanda's splayed buttocks shifted on my hips.

I was trying desperately to think of something, anything, else. The way the refrain of an old song will sometimes haunt you, refuse to get out of your mind, a line – a single line – of some poet or other repeated itself endlessly in my head. *But though I do not wish to wish these things . . .*

Well, one of the things I certainly didn't wish, right now, was to have an erection. Still less to have myself jacked off by a tall female athlete wearing a rubber blouse, whose cunt, at this moment, must be flattened against my pubic— Stop! For God's sake think of something else.

Back to the rag-trade. To the shoulder pads and gussets – Gusset: a piece let into a garment, esp. underwear, to strengthen a portion (usu. between the legs) [Shorter Oxford]— Quit that! Change direction at once. *In the Financial Times Index the dollar rose three points today . . . so how much would this bitch be pocketing if she was on the game and I was an SM punter . . . ?* Danger ahead! Try harder. *Desmond Leslie, the UFO expert, erupted last night onto the set of a TV satire show and attempted to knock out critic Bernard Levin because his review of a one-woman revue by Leslie's actress wife 'was not the act of a gentleman'.* Better. So what about gentleman, then? *Gentlemen prefer blondes . . .*

And the unending, unnerving, pistoned pumping of my bursting cock by the blonde astride me was sending me . . . was making me . . . was agonizing the head of my grip-wrapped tool and . . . *Think of something. Concentrate. Think of meditation, of the Bhagavad Ghita, of the Beatles. No don't think of the Beatles. 'She Loves You'. 'From Me To You'. 'A Hard Day's Night' . . . Enough. Concentrate on the largest, nearest, unvaried, homogeneous mass . . .*

In front and above me: a broad and shining expanse of tight red rubber, fanned by tiny horizontal creases beneath the moving arms.

And, yes, the blonde hair preferred. Hanging forward over her face now as she bent her back to concentrate on *her* work, the rubber gloves sliding, gliding, riding with greased ease the *fulminating* tension of my aching and throbbing stem, and the wet cock-head teased by that cascade of glossy gold.

Concentrate, hell. When you came to think of it, what the fuck did it matter? *Relax*, man. Just go with it.

The two clenched, lubricated, rubber hands fucking me, sucking me, drawing me on . . . out . . .

And then, abrupt but inevitable, the beginning of the depthless, soaring plunge . . . the Gadarene swine . . . the downstairs rush to make the last Underground to Edgware . . . the roaring wind of the delayed, no longer delayed, parachute drop . . .

I came.

The whole of my body, from the waist downwards, convulsed. As she had wanted, my savaged cock jerked and spurted, spilling the proof of my defeat between her black and shining fingers.

Aftermath – there's always an aftermath, isn't there? But I have to say Agatha handled ours with both tact and delicacy.

From the instant my loins spasmed and I heard the strange orgasmic noises gasping from my mouth, she had begun subtly to disengage. Not crudely, hastily, no suggestion of *Well, that's that! So now let's get the hell out!* But with the sensitivity to leave well alone, to avoid the boast, avert any quesion of humiliation and leave me to gather such dignity as I could find.

By the time I opened my eyes she had released me and vanished. And, after all, I had nothing to do but find a towel, some kleenex, and do up a few buttons before I resumed my own idea of me.

When she came back from the executive washroom, Agatha was once more dressed in the flower-print Dulok special. Her hair was drawn back and put up. She was smoking. Her smile was conspiratorial . . . but friendly. 'You're humming something,' she said. 'A dactyl and two spondees; followed by two spondees, repeated. It's a tune; it

159

seems to tell me something, but I can't quite . . . what is it?'

'It tells you everything, Eng. Lit. lady,' I said. 'It's an old song, probably from the forties, with a brand-new meaning – as of today! The first line goes like this.' I sang, with emphasis:

'Well, all-*right* . . . oh-*kay* . . . you *WIN* . . .!'

Agatha laughed. 'The point,' she said, 'was that it had to give you pleasure. Honestly, did it?'

'Yes,' I said. And I don't think it sounded as shamefaced as I felt.

She nodded, honour satisfied. 'See you Monday at eight,' she said.

'Just a minute.' Something had occurred to me. 'Look – we had a bet. I accepted the wager. I lost. But although we agreed what we were betting on, we never established for how much; we never quoted the stakes!' I grinned. 'So, okay, you won – now tell me what prize you are going to claim for yourself as victor?'

The smile this time was a shade more than conspiratorial. 'The opportunity,' she said, 'to meet you again, person to person, out of the office, in private. Perhaps to play for higher stakes – double or quits, for instance?'

'Dinner will bloody well have to wait,' I told Elvira when at last I got home. 'Confession-time in the television-room is like *now*!'

'It's a cold dinner,' Elvira said. 'I'm already on my way to the TV-room myself! I made contact today with your old workroom supervisor.'

'Snap!' I cried. 'I made contact today with our new one.'

'Great. And so?'

'I think it was the actor Ian Carmichael who said once that he'd always dreamed of being a Sheikess's plaything,' I said. 'You know: full of Eastern promise. I can't match that, but I'm here to say that, this very evening, I became the plaything of a Carnaby Street window display model!'

160

15

This time I couldn't resist it. I'd veered off the usual rails by suggesting Gladys Carter, the nubile redhead, as a possible conquest for Elvira. Purely for business reasons, of course. Now I reckoned I might as well go the whole con-man's hog. I would, for this one time, act the voyeur and spy on them. Strictly for personal reasons, if you must know.

I wouldn't break The Rule, though. I'd own up to Elvira afterwards.

The first shots in the campaign to seduce Gladys were to be fired in public. They were to meet for lunch in a Soho restaurant not too far from the Preckner workshops. Afterwards it would be back to our place – easy enough because it was a Saturday and nobody was working. Hubby of course had been given strict instructions to stay away from home at least until dark.

But Hubby was particularly anxious to eavesdrop on the tête-à-tête lunch party . . . simply because it gave me a hell of a kick watching Elvira do her personality number, waving her magic sexual wand. And especially when she didn't know I'd be watching.

Okay, okay: I know I said I was no voyeur. But if one's going to cheat at one's own game, there's no point trying to draw the line: no lines exist in this kind of situation.

For an efficient eavesdrop in a crowded restaurant, though – when one's known to both of the subjects – there's one evident essential: some kind of disguise.

I know something about disguises. When I was a lad, I worked for a top theatrical costumier. And the golden rule here is: keep it simple. Absurdities such as false beards, toupees, dark glasses or a crutch are out. All they do is draw attention to you. And the disguised person will be ill at ease too, and make himself all the more noticeable. Speech, dress, stance, hair-style, walk – these are the features most distinctive of the individual. And, given some know-how, the easiest to alter.

Normally, I take pride in holding myself particularly upright. To be slightly round-shouldered, a trifle stooped, would therefore be the first element, especially when sitting at table. With this, of course, there must be a suitable walk. My usual stride is springy, almost bouncy – kids were always mimicking it when I was at school – so now we adopt a gait that drags the feet a bit. Something that stops short of being a slouch but goes with the altered posture.

Dress helps here: a jacket that stands away from the nape rather than fitting closely; a shirt with sleeves a little too long; trousers that stop above the ankle. Shoes that are two sizes too large help with the foot-dragging walk and contribute here to the general air of slovenliness. I emphasized this with the clothes I actually wore. Normally it's the dark two-piece, white shirt, silk tie and black highly polished shoes. Today it was a shapeless wool-jersey jacket, worn over a long-sleeved vee-neck pullover, plum-coloured, and a sloppily knotted tweed tie. The trousers were corduroy and – horror of horror! – beneath them were sandals with wool socks . . .

The most vulnerable parts are the facial features and the head in general. With of course the voice.

The *register* of the voice, of course, cannot be altered. But, to some extent, the tonality, the articulation and especially the pronunciation can. The last of these is purely a matter of concentration (a sprinkling of American – tomayto, gotten, elevator, My Gard! – helps here). One or two easy tricks can affect the others. Two small pads of cotton-wool – the harder, not the fluffy kind – lodged between gum and cheek on either side of the nose can fatten and change the outline of a lean face like mine and marginally change the resonance of the voice; small wooden rings inserted into the nose can flare the nostrils and make the voice more nasal. If your speech is fast and clipped, like mine, you must remember to drawl.

But accents, regional or foreign, are out. Much too difficult to keep up.

None of these trivia is decisive, but together they turn the attention away from the known you. When it's a question of remaining unrecognized by people who already know you, the essential is *not to give them what they expect*, visually. Basically this boils down to (1) general appearance of the face, and (2) body language.

I have a habit of sitting with my ankles twisted together and my feet stowed beneath the seat of an upright chair. At a desk or table, I often rest one elbow on the flat surface and pinch my chin between the forefinger and thumb of that hand. I play with an escaped lock of hair behind my left ear. I catch my lower lip between my top teeth when making a decision. I scratch one side (the left) of my nose. So: *sit foursquare with the feet planted apart, in front of the chair legs. Keep the hands in the lap when not occupied with knives or forks. Leave nose and hair alone.* And like that.

In my case the hair was already taken care of. Like most men in the past couple of years, I wore mine brushed forward from the crown, slightly overhanging the brow. A spin-off, I suppose, of the ridiculous styles of Presley and Tony Curtis. Today, however, with the aid of hot water and brilliantine, it was brushed straight back, as severely as Agatha's, and tucked – no parting – behind the ears. This, together with wide owl-frame spectacles (plain glass), gave me a much higher forehead and made me look, I hoped, like a history lecturer from one of the smaller red-brick universities.

I was installed, three tables away, before Elvira and Gladys arrived. I knew where they'd be sitting because I'd heard her make the phone reservation. I was studying an *Evening Standard* over a Campari-and-soda (Italy was in for intellectuals) because I'd told the waiter I was expecting a lady and would order when she arrived. There was no question of my listening in to the conversation. In Soho at lunchtime that would have been impossible even at the next table. I wanted just to take in the mime, as it were, and guess how far my wife had got. Sorry – gotten. It would be, for me, rather like watching a ballet of which I knew the story but

163

was ignorant of the individual steps and leaps and entrechats.

Elvira was doing her number, in top gear at that, even before their ladylike buttocks had subsided onto the chairs held for them by friendly neighbourhood waiters. She was very skilfully made up, quite radiant, her slender frame indescribably *feminine* in a pleated, pecil-slim white skirt, dull gold slingbacks, and an ultra-lightweight, sea-blue Pringle or Braemar woolly with silvered threads. Her bra-less breasts shimmered the marine facade each time she laughed.

Gladys was dressed in a pinkish sweater moulded to her ample breasts, the shape of her wired bra evident through the tight material. Her skirt was wide and flared, over-printed in a Paisley design mainly violet and blue. She wore black tights with clocks halfway up the calf, and there was a checkered stole draped over her shoulders in zigzagged stripes of black and yellow. With that dark red hair and creamy complexion, she could have been a fashionable Irishwoman displaying her catholic taste.

'My dear,' Elvira said sweetly as they settled at the table and reached for the menus – this was one of the few exchanges I did hear – 'My dear, how clever of you to choose such a *pretty* colour for your sweater! So daring with your red hair, and *such* a complete success! Burnt orange is it – the colour, I mean?'

'Melon, actually. It was one of this year's *House and Garden* choices, and I thought—'

'Yes, of course. Melon. The Charentais variety rather than the Canteloupe, I fancy. Quite ravishing. A splendid contrast to the yellow in the stole. But then your resplendent *poitrine* is itself such a contrast to the waist—'

'Potween?'

'The French, dear, for the whole – shall we say? – upperworks. Only used, normally, when these are impressive. As indeed yours most certainly are!'

'Oh, the tits!' Gladys smiled. 'Well, you know – I find blokes do tend to concentrate there, and it does help if a girl keeps them, you know, in shape.'

That was all I could hear for the moment, as they went into a huddle with the Maître D over their luncheon choice.

Champagne cocktails as an apéritif, I noticed! Oh, well – it was all in a good business cause if my wife could wheedle out of Gladys everything she knew. Her fingers had already rested twice beside the gold bangle on the redhead's plump wrist as they chose.

I watched with fascinated interest the effect of the subtle waves of Elvira's sexual wand. In no time, Gladys was all shining eyes, hanging on her seducer's every word. My own sexual wand, indeed, was already exhibiting a stir of interest, knowing what was – almost certainly – going to happen in my own house later that afternoon.

I can't describe the lunch in detail, gesture by gesture. All I can say is that the fascination exercised by my wife was, as usual . . . well, fascinating. And it wasn't the rabbit and stoat kind either: Gladys was in no sense spellbound; she was vivacious, she reacted, she joked. It was evident that both of them were having a ball. Elvira really could have made an execution mutually pleasurable!

My attention was in any case partly divided by the arrival of my own lunch guest. A couple, I had reckoned, would be less obtrusive than a single oddball male. My mistake. Not with this guest.

She was riding on a cloud of Lancôme *Magie* – a swirl of swathed breasts and flying panels in violet tulle, the original blonde bombshell turning every head in the place.

Maureen.

I had called her, using the 'friend of a friend' opening and using the name of my night-watchman, Albert Shields. A nice lunch first, I had suggested, and then we could 'get down to business' during the afternoon. She had agreed at once.

I hadn't realized that we would make *quite* such an oddly-assorted couple, and the second facer came when the head-waiter showed her to 'Mr Shields's table'. She undulated into the chair next to mine and exclaimed: 'Edward! How very nice to see you! I always prefer old friends.'

'How did you know?' I gulped when I had recovered my breath.

165

'But your voice,' she trilled. 'I recognized it at once when you called. I'm good on voices.'

'Among other things,' I said gallantly. 'What are you going to have – a champagne cocktail?'

Facer Three – bad news is eternally a triangle, they say – came when Elvira and Gladys were ready to leave. Still disseminating that 'greater love hath no man' aura.

My wife was on her way to the powder room to repair her still faultless make-up.

She chose a route that took her past our table. Looking straight ahead as she walked. She was almost past when her heavy handbag – it was beautifully judged – swung against the rim of my soup plate and tipped half a litre of hot *minestrone* into my lap.

'Oh, my goodness!' she cried as I leaped to my feet clutching my crotch. 'Oh, how *awful*! My dear sir, how can you ever forgive me?' And then, as waiters rushed up with hot water and towels: 'I'm not quite so clumsy *as a rule* . . .'

Okay, okay: I got the message. She didn't have to use the italics. I was cheating. Period.

So much for disguise.

By the time I was partially cleaned up, both of them had left the restaurant.

'Rather a common woman, I thought,' Maureen observed. 'And reely, did you see the person she was with? All those colours: she looked like a barmaid!'

The next time I saw the happy pair, everything was flesh-coloured. Everything, that is, but the wired, black lace bra that Gladys was wearing – and Elvira was busy unfastening that.

I had told Maureen that I had to go home and change. Naturally. 'Of course, I shall pay for your time in the afternoon,' I said. 'But be back at the Cumberland by five. I'll be dropping back to earth from the sixth floor round about then. Okay?'

'That will be naice, dear,' Maureen said.

I didn't go home to change. I let myself into the office, where I had left my normal clothes and effected what I'd hoped would be my transformation. It was after I looked like me again that I went home. I took a taxi, paid it off a block away, and stole in secretly the back way, via the woodshed and the laundry room.

Elvira and I had two or three secret viewpoints and spyholes which we used occasionally for agreed voyeuristic purposes. I didn't think she'd expect me back since she'd seen me herself with a sexpot blonde, but I knew she'd have covered these up anyway . . . just in case. There was, however, one vantage point even she knew nothing about.

The big guest room, where she usually consummated her conquests, was fitted with a huge looking glass, cemented in, which took up half the wall opposite the bed. And this glass, if you happened to be stashed behind the rails of model dresses in the built-in cupboard of my stockroom-study next door, happened to be a two-way mirror . . .

I'd bought it once on the off chance – an impulse buy – from a rich old idiot called Raymond Large, who had apparently stripped half the bawdy houses in Paris when they were ruled illegal after the war. And this was one item he didn't have room for in his own country place.

I had it installed when the house was being redecorateed and Elvira – oddly enough – was spending an illicit weekend in Paris with a young actor she fancied.

That was one of the ones that didn't work out. And I could never find out why because it was all over before she came back and I inaugurated the mirror.

The investment was nevertheless well worthwhile. The glass was so wide, and in such good nick, that it really felt as though one was sitting in a chair about three feet from the bed!

The wall was thick, so there was no dialogue. But the picture – man, that was something!

Elvira, of course, loved it as a regular mirror. She was always turned on by seeing her conquests from a variety of angles – and seeing herself seducing them. During her secret sessions, therefore, she was constantly staring straight at the glass. Usually with the spaced-out expression of one about to take off. And to me on the far side of the two-way mirror it was exactly as though she was staring straight at *me* . . . sharing her lewdness and lust in unknowing complicity.

I don't know why this should have been such an extra turn on for me – perhaps because, being in secret, it was forbidden fruit? – but it certainly had the flies open quick as a B-girl's wink.

One of the advantages of the two rooms being acoustically sealed was that the person on my side of the mirror didn't have to tiptoe in, ease open doors, hold the breath, and in general respect Ømerta – the law of silence. I slid back the cupboard doors, rasped dresses back on their rail, and plonked a straight-back chair down in front of – or rather behind – the glass. I sat down.

They were both on the bed, Elvira kneeling, Gladys reclining on one elbow. Clothes were strewn all over the floor. Not, I thought, as the result of struggles; more through eagerness. The first movement I saw was the deft twist of my wife's hands, unsnapping the rear fastener of the black bra to spill Gladys's heavy breasts out over her heaving chest.

Immediately, Elvira was facedown beside her, both of these swelling, fleshy mounds cupped in her hands as she transferred glistening lips from one erect and budding nipple to the other.

Gladys's smile was dreamy. She lay flat, shifting her big hips slightly. One of her knees made an appearance between Elvira's slightly parted legs – a third smooth prominence neighbouring the twin hillocks of my wife's tight little buttocks. I couldn't see where Gladys's hands were. Between their two bodies certainly. Probably with the fingers laced through Elvira's pussy. Elvira was in any case grinding her mons against the upthrust thigh between her legs. Sunlight slanting through the open window dusted the down furring the base of her spine with gold each time she squirmed her hips.

I cannot lay my finger (sorry, no pun intended) on the difference, but difference there is – and an appreciable one too – between the fashion, the manner, the actual *way* in which men and women make love. I'm not making a distinction here between love involving those united by the grand passion and those taking pleasure out of a fuck for its own sake. The point is valid in both cases. Watch a man and a woman together, then watch two women.

Okay, I'm no voyeur. But – as you see! – it is not unknown that I do watch.

When two women are together, each gesture, every stroke and squeeze and pressure, any tiny flicker of no matter what muscle seems totally spontaneous – so much so that it's almost as if the delight of those making or experiencing them was mingled with surprise. With the man, though, however skilled he may be, it's more like he's working to a formula, a plan. The thinking is Pavlovian: *this* pressure *here* will have *that* reaction; if I play it *this* way, she should react *that* way. As a jazz musician might put it: the guy reads the dots, the chick improvises.

This may be why a lady, not being programmed in the same way, is disappointed – and in turn disappoints – sometimes when she's with a man, not experiencing a tenderness in the same league as her own. I'm not saying this one's better or that one's worse, mind you: just different. So let's make allowance for that from time to time, eh?

On the far side of that mirror on that Saturday afternoon, though, it was all there, every bit of it. The togetherness, the tenderness, the action and reaction, spontaneity allied with the inevitable, all in two fleshily voluptuous packages, neither of which had ever been in contact with the other before! I told you my wife was a genius.

Do-it-yourself psychology apart, this was a knockout scene.

Already each of those girls was lost in a rapt and dreamlike concentration on what she was doing – and what was being done to her. Each was so totally immersed in the other that nothing existed outside that bed and the vibrating thrill of their two naked bodies.

A very private world, I thought, peopled – for an hour? for two hours? for eternity – only by four hands and two mouths.

They had changed position now. I was certainly aware of that, but I'm not sure they were.

Gladys still lazed on her back, but Elvira, moving into place to ready herself for the serious stuff, had executed a smart – and swift, to forestall possible protest – one hundred and eighty degree turn. She knelt, legs splayed frogwise, with her buttocks cushioned on the redhead's big breasts. Her upper half was supported by elbows planted on either side of Gladys's hips, and her face was poised above the auburn-tufted mons.

As I watched, she swung both forearms up and over, allowing her wrists and long fingers to settle gently on her lover's belly. Smiling with a beatific content, she started to stroke, from bottom to top and then back again, with a monotonous, hypnotic precision, the outer lips of the cunt bedded in its thatch of springy pubic hair.

Gladys's hips arched fractionally off the bed, quivered, arched once more . . . and remained lifted, raised to welcome the intrusive fingers.

Her labia, visible at first as a sinuous, coral-coloured slit gashing those hairy loins, were flowering open under Elvira's caress as sweetly as a rose in the sun. Separating under that beguiling touch, the creased outer folds drew apart to expose the cushioned pads of the inner pair, darker in colour and glistening – now! suddenly! with an electric thrill! – as moisture from the sexual secretions started to flow.

Sliding easily now, the exploring fingers probed, ravishing each crevice and every tremoring curve until the whole wet cunt with its darkly tunnelled heart seemed to be pouting outwards, eager to receive those raping hands.

At the apex of this lewdly revealed vulva, distended already and inflamed, the swollen, throbbing button of the clitoris appeared. Sly fingertips tweaked and massaged the supersensitive organ as half my wife's hand plunged into the streaming inner depths.

Gladys's hips and belly heaved convulsively. Her whole body quaked as the invading, massaging hands quickened their thrusts and teasing to thrill the nakedly exposed secret flesh.

The redhead's torso, imprisoned between Elvira's clenched thighs, threshed wildly from side to side. Her own

170

thighs jack-knifed to clamp vicelike on either side of Elvira's head.

I couldn't see Gladys's head, which was hidden behind my wife's backside, but her hidden hands were certainly furiously busy under there, because I could see the compulsive gyrations of Elvira's hips and buttocks as she was buoyed up on her victim's straining, fleshy frame.

I saw, too, the abrupt, snakelike dart of Elvira's pink tongue as it flicked down once, twice to lash the clitoris head free of its fleshy sheath. I saw Gladys's most galvanic heave yet as her arms flew out and around to wrap tightly over Elvira's waist. I saw the tongue tip's second assault, a quick flash in and out of the vaginal passage. And then I saw no more – at least of the cunt and its bewitching digital treatment.

Jerking it free of Gladys's clenching thighs, Elvira had lowered her head to cover the loins entirely as she started to suck and tongue in earnest. Instead of an auburn genital cleft, I was staring, between those cliff-like thighs, at the short and shallow waves of my wife's dark hair.

For an instant the two of them became, from my viewpoint, no more than a complex articulation of limbs. Then Elvira moved again – more decisively still.

Very slowly, she un-doubled the kneeling legs, raising her body to straighten them, sliding each one backwards to frame Gladys's head. Then she lowered herself again, but inched her pelvis back until her own cunt was within easy reach of the redhead's mouth.

Gladys straightened her own legs. Now they were locked together in the classic position vulgarly known as sixty-nine. And the two bodies – the original two-backed beast – began to move as one. Slowly, dazedly for the bellies and breasts, quickly for the buried heads – arms clenched and legs shuddering as they scaled the heights towards their shared ecstasy.

Gladys was the first to come – a titanic, long-lasting orgasm that almost threw Elvira off the bed and took minutes to die away in shuddering spasms of agonized delight.

Elvira wasn't far behind – although in her case it was less

the extravagances of the flesh than the mental joy that triggered her release. Success was the stimulus that really turned her on.

The second time, they came precisely together – and that was a whirlwind of expertly mated bodies if ever I saw one!

I stayed for the third. Then reluctantly I had to steal away. I had after all promised Maureen I'd be at the Cumberland at five.

On the way, I figured I might as well make a night of it. I was going to catch it when I got home officially, whatever time it was. The luncheon showdown had proved that I had broken The Rule: I'd not only kept a date secret; I had effectively lied about the fact that I was going to spy on Elvira by attempting to disguise myself!

Oh, well. What the hell.

There was a song – most relevant to the present situation – in one of the last Astaire-Rogers musicals in which Mr Astaire regretted the presence of trouble ahead and of teardrops to shed but nevertheless urged Miss Rogers to face the music and dance.

The movie was called *Swingtime*.

So, once more, what the hell? We were supposed to be the swinging sixties, weren't we?

Okay, so I'd swing!

After that I'd be prepared to face the music. But first came the dance . . .

PART FIVE

Points of View

16

Luke Hornby could never understand why it was that he found fucking so much more satisfactory when he was standing up behind the girl and she was bent double in front of him, elbows on knees or resting on a desk, allowing him into her cunt from behind.

Could it have been visual? That his huge, untidy frame splayed out on top of a woman acted like a candle-snuffer extinguishing a flame? He thought not, although he could in fact see much more of his partner if she was bent over in front of him – and allowed her breasts, if heavy enough, to fall into his hands (if these weren't busy steadying her hips).

No, it was much more, he finally became convinced, a matter of depth, touch and *pressure* on the sensitive nerves of his tool – which, although thick, was not especially large for his size.

The secret, he believed, was gravity.

If a girl lay on her back, flattened beneath his weight, every ounce of his frame was indirectly – via the vagina walls – pressing all the innards beyond, intestines, bladder, liver, etc., down hard against her backbone. Effectively, he thought, dragging the vagina walls *away* from his inserted cock. If, on the other hand, she was standing up and leaning forward, with her torso horizontal, gravity *acting on the mass and weight of the organs themselves* would draw them down and compress the vaginal cavity, thus forcing the upper wall harder against his shaft.

The few friends to whom he had ventured to suggest this theory had ridiculed it. The fact nevertheless remained: a missionary coupling to him too often resembled those stories of fellows who claimed they'd gone in and couldn't touch the sides; whereas, standing powerful behind, he felt more often than not that his cock was literally being *sucked* by the lips of a pussy whose inner surfaces were already clamped together the better to clasp the penetrating shaft.

To be honest, Luke didn't waste too much time on the theory. He was more concerned with the practice. He was a man who enjoyed taking decisions. And once they were taken, he acted on them. So, theory or no theory, most of his fucking now was done while he was standing up.

Since he was unmarried, this saved him the expense of buying a king-size bed, for most of his coupling was effected either in his office or at the apartments of the girls prepared to bend over and receive him. The stance was particularly convenient in the case of an office session, because both parties could resume the perpendicular and adjust their clothes in the time it took an unexpected visitor to bring the lift up to the second floor from the building's entrance lobby.

The building was new, a concrete block overlooking the equally new Holborn traffic roundabout. The office, a three-room suite comprising reception, Luke's sanctum and a combination workshop, art room and studio, was very modern: chairs of black leather stretched over chromed steel frames, teak desks, double-glazed picture windows and flock-sprayed walls in different 'contemporary' colours. Thanks to Raymond Large's money it was very different from Luke's old eyrie off the Tottenham Court Road.

At the moment, however, with the official launch of the new lingerie magazine only a week away, it was as chaotic as the old one had ever been. Colour proofs, separations, paste-up dummies and bundles of press cuttings lay scattered over Luke's desk. Glossy publicity brochures were stacked high on each visitor's chair. Galleys black with text in different type-faces overflowed the waste bins and curled like paper surf across the floor.

The inner studio was untidier still. Proofs of most of the magazine's forty-eight pages hung from clips fixed to battens on each wall. The inclined draughtsman's desks used by Brigitte Dubois for her make-up sheets were loaded; ten-by-eight photographs littered the floor – some crumpled up or torn across in rage, others scarred by savagely scrawled chinagraph instructions to the block makers. The designer herself had gone to see Large to discuss the cost of the initial print run.

The sole space distilling an air of tranquillity was by the big window overlooking the traffic circus, immediately behind Luke's desk.

Luke himself stood there with Sandrine, the Jamaican model who had been one of the original quartet photo–graphed to display the Preckner-Curnow sexy underwear collection. The window was open and they were looking down at a noisy altercation between mounted police and a couple of hundred anti-nuclear demonstrators whose un–official march had snarled up the traffic on the roundabout.

Sandrine was very beautiful. Her features, like those of many West Indians, showed traces of Chinese and Spanish as well as African ancestry – with the finer points of each. Add to this a resilient 35–25–35 body that was nubile enough for undie ads yet sexy enough for pinups and there's no need to question why Luke, with the agreement of Preckner and Large, had decided the moment he saw her to make her the cover-girl for the first issue of his magazine.

Sandrine in fact smiled enticingly from every wall in all three rooms of the office suite, her dark body seductively visible within a low cut bra, skimpy panties and a hip-length négligée in the sheerest semi-transparent white tulle that Shirley Sabbath could find in Europe. It was an arresting cover, its impact by no means diminished by the fact that, ever since the Notting Hill race riots in 1958, black had obliga-torily become very beautiful indeed – especially in the press.

There had been a special photo session for that cover. Luke remembered asking Sandrine what she had thought of the photographer, Warne-Johns. 'Screwy, man. Halfway to nutters' corner,' the model had replied. 'I mean, hell, he takes good pictures. But afterwards is another story. Man made a heavy pass, if you like!'

'Sandrine!' Luke had protested. 'Look at the pictures. Can you blame him? Guy's not a queer, after all.' He grinned. 'Be very tempted to make a heavy pass myself, one of these days!'

'Yeah, well, that's different,' the girl said. 'Maybe I'd say yes, maybe no – but, shit, the relate is different. You give me work, after all.' She shook her head, the black hair, silvered for the photos, a halo framing her chiselled features. 'This guy, though – what he wants is, I wank myself in front of him while he jacks off! Hell, man, I only do that when there's no one else around!'

'You refused?'

'"Damn" sure I refuse. A girl has to draw the line someplace.' Sandrine laughed. 'He was furious. All I could do to stop him tearing up the negs!'

'Thank the Lord you did,' Luke had said, eyeing the cover proofs.

His own requirements, when it came to the pass, were simpler and less idiosyncratic – well, a little less anyway. They were each leaning on the marble sill beneath the open window. Police whistles shrilled through the angry shouting now, and there was a rising cacophony of horn-blowing from impatient motorists and cab drivers. Sandrine was smiling broadly, but she wasn't particularly amused, at least not by the traffic jam.

Luke was beside her and slightly behind. He had an arm around her waist. To a watcher below, they were a couple leaning out of an office window to see what all the fuss was about, to join in the fun. Just like the lunchtime crowds already jamming the sidewalks bordering the circus. This was not the whole story though.

Lucy, Luke's new secretary, receptionist and switchboard girl, had been sent down to the printer's in Balham to deliver some photos that were urgently needed for a display panel presenting the magazine's contributors. Luke and Sandrine were alone in the office.

He was wearing an open-neck, short-sleeved, green and yellow striped summer shirt by Pierre Cardin. And nothing else.

Sandrine was bra-less beneath a Hawaiian shirt printed with huge tropical flowers. Her jade-green cotton skirt had been hoisted above her superbly rounded buttocks and draped neatly over her waist. From there she was naked all the way down to the floor.

Between her plaint thighs, Luke's bulbous cock-head was firmly embedded within her cunt.

Someone had told him once that there was a similarly sited secret fuck in Flaubert's *Madame Bovary*, and the concept had excited him ever since. Apart from the fact that the position was in tune with his theory, there was the additional turn-on that, here he was shafting a woman virtually in public – and not a man, woman or child among the spectators had the remotest idea that he was doing this. The secrecy, the indecency, the obscene contrast between the conventional view of them outside and the lewd spectacle within – this, together with the sheer *naughtiness* of the concept, was to him the stuff that dreams were made of. 'Wet dreams anyway!' Raymond Large had replied maliciously when Luke confessed this epicene taste to his new Croesus.

The opportunity, nevertheless, was not to be missed. The rowdy traffic jam was an ideal in.

It had passed off right from the beginning almost as though they were following a blueprint.

She had come to the office to see the cover proofs. The printer's urgent appeal for Lucy's pictures had been a happy coincidence. Sandrine had run to the open window at the first trill of a police whistle. Luke had followed, eyeing her leaning form and thinking 'If only . . .'

The thought had at once made him hard. And he had then leaned over her to share the fun – but but permitting the rigid outline of his excited cock to nudge the mellow curves of her cottoned backside. She had sensed it at once – and responded with a tiny, shifting twist of her hips against his hardness.

After that it was all plain sailing. She continued to lean out of the window, enjoying the scene while he took the necessary steps. She didn't even turn her head when he lifted the skirt and dragged green satin briefs down to her ankles. He ripped off trousers and underpants and stepped his big frame up behind her.

Somewhere along the line, Sandrine had fractionally spread her legs – enough to reveal the hairy cleft separating her taut buttocks and the tight little cunt nestling within it.

Luke caught his breath. Between the ebony globes so indecently exposed, the flesh of her labia, glistening already with anticipatory moisture, was so dark as to be almost violet in colour.

Feeling the blood hammering within him, Luke edged forward again, his short, thick, hard tool in one hand, and stroked the throbbing tip, lightly as a feather, down and then up the outermost margin of that enthralling, cushioned cunt.

Sandrine uttered a small, wordless noise. Her hips moved an inch, this way, that way. But she remained staring down into the street, apparently fascinated by what she saw.

Luke too was fascinated by what he saw. He watched himself stroke again – and then plunge.

What bliss, what joy!

He tilted back his great untidy head and released a long sigh of pure ecstasy.

The length of his cock, quivering with eagerness, was . . . well, received was the only word. He was aware of warmth and wetness closing over him. He sensed hot walls of inner flesh, giving way, parting easily under his thrust, permitting the shaft to advance, then tightly closing around him once more, engulfing him in the close, pulsating heat of the black girl's belly.

He withdrew and pushed again, exulting in the heat and smoothly swelling clasp of those fleshy interior walls, conscious of the burning depths he was exploring.

Out . . . then in again. Luke's mind was spinning with desire. Now he could feel the grip of ridged vaginal muscles contracting to grasp the whole rigid length, the entire throbbing circumference of his skewering tool. Dear God, this sensation was Elysian, it was paradisiac, it was . . . What exactly was it like? It wasn't *like* anything on earth – and probably not in Heaven either – but the nearest he could come to an actual description, a simile . . . well, it was a metaphor really. Some years ago, increasing weight had provoked circulation troubles in Luke's legs, and he had for some time been obliged to wear elastic stockings. That was the nearest he could get: shafting this beauty was like pulling a tight elastic stocking up – and up – the leg! Although that, of course, had nothing of the wet and searing thrill of this gliding advance and retreat.

This was it, Luke thought dazedly; this was undoubtedly, incontrovertibly, indisputably it! Forget all that splayed out bedtime stuff, the updoubled gymnastics of handbook sex. Forget the awkward disposition of his heavy frame. Forget even the thrill of this girl's body beautiful. What they had now was sex fined down to its ultimate, concentrated essence. Hands and mouths and breaths and bodies as a whole had finally been dispensed with, leaving every muscle, each nerve and every fragmentary thought, centered on the breathless, eternal moment of truth – what someone had once called the still centre of the turning world.

This, when you came down to it – the private, mating dialogue between cock and cunt – was what it was all about!

His weight was on his elbows on the windowsill. He leaned his cheek momentarily against the silvered curls of Sandrine's hair. Very gently, he started to oscillate his hips, moving the hinged pelvis just enough to withdraw and re-insert the pulsating length of his shaft, from just below the cock-head to the base, within the moistly sliding caress of the cover-girl's pussy.

Sandrine herself – she was already breathing a little hard – did not back up to meet Luke's every thrust, but contented herself with a slight but subtle rotation of the hips which had the effect of canting and minimally twisting the vaginal canal so that its rolling grasp added an extra dimension to the tingling inner grip each time the impaling staff stroked in and out.

Luke felt as if his cock was literally humming with desire.

There were people leaning out of the windows of adjacent offices now. A man Luke knew by sight – a quantity surveyor, he thought – waved cheerfully, then rolled his eyes heavenwards as a commentary on the chaos below. The noise was becoming deafening. Some of the police had dismounted. Several scuffles had erupted between marchers and angry motorists.

On the other side, a man and a blonde had turned their

heads to say something to Sandrine. The girl laughed and the man said something about the difficulties these days of keeping the peace. Sandrine murmured a suitable reply.

Shafting rhythmically in and out between her quivering buttocks, maintaining his slaving, monotonous assault on her gaping loins, Luke thought: 'If only they knew!'

The thought excited him still further. If only any of them knew – accelerating the pace of his pistoned intrusion slightly – if only anyone, above, beside, in the block across the street, could see through walls, had X-ray eyes, long-range cameras with periscopes, a crystal ball . . .

Sandrine uttered a small, smothered cry as an extra hard thrust rammed the distended velvet glans unexpectedly against the neck of her uterus. Smiling secretly, she allowed herself a tighter than usual contraction of the vaginal muscles and Luke in turn caught his breath, ploughing in and out with increasing force and speed.

Supposing all those other people, instead of being amazed at what he and Sandrine were doing – suppose they too were taking advantage of the scene below and . . . yes, and fornicating . . . fucking stealthily, in secret, wondering the way he was what other people would think. . . ?

Suppose every couple, in every window, in all the blocks around the circus, were hard at it the way he was? Luke thought dizzily.

The hell with it. Suppose they were? Let them deal with their own problems! So far as he was concerned, the row in the street below was without importance. What mattered was – how long dared he himself keep it up? How long had they got before Lucy returned to the office?

Perhaps – a momentary flash of hope – perhaps, if she had taken a taxi, she too would be blocked someplace in the tail-back of the traffic jam?

If not, could he risk betting on the idea that she might have stopped at some coffee-bar on the way back and treated herself to a cappucino?

On the house, on the house: I'll gladly pay! he groaned mentally as he thrust and withdrew.

'It seems,' Elvira Dulok said to her husband, 'that Curnow

simply wanted information on your new ranges because they were planning something and didn't want it to be in any way in the same line as yours.'

'Evidently,' Edward said, 'this underwear nonsense. Trade press has been full of hints for bloody weeks! As if I cared. We make dresses; such lingerie as we do is available, as it were, as an extra service to clients – something that won't conflict with their good sense. And dress sense.'

'There's apparently a new mag too – much more hush-hush than the undie collection. Aidan did a piece on it, oh, a few weeks ago now.'

'In his column, *The Carriage Trade*, yes I saw it. So what? All publicity is good publicity. No bad thing, an extra trade paper.'

'But, darling, if they're connected? Won't the mag favour Preckner's new lingerie collection?'

Dulok shrugged. 'Suppose they do? We're not direct competitors,' loftily, 'in *that* sort of line.'

'Apparently they think so. Otherwise why go to that trouble to organize a break-in?'

Dulok ignored the question. 'So that's all your incendiary redhead had to do?' he asked. 'Tell the man where to find what he wanted? I *suppose* you could call that industrial espionage!'

'Industrial . . . ?' Elvira laughed. 'Come on, sweetie! Let's not exaggerate. Apparently he was also anxious to know how – and when – to *get* in. And apparently she came across with that too.'

'Came across? How? What would she know? She leaves – left – at six with the others.'

Elvira shook her dark-waved head. 'Oddly enough, that was the one thing she was cagey about. I pressed her like mad . . .'

'No kidding!'

'. . . but all she would admit was that she "gave him some information".'

'Well, thanks anyway,' he said. And then, slyly: 'I trust it was worth all your . . . trouble?'

'Oh, yes,' Elvira said. A few minutes later she remarked

carelessly: 'I don't know how often you experience a mad desire to lunch with whores in Soho while wearing sandals, but if it ever happens again . . . well, isn't there anything *else* you'd like me to find out from your voluptuous, red-haired, ex-workshop supervisor?'

Raymond Large telephoned Pete ('Try anything once') Sampler, the art director of what he now thought of as 'his' magazine.

'It's been decided,' Large said. 'We're going to launch the mag in style. No point just having it appear on the newsstands one week, however much advance press we've had. We're going to have the year's big launch – at my place in the country. Everybody who's anybody – press, radio, television, gossip column jet-setters – they'll all be invited.'

'Good idea,' Sampler approved. 'And the details?'

'Champagne reception, cold salmon in a marquee on the lawn, music, dancing, the lot. No speeches as such . . . but the big promotion deal in the early evening.'

'Which is to say?'

'In a sense it's a dress show – but a very special one. We're going to have the whole bloody magazine come to life. Page by page, photo by photo. On a specially designed stage set, with the same format as the magazine itself, the audience will see in three dimensions what the pages show in two. Every item, each article of lingerie featured there, will be modelled live, in the same order, by the same girl who posed for the photo in the magazine!'

Sampler whistled. 'Boy, I reckon you really got something there!'

'Don't you think?' Large sounded delighted. 'Jo Prozyck, that Polish genius doing *Coppelia* at the Garden, is directing the show as a show, but, naturally, I'd like you to collaborate on the set design, since you're responsible for the mag.'

'Count me in,' Sampler agreed. 'This is a great idea. There is just one thing, though.'

'Namely?'

'Your magazine hasn't got a flaming title!' Sampler exploded. 'Everything is ready for the trial print-run – except

184

the fucking title page! How the hell am I expected to design that if I don't even know how many letters to blank for? Nobody's even mentioned—'

'All right, all right,' Large soothed. 'I know we've been very unprofessional, but the title is so important, and there have been so many different ideas, that—'

'Have you fucking *decided*? That's all I want to know.'

Large sighed. 'This morning, yes. The final short-list was between *FRILLS* in caps, *Buttons and Bows*, a second go at the frillies with *Frills and Furbelows*, and, finally, *Frou-Frou*.'

'I know which I'd choose,' Sampler said. 'In fact for me there's no choice.'

'And your decision?'

'*Frou-Frou*. Unquestionably. It's short, it's snappy, it's easy to say – most importantly, it tells you what the magazine's about, it describes the contents . . . with just enough hint of your actual French naughty-naughty to attract the casual reader. For me that's the only runner in the race.'

'I'm glad you think so,' Large said, 'for that's the one we decided on. At one time *Sheerline* and *Sheer Delight* were in the running, but Shirley figured people might think it was about stockings only. Or at any rate specializing in clothes made of silk.'

'*Sheer Delight* is a great title,' Sampler said, 'but in this case I think she was right. Likewise *Frills and Furbelows* – apart from being old hat – could be interpreted by the dirty-minded as *FARbelows*, which would have you on the booksellers' top shelf, along with the beaver glossies and the soft porn material.'

'That's why we junked it,' Large said. 'But – er – talking of which . . .' He allowed the sentence to die of its own accord.

'You're talking about another kind of show altogether? This . . . pageant, didn't you say? . . . that you wanted me to design, well, kind of privately?'

'Exactly. Nothing to do with the dress show – although I have hopes that there may be one or two trusties who can be persuaded to take part in both. No – this will be late in the evening, after most of the launch guests have gone home.'

185

'Fine. How, by the way, will they go? How far from town is this place of yours?'

'About thirty miles. But I've done a deal with a private hire company. Every single person with an invitation will be called for and delivered to my house. And the cars will wait and take them back again when they're ready to go.'

'Man, this is going to be some shindig!' Sampler enthused. 'Now, this . . . private deal; the late-night stuff. I reckon the best thing is for me to come out to your place, no? Then you can put me in the picture, explain what you want, and we'll dope out the details together. Okay?'

'I'll send the Rolls for you,' Raymond Large said.

Sampler put down the phone. 'Rich guys don't half rabbit away,' he observed to the blonde sitting next to him on the low divan in his Chelsea apartment. 'You ever notice that, honey?'

'Frankly, I'm not familiar with too many rich guys,' said the blonde, whose name was Eve. She was one of the first four lingerie models who had posed for the original studio photo session designed to showcase the Preckner collection. And the only one Sampler hadn't yet seduced. 'On the other hand,' she said, 'I know plenty of not-so-rich guys who don't half rabbit away – mainly because I refuse to be familiar with them too!'

'Meaning, or mostly meaning, me?'

'If the cap fits, as my Mama used to say.'

'Fuck your Mama,' Sampler said genially, splashing Beaujolais into the girl's glass. 'I want—'

'Ah! So now it's the generation gap already! And I thought it was my favours you craved – still, so long as we keep it in the family—'

'Eve, for Chrissake!'

'No, Pete, for my sake, please. It just so happens that – like yesterday and the day before – I don't happen to want to fuck. Not with you anyway. End of story.'

'Ah, so it's personal, is it? In that case, baby, this ain't no story end. This is just the prologue!'

'Of *course* it's personal, Pete. Anything . . . physical . . .

186

between two people is personal, dammit.'

Sampler was striding up and down the big living-room of his attic apartment, a glass in one hand. Like most designers and directors, he himself lived in a chaos of disorder and indiscriminate taste. 'What's the matter with you?' he cried. 'Did I mortally offend you? Or something?'

'Not yet, but you're coming near.'

'Do you know what those French clients called you? *Eve le Givre*. And the word *givre* means frost in French . . .'

'Thank you, I did one foreign language at "O" Level too.'

'. . . so it's Icy Evie. But I want to know why. I know damn' well that you're no dyke. I asked around. You're frigid?' He eyed her curvy, compact figure. Splendid breasts thrusting out a loose blue sweater. Small waist, good hips, nyloned legs to dream about. 'No way, duckie. So just give me one good reason why not. I mean – here comes a French idiom again – if, as they say, I "displease" you; if I smell bad or the thought of me naked makes you want to puke, just say so. I'd understand that. Christ, it can happen to all of us. Bad vibes or poor chemistry. But I'd thought—'

'Will you please stop this now?' The blonde cut in. 'Please? . . . Look – I *like* you, Pete. I really do. I like being with you. You're fun: you make me laugh. But you're not going to make me. Not just like that.' She drained her glass, held it out for more. 'And if you persist in wasting the entire morning crying why, why, why? – then I'll tell you again: Because I don't want to.'

'But *why* don't you want to?' Sampler brushed a scatter of long-playing record sleeves off a bentwood chair and sank onto the seat. 'Christ, even women don't function totally on instinct, like a bloody amoeba reacting to a light source. There must be a *reason* why you don't want to. All I ask is to know what it is.'

Eve didn't reply. Framed by the pale, cropped hair, her wide grey eyes were bright. Traffic noises from the King's Road five storeys below rumbled through the open window. 'Now I've made you cross,' Sampler said regretfully. 'You're angry with me.'

'Not yet,' Eve said again, 'but I'm still working on it.'

'Look at the bloody records!' he burst out, stabbing a finger at the sleeves on the floor. 'Ella, Sinatra, Mel Torme, Como. Look at the fucking songs they sing: "Everybody's Doing It", "Anything Goes", "Who's Sorry Now?", "Let's Do It!" Why in God's name is everybody in the whole world in bed except us?'

Eve laughed in spite of herself. 'You're mistaken in one thing, Pete,' she said. 'Those are not, as you so elegantly said, fucking songs. That's the whole point. They're *loving* songs. The payoff at the end of each verse in the Cole Porter piece – which qualifies in each case every one of the preceding examples – is "Let's do it: *let's fall in love!*" Are you reading me, Sampler?'

He stared at her, absently refilling his glass and then her own.

'Do you know that creep Donald Warne-Johns?' Eve asked.

'No – but whistle the first four bars and I'll vamp in the rest,' Sampler said.

She ignored the crack. 'A weirdo,' she said. 'Half flasher, half voyeur, and one part wanker.'

'That's more than one hundred percent.'

'Exactly. More than a hundred percent weirdo. There's your answer: I ... do ... not ... want to be like one of Donald's dos; I want to be my own don't. I am in no way prepared to be nothing more – as the man said – than a convenient aperture for penile gratification! Do I make myself clear?'

He didn't answer directly. 'Do you know the Trans-Siberian Railway story?' he asked.

'No – but whistle the first four bars and I'll—'

He held up a hand to stop her. 'Once is enough, sweetheart – especially when it didn't get a laugh the first time.'

He stood looking out of the window. It was a dull day. Drizzle had fallen, and tyres were already sucking greasily at the damp street below. 'There's this compartment on that train,' he said. 'In it, there's just this young woman and, sitting opposite her, a Cossack. After the first couple of hours, the Cossack says: "Have you ever been to Omsk?" and the girl replies: "No."

'Three hours later, the Cossack clears his throat and asks: "Have you ever been to Tomsk?" And once again the girl replies: "No."

'Later still, dusk is falling over the steppes, the Cossack queries: "Have you ever been to Tobolsk?" After a short silence, the young woman shakes her head. "Never."

'The Cossack rises to his feet. "Enough of this love-talk," he says. "Remove your drawers." '

The blonde laughed again. 'A cautionary tale?' she enquired.

'Meaning that, like the rich guys, I rabbit too much. I guess lots of men do.'

Sampler swung around. There was something curiously purposeful about his stance, something that caused the girl involuntarily to widen her eyes. 'If you mean,' she said hastily, 'that, like the dread Donald, you seem to make a pass at every girl you meet, then attempt to *talk* them into bed, then I can only say . . .'

But what she could only say remained unheard. Her words died away as the art director strode towards her – steadily, forcefully, almost menacingly but certainly with a very positive air.

'Pete,' she began, 'I really do think . . .'

He halted by the divan. His lips were compressed. Everything about his crew-cut, rather bulky form exuded confidence and determination. Bending swiftly down, he seized her upper arms and dragged her to her feet in a single powerful movement.

'You sexy little bitch,' he said hoarsely, 'I've had hot pants for you since the moment I saw you in that filmy mauve crap at that first photo session! I only made the others as a way to get closer to you, the fucking ice maiden. But it's you I want, damn you. Do you hear me: I don't give a shit whether you want to or not. Not any more. I want you, I need you . . . and by God, if it's the last thing I do, I'm going to have you! Can you get that into your darling blonde head?'

He seized the short, cropped hair in both hands and tilted

her head back so that he could stare down into her eyes. She gazed back wide-eyed, her face expressionless.

Sampler released her head and reached down to grab the blue jumper. His fingers clenched over the hem. The heave with which he yanked it up was so violent that the garment also displaced her bra and rode with it as far as her armpits, allowing the taut warmth of her perfect little breasts to fit snugly into his ready hands.

He was panting, the hot breath jetting onto her half-open mouth. Ducking his head he parted his own lips and kissed her ferociously on that mouth.

Her whole body melted against him. To his amazement she responded wildly, passionately to his kiss, tongue darting hotly between his lips. He felt arms tightening around his waist; her nipples were hard against his palms.

'And this, baby,' he groaned when at last they disengaged, 'is like that other song says: not for just a month, not for just a year, but always!'

By the time he had lowered her to the divan, ripped open his fly and hoisted her skirt so that he could touch the top of her thighs, her blonde pussy was streaming wet and trembling with avid anticipation.

'That's more like it,' she murmured as she felt his fingertips brush the folds of her inner flesh.

It was later, much later, that she remembered she had an appointment with her agent, should indeed have been there before dark. Sampler ran her downstairs and out into King's Road to hail a taxi.

He had installed her in the cab and was about to hand money to the driver when she reached through the open window to lay cool fingers on his sleeve and push his arm down.

'No, no,' she said. 'That's gallant and I appreciate it, but I have to refuse.'

'Have to?' Sampler repeated, frowning. 'But I don't . . .?'

'I may be known as Miss Frost,' Eve said, 'but I'm damned if I'll be called a whore Frost!'

17

If a celestial mastermind had made a list of all those persons connected, directly or indirectly, with the magazine *Frou-Frou*, then taken a pin and chosen half a dozen – three of each sex – to make up unlikely intimate couplings, he could not have chosen less believable partners than those who actually found themselves together two days before the review's official launch.

The first of these unscheduled meetings – if indeed anything is really by chance – was the result of what seemed at first a triple coincidence. And a coincidence which, although it appeared to give pleasure to the parties concerned, arrived despite the fact that each of them had organized a totally different timetable for that particular evening.

The coincidence – if such it was in terms of the space–time continuum – related to individuals in or around the West London mews flat owned by the designer Shirley Sabbath. And its function, insofar as this varied directly with the libido, blood pressure, pulse rate and carnal impulsion of those concerned, could fairly be said to be exponential.

Three contributory factors – all negative, each involving anger or disapproval – coincided geographically here to produce the positive result which fixed the process in the form which was to become final.

They were: a bad-tempered outburst from Roger Curnow's wife, Marjorie, accusing him (accurately, as it happened) of adulterous conduct with young women connected with the lingerie collection to be marketed by him and his partner; the realization by Shirley Sabbath that the complimentary stall given to her for Fonteyn and Nuryev at Covent Garden had in fact been for the previous week;

and a telephone call to young Tom Silver at his Knightsbridge office from the blonde model Eve. She was sorry, she told him, but their date for that evening was definitely off. And no, coldly, she was afraid she was not prepared to suggest an alternative day.

Tom was furious. He stormed out of the office – the hell with the proofs of the *Frou-Frou* ads destined for next week's nationals – and strode angrily towards Old Brompton Road. He had been convinced that, if anyone could thaw the ice maiden, he was the man to do it – and her blunt cancellation of their date (which evidently meant some other bastard was in the running) was a blow to his pride. All he could do now was hurry to the caterers from whom he had ordered an expensive home-delivery meal and hope he'd be in time to cancel the order.

Roger Curnow was furious. Nobody appreciates a nagging wife, nobody likes to be found out, and the worst insult of all rankles most if the accusations are true. After the usual shout-up, he had flung out of the house in a violent rage. Very well, if the bitch was going to be like that, he bloody well *would* fuck off and 'dip his wick with some little tart'. The trouble was, it was too late to call anyone he knew: he would have to go up to the West End and troll for a pro he could fancy. He headed for the nearest Piccadilly Line underground station.

Shirley Sabbath was furious. She was in fact sick with disappointment. It would be impossible to obtain another ticket: the Opera House was booked solid for the entire season. She had been given her complimentary some time ago: how incredibly, insufferably, *bloody dumb* to have double-checked the repertoire – but neglected to verify the different dates of each performance! There were still tears in her eyes – though they were of anger now – when she left the train from Covent Garden and surfaced into the rainy dusk at South Kensington station.

At the top of the steps leading up from the booking-hall, blindly hurrying, she collided with a well-built, slightly swarthy man of about forty who was about to go down. He was scowling.

'Christ, can't you look—?' he began. And then: 'Shirley!'

'Roger Curnow!'

A tall, lean, young man with a fringe of beard, passing through the station arcade to shortcut the rain, had stopped dead in front of them, eyes widened with surprise.

Tom Silver.

'Good God! What on earth are *you* doing here?' each of them exclaimed at the same time.

'I could kill myself for being so stupid!'

'I'm pissed off with my bitch of a wife!'

'Some two-timing slut has stood me up!'

They laughed. A sudden relief of tension all around. 'Sorrows,' Curnow said, 'should be drowned! Since we've met, let's for fuck's sake have a drink. There's a wine bar across the street.'

They went across the street. In a basement bar redolent of the woody hints of port and madeira they drank an ice-cold bottle of slaty Gewurztraminer from Alsace. The bar – bench seats, tiled tables with wooden frames – was almost full. A serious, seated crowd, seriously drinking and savouring what they drank. A civilized place with low-key lighting. By the time the bottle was finished each of them felt better. Much better, in fact. 'We'll have another!' Curnow decided.

'I've a better idea,' Tom Silver said over the subdued hum of conversation. 'If you agree, that is.'

Curnow and the girl looked at him enquiringly. They had nothing else to do anyway.

'There's a super meal going to be delivered to my place within the next half hour,' he said. 'It's in Elvaston Place, off Gloucester Road. Less than ten minutes' walk.' He grinned a little shamefacedly. 'It was part of the big seduction scene. You know: soft lights, sweet music, dry champagne. Your actual candlelight couple. But it can easily be cut three ways – the food's Greek: kebabs, rice pilaf, stuffed vine leaves and suchlike. Why don't we go back there for a nosh-up and tell each other the sad stories of our lives?'

They went back there, laughing a little at the rain, which was falling heavily now. On the way, Curnow ducked into an off-licence and re-emerged with two bottles of champagne.

The dinner was admirable. And so, very soon, was the company.

By the time they had finished Tom's champagne and were within an inch of the bottom of Curnow's first bottle, the regard with which each of the trio viewed the other two was very high indeed. Much the same could have been said of the diners, though none was aware of that.

Unexpectedly, they were in the middle of a happy happening. They were having a lovely time.

'The hell with dancers and delin— delinquent dates and damned and damning wives!' Curnow cried, reaching for the last bottle. 'We're going to have ourselves a bloody ball!'

He shot out the cork, frothing champagne over the cheeseboard and what remained of his raspberry mousse.

Shirley was looking spectacular. She had after all been expecting to spend the evening at the Royal Opera House. Her waisted, wide-skirted cocktail dress, with its bare back and swathed, crossover top, was in heavy jade-green dupion (Jacques Fath, Curnow had guessed), and her high-heeled court shoes married gold with the same shade of green. A single pendant of jade hung from a heavy gold chain around her neck.

What was already evident to her – although not yet to either of her escorts – was that, inevitably, at some time or other, the sexual allure which she was well aware she exuded would stir each of them to male awareness: at best to pawing and hot pants, at worst to a drunken rivalry that could end in unpleasantness if not in actual violence. She herself would cease to be a mate, a chum, one of the boys; all at once she would be A Female, prey to be fought over.

Unless she allowed them to drink themselves insensible.

Shirley's own sexual awareness was not prepared to consider this as a solution.

She glanced quickly around the bachelor apartment – Curnow was pouring from the new bottle – and took stock. The rooms, converted from a large Victorian terrace house, were spacious and well furnished but a trifle spartan. Through a half open bedroom door she could see a single divan bed.

Shirley made up her mind.

'This time it's my turn to have a better idea,' she announced. 'If you agree, that is! I say, yes we'll have a ball – but why don't we go back to my place, just round the corner from the station? I've just had Jackson's deliver me some super Turkish coffee. We could take what's left of this bottle with us, and then switch to brandy as an afterthought. What do you say?'

They thought it was a wonderful idea, a stroke of genius, the most unimaginably imaginative . . . well, yes, a super-duper idea. When should they leave?

'Now,' Shirley said, pushing back her chair. 'A splendid dinner, Tom, and thanks a million. But from what I hear outside, I think the rain's eased off. If we hurry, maybe we could even make it dry.'

And it was then, to her astonishment, that instead of the expected jockeying, glare-eyed, sullen I-saw-her-before-you-did rivalry which can be such a drag for a woman, this time the demon drink had wrought a contrary miracle within its acolytes. Each of them, instead of becoming mulishly argumentative, had turned excessively polite, considerate and self-effacing to the point of absurdity. It can happen like that. Sometimes. Not often enough, Shirley thought.

They were all standing up. 'Look,' Tom Silver began awkwardly, 'it's been a splendid evening, really smashing. Enjoyed every minute of it. I mean, splendid people . . . but why don't you two – er – go ahead? You know each other anyway. That is to say, frightfully kind of you, but, much though I'd love to . . . well, I don't want to butt in, and—'

'My dear chap!' Curnow's interruption sounded practically affronted. 'I wouldn't hear of it. No question. No . . . not a word, old boy! After all, I have a wife, dammit. You two finish the evening together . . . sample a spot of the Turkish. I'll see you as far as the door. Then, with luck, I'll make the last Hounslow from South Ken.'

Shirley laughed. 'Marvellous!' she said. 'Anyone wonder what the lady would like? Come on: let's quit horsing around. I'll take the two of you on! You can run me down to my place first.'

They did exactly that. With a single glad cry, they swooped on her, lifted her off the ground, supported under each elbow, and ran her out of the flat, downstairs, and into the street. It was still raining. They ran her, feet off the ground, along Elvaston Place, down Queen's Gate, and as far as her own front door in the mews. They finished the opened bottle, by the neck, on the way.

They were lolling in armchairs, still panting, when she brought the coffee in from the kitchen. Curnow, at any rate, had been there before. He was not surprised to see that she was totally nude.

'Liqueurs,' she said unsteadily, 'will be served only to gentlemen in the altogether.'

The two men, so dissimilar in shape – one solid, compact, swarthy, a clean-shaven forty; the other tall, lean, pale, a bearded youngster – leaped at once to their feet. 'Bet you I'll be down to socks and underpants first!' Tom Silver challenged.

'Try me!' Curnow replied, tugging at his tie.

They did not, of course, stop at that. Shirley made sure of the point. When they were both naked, Tom said: 'Who won?'

'It was a dead heat,' the shapely blonde said diplomatically. 'And I do mean heat!'

She was gazing with approval at the two pairs of hairy loins, each of which – despite the amount of liquor consumed – sprouted a dark, rigid and very serviceable erection.

Despite the liquor, yes – but it was *because* of the euphoric effect of the champagne that what could have turned into an awkward or embarrassing situation between the two males in fact remained jokey and even joyful. After all, apart from the age difference they hardly knew each other – and neither one nor the other customarily found himself in a group-sex environment. But with Shirley's totally unforced enjoyment and natural appreciation of the scene to help, the two nude men and the naked blonde sat sipping coffee and brandy as if it was the most natural thing in the world.

'It should be natural too,' Curnow observed in a professorial tone. 'Our hostess, dear boy, firmly believes' – a sly look at Shirley – 'in doing what comes naturally!'

196

'Of course I do!' the girl said passionately. 'And why not? Christ, we've been given all this marvellous equipment, these thrilling zones, these exciting opportunities to feel and touch and stroke and explore – why on earth not use them while we can?'

'That's my girl!' Curnow enthused. Tom said nothing. He was allowing his eyes to rove the area of satined flesh between Shirley's firm, pointed breasts and the pert tuft of public hair between her bare thighs.

When the coffee was finished, she rose to her feet. 'All right, you studs,' she said lazily. 'The hostess has had enough of the academics, the theory – now she's baying for the practical!' Grasping an erect cock in each hand, she led them through the archway into the studio.

When the big divan bed was in place, she said with deliberate, clinical matter-of-factness: 'Now as you know, I have two hands – which are going for the moment to be restricted to accessory use – and three means of entry. Since, especially after that excellent dinner, I don't feel right now like a sandwich, it's got to be a choice between the upper and the lower.' She looked from one man to the other. 'So who's going to be' – a suppressed giggle – 'the lucky fucker?'

Each of them, glancing at her belly as she spreadeagled herself on the bed, spread a polite arm in a caricatured after-you gesture. Then Tom said: 'You go first, sir. After all, age plus length of service!' – quoting the formula determining the order of demobilization from the army – 'And of course . . . first in, first out!'

Curnow nodded, grinning. 'My pleasure.' And to Shirley: 'We rely on you to blow the whistle for half-time, intermission, musical chairs or whatever.'

'A whistle won't be the only thing I'll blow,' the blonde said coarsely. 'Come right up to this end of the divan, young man . . .'

The slight stiffness and self-conscious awareness of being daringly 'different' which, willy-nilly, had been affecting them all vanished quickly as a waking dream once the sense of touch intruded.

For Roger Curnow, perhaps, the next step was the most difficult. With his powerful body face-down between Shirley's invitingly splayed legs and his hands on her hips, he was suddenly aware that he was, so to speak, facing the goal without having run through the opposing field; he had arrived at the destination without making the journey. Yet it would clearly be absurd, at this stage of the game, to start a subtle and elaborate foreplay full of lovey-dovey endearments. The girl had bypassed all that with her frank admission that she wanted to be fucked. On the other hand, just to ram it in without a word seemed, well, to put it brutally, not only crude but entirely lacking the finesse he liked to think the good lover should always show. Especially if his name was Curnow.

Effectively, he thought, young Silver at the moment had the best of it: he had no choice to make; all he had to do was stand and enjoy. But Curnow, in the other sense, must stand and deliver! Silver was having something done *to* him; Curnow was going to have to do the doing.

He glanced up the lovely length of Shirley's supine body. Beyond the taut swell of her breasts, he could see the blonde head turned sideways, one hand raised up to guide Silver's long, hard cock into her open mouth as he stood by the bedside. Her cheeks hollowed rhythmically as she sucked the throbbing staff deeper and deeper in. Silver's breathing, rapid and shallow now, was loud in the silent room.

The hell with it, Curnow thought. He lowered his gaze to the girl's tuft of genital hair, the slit-like scarcely visible opening below it. He moved his hands from hips to belly, from belly to labia, fingering the soft cushions of flesh apart. And, right enough, she was wet as hell.

Very well. He had the stand – it was aching, the whole shaft begging for comfort. So steel yourself, baby: here's a Special Delivery!

Hoisting himself up higher, he splayed those lips wider still, took his pulsating cock in his other hand, and sank violently down, slamming the whole stiff length deep into the sucking clasp of Shirley's pussy.

The girl's hips arched convulsively off the mattress as

she felt the iron-hard penis shaft hotly into the fleshy embrace of her own burning belly. For an instant she freed her mouth to cry aloud: 'Oh, God! Oh, yes, yes, yes . . . Oh, *Christ, yes!* Put it in, give it to me! I want it right up inside, as hard and as high as you can go! Fuck my cunt, lover man, *fuck!*'

And then, as Curnow, his pulses hammering, started to piston relentlessly in and out of her with forceful plunging strokes, she turned and choked out to Silver: 'Come over me, sweetie . . . kneel on me, squash my tits, let me take your balls in my hand . . . but give me, give me again, that long and luscious, hard and horny cock to suck!'

And seconds afterwards, once more freeing swollen lips from the gagging bulk of that throbbing tool: 'Jesus, how I love to feel those dilated veins against the swirl of my tongue! . . . How the huge, hot bulk in my sucking mouth excites me!'

It was later, the slender body threshing wildly on the bed as the two cocks fucked madly in and out of her mouth and cunt, the two muscular bodies convulsed and quivering above her, that Shirley came for the first time. The second was when Silver's bearded mouth was slavering at her cunt and she herself was sucking Curnow's throbbing tool. In between, the two men – in a special command performance – had allowed themselves to be milked to orgasm by her expert hands while she stared bemused at the burning, hot white spurts of semen splashed over her belly and breasts.

And somewhere, sometime – nobody could quite remember when or how – there had indeed been an intermission, with more coffee, more brandy, more talk, of a randier nature now.

It was during a brief – uncharacteristic – lull in this conversation that Shirley, hands cupped over her plundered loins, had posed the question.

'Tom,' she said, 'suppose the girl who stood you up had made the date. You said there'd be soft lights and sweet music, no?'

'That's right.'

'We saw the first part: the lighting was fab. But what was the record you'd have played if she'd been there instead of us?'

Tom laughed. 'Sinatra's *Songs For Swinging Lovers*,' he said. 'What else?'

18

Sinatra was in the news anyway that summer. His teenage son had been kidnapped. When the boy was returned unharmed, a newspaperman asked what the deal had cost the singer. Sinatra replied matter-of-factly: 'The ransom paid was two hundred and forty thousand dollars.'

At Leatherslade Farm in Buckinghamshire an unusual collection of wrongdoers, including an antique dealer, a motor-racing driver and a fashionable hairdresser were planning the abduction of an entire train. In a brilliantly organized operation they stopped the Glasgow–London mail train and absconded with £2,500,000 in used notes – the biggest haul in British history. Only one person, the engine driver, was injured by a knock on the head, and that was through a misunderstanding. But because that god of the sixties, money, was involved, the train robbers when they were caught were given the most savage sentences ever awarded by an English court: twenty-five years' hard labour. In the same period a man who kidnapped, violated and killed a little girl of eleven – no money was involved – was sent to prison for eleven years.

Money was, however, involved in Raymond Large's business. A fair proportion of his not inconsiderable fortune was being dispensed in favour of the new lingerie magazine *Frou-Frou*, and a much larger sum for the temporary conversion of his Georgian house in Essex, devoted to the official launch of the new publication.

And of course to the gratification of Large's peculiarly personal desires in the matter of sex – though any anti-vice strictures levelled here would have to be based on moral rather than criminal grounds.

An army of caterers, electricians, carpenters, scenic

designers and 'Italian warehousemen' – as suppliers of booze were still officially designated – infested the old house daily for a week before the ceremony. Stairways, corridors and galleries were alive with frowning executives accompanied by secretaries with clipboards frenziedly taking notes. Overalled workmen manoeuvring huge sheets of plate glass obstructed lady banquet organizers trying to work out seating plans.

The only absentees during this hectic period were members of the press. Their turn would come on the night of the launch. But not before. A private security firm patrolled the estate day and night to discourage trespassers, particularly those with cameras. Secrets, however, cannot eternally be kept when large numbers of persons are employed, however well-paid they are. And press speculation was, as they say, rife – especially in the tabloids and popular Sundays. It was rumoured that the Beatles were to provide the music. Princess Margaret would break a bottle of champagne against a printing press to christen the mag. Ella Fitzgerald, Pearl Bailey and Dean Martin were to be flown in from Hollywood to perform a close-harmony act. Danny Kaye would be toastmaster, Nureyev was to sing . . .

'That's my all-time favourite, the Royal launch!' Luke Hornby laughed. 'Can you imagine?' And then, in a falsetto voice: 'I neem this undehwah publication *Frou-Frou* – SMASH!'

'And God bless all whose sales are in her!' Sampler added.

His own activities – restricted to what Large still called 'the pageant' – were of course the most secret of all. Apart from a qualified use of the owner's existing two-way equipment, they involved the installation of hidden film cameras, microphones and sliding panels, the construction of unseen walkways within false walls, a complex audiovisual hookup manipulating all these from an attic control-room, and supervisory production control of certain cakes and sweetmeats designed to incorporate a substance grown in North Africa and Columbia but not customarily found in the pastrycook's recipes.

To his surprise and pleasure, Sampler was provided with

two unexpected helpers: the French typographer and page-designer Brigitte Dubois, who was apparently to share the control system with the host, and Shirley the designer herself. She, it seemed, would be the only guest to know she was part of a pageant – the Chief Exhibitor-Persuader, she called herself!

Sampler was happy to have both of them, since his own work – with a couple of trusted engineers – had necessarily to be carried out in the evening and at night, when the workforce concerned with the launch had left for the day.

It was while he was strolling in the grounds, waiting to make certain that the coast was clear, that he himself became an inadvertent witness to the efficacy of Raymond Large's existing installations – and to the second of the unlikely threesomes to burgeon that week.

Sampler was approaching the further end of the twelve-acre estate, not far from the gazebo on the fringe of a copse which Large had mentioned. There was, the art-director knew, a camera obscura concealed within the building ('Useful after garden parties,' Large had said), but they had decided not to use it for the pageant. The target areas did not coincide with the general indoor plan, quite apart from the lighting difficulties, even with floods blazing near the house.

He might as well, nevertheless, take a look, he mused. It would be interesting to see how the device worked . . . and how efficient it was. He climbed the steps to the wooden verandah surrounding the octagonal building.

The folly had been designed almost exactly a hundred years ago, in the eighteen-sixties. Rising from the centre of the steeply tiled roof was a first-floor eyrie surmounted by a domed bell-tower of the kind usually seen above stable blocks. It was within the open columns supporting this dome that the mirrors and outer machinery of the camera obscura were housed.

The slatted double doors at the entrance were unlocked. Sampler opened them and went inside. Late afternoon sunlight slanted through two of the windows, illuminating the dust motes rising from the wooden floor. Apart from a rustic bench, a table and two garden chairs, the place was empty. Sampler climbed a rickety stairway and pushed open a trapdoor leading to the tower room.

Here at once he struck paydirt: an outsize ground-glass screen rising from a desk, an assortment of wheels and levers to operate the mirrors above, a swivel chair.

Sampler sat down in the chair. He remembered the dictionary definition of a camera obscura: *An internally darkened space with an aperture for projecting the image of external objects onto a screen within it.*

There was an image on the screen but it was indistinct. Foliage, branches, the corner of a wall?

He drew curtains over the slitted windows. The gloom in the room deepened, the image became clearer. But not interesting. He seated himself again, experimentally rotating wheels, tugging at levers. Pulleys creaked and metal groaned as the ancient mirrors above re-angled their surfaces. Lines and waves and nebulous shapes chased one another across the screen, some dense and blurred, others so bright as to be dazzling. Until suddenly, unexpectedly... there!... no, no: gone away, vanished ... roll back the wheel ... gently, gently... that lever sharpens the focus; this lets in more light ... *There!*

A perfect image, diamond-hard, admirably lit: a flagged rose garden with a central fountain playing. Sampler knew where it was: outside the French windows to the ballroom. Empty of course. He had found the controls to displace the image sideways, rather like a pan with a movie camera. He rolled and pushed. An avenue between yew hedges. Acres of lawn. The rear wall of the house's eastern wing ... the corner of a tiled outhouse with a gardener putting away a wheelbarrow, a rake, a hoe.

Sampler extended his range, sweeping wider, further afield. Cars in the drive. A minibus passing security men on the way to the gates. A balustraded terrace – yes, and there was old Large himself, carrying a tray of drinks to Shirley Sabbath, sitting at a table with a parasol! Really, this Victorian toy was a find: he could practically distinguish separate hairs amongst the golden cascade streaming down the slender blonde's back!

He watched her drink, smile, produce a cigarette. Large flicked a gold lighter. Extraordinary!

He re-angled the planes of the camera obscura, taking a wide view, towards the far side of the estate. Ornamental gardens, shrubberies, tennis courts, the corner of a swimming pool with a barbecue house flashed past. And then it was—

Wait.

There had been something . . . carefully, he juggled the controls to pan back, back past a croquet lawn towards the barbecue house and the pool . . . yes, towards a summer-house a little further away: a smallish, thatched structure with miniature wheels rotating it on a circular rail, so that it could always face towards – or away from – the sun. At the moment the back of the summer-house was towards the main block, but the open front faced the camera obscura, and . . .

Christ!

He had thought at first it might be statuary – Large had the oddest tastes – but now he saw with blinding clarity that there were three people entwined in that summer-house. Two women and a man, and each of them was stark naked.

With infinite care, Sampler stroked the controls to obtain the finest, sharpest image possible. A short, compact brunette, a girl with very dark red hair cut short as a boy's and – Good God! – of all people *Edward Dulok*, the dress manufacturer and arch rival of Large and Preckner!

But how and why in Christ's name . . . ? Sampler settled down to concentrate on his screens.

Entwined they certainly were. Like Roman or Greek statuary? Maybe. More like the North American Indian equivalent, perhaps: the traditional totem pole. Like those carved wooden deities, the nude palefaces were undoubtedly stacked one above the other. A female sat on a bench seat just inside the shallow shelter, feet on the floor, buttocks on dusty wood. The male stood on the same seat, facing her with his feet on either side of her hips. From between his own hips, jutting through a hairy triangle, an erect penis was

205

buried between her parted lips. The third woman straddled his shoulders from in front, her legs hanging down his back, her hands on his head and her genital area jammed against his gobbling mouth. The face of this girl – it was the shorthaired redhead – topping the moving human column, was hidden behind the guttered edge of the summer-house's thatched roof.

A watcher observing this unusual trio – and of course somebody was – might well have wondered what strange series of events had led them to be there, like that, at this particular time.

There was a series of events, sure. But none of them was strange in itself. What was perhaps unusual – at any rate unforeseeable – was that their separate paths should have crossed in the way they did. As for the rest . . . well, it was just something that happened.

Suzanne Towers, the brunette beauty who was handling the publicity and promotion for the magazine once it was launched, was prowling Large's estate in the hope of finding some outside angle, some fresh approaches which might make a piece or a mention, after the launch itself had been covered, which she could sell to some of her many Fleet Street conquests. There might be something to do with the house itself, the grounds, the history of that cute little folly in the wood.

Edward Dulok – despite his lofty put-downs and denials to Elvira – was in fact consumed with curiosity, a savage desire to know exactly what 'the Preckner lot' were up to. And, for private as well as professional reasons, this burning sense of need-to-know was being fuelled daily to white heat by innumerable hints and rumours and trailers he saw with increasing frequency in every newspaper or magazine he picked up. Finally, unable to find anything factual from the contacts he had, he decided to try a little 'industrial espionage' himself. He would take a trip out to this goddam country house and see what he could uncover.

He left his car in Great Bardfield and walked the two miles to the property. The house itself was a red brick Georgian pile with an E-shaped ground-plan, balustraded roof-lines, two wings and a pedimented central block. But apart from an unusual collection of minibuses, delivery vans and unloading trucks parked among the cars crowding the circular driveway, there was nothing of any interest to be seen from the black and gold wrought-iron gates. And any idea of penetrating the estate on some pretext or other – he soon found out – was a non-starter. The security service was much too efficient and too well-staffed. Dulok determined to circle the property on foot. He was half a mile along an unmetalled track leading to a farm – also Large's – when he found by a small wood a place where he thought he might succeed in making an entry undetected.

Red-headed Marie O'Riley, the fourth of the lingerie models originally booked to show the Preckner-Curnow collection, had not gone back to London with the rest of the crew when the day's work was over. Like Eve and Zita and Sandrine, Marie knew very well that there was 'something on' in the house once the grand launch was over – 'Kind of a private party,' Mr Large had said, 'to which you are all invited.' She knew that engineers and electricians of some kind worked late every evening on this, whatever it was. She would cadge a lift back to town with one of them. Meanwhile she loved the park, she had found it a shame to work indoors the whole beautiful summer day, and there was at least an hour and a half of sunshine still to enjoy.

She made her way to the small, secluded summer-house she had discovered half hidden on the edge of the wood. It was the ideal spot – for, unlike Sandrine and Zita and Eve, Marie was an enthusiastic naturist.

Again unlike her three co-workers, Marie was also, as it happened, a nympho.

Suzanne came across the summer-house after she had rounded the pool and barbecue. She crossed an orchard and approached the small thatched shelter from behind. Seeing that it was mounted on a sort of turntable and that the rail was shiny and not rusted, she gave the wooden wall an experimental push.

The summer-house swung easily around. She heard a

sudden exclamation . . . and to her astonishment Suzanne found herself face to face with the naked young woman who had just slid into her field of vision. 'Oh,' she gasped. 'God, I'm so sorry! I mean, I'd no idea . . . Marie, isn't it? One of the Preckner models?'

'No harm done,' Marie said lazily. 'At least I'm alone!'

She was, Suzanne saw, really very prety. The body – tanned all over – sprawled on the seat with its smooth curve of belly, its auburn genital triangle and the soft but well-formed breasts heavy on the chest, was voluptuous without being over-weight, sexy without any hint of tartiness. From the boyish haircut with its side parting, a dark red wing hung down to hide one of her eyes. The other, bright green and glistening, was slightly screwed up in a quizzical expression that mirrored the wry twist to her mouth. 'Be a love and push me back into the sun,' she said. 'And, look – why not join me? The sun's still gorgeously warm. Do you good after all that running about, being pushed around by that sweaty crowd inside.'

'That's sweet of you, but I really couldn't,' Suzanne began. 'That is to say, I have so many things still to . . .' She stopped. All of a sudden she thought: After all, why the fuck not? The redhead was nice, the sun *was* beguilingly warm, and she did love to feel that warmth, and especially the breeze, caress those parts of her she was normally obliged to cover up. She grinned. She said aloud: 'As you say, why on earth not?'

Rotating the summer-house back into its original position, she climbed the wooden steps and unconcernedly stripped off jeans, tee-shirt, panties and bra. She kicked away a pair of white trainers and perched herself on the seat beside Marie, legs stretched gratefully out in the sun. 'Mmmmm! Quite gorgeous!' she agreed.

It was a little later – they had talked of this and that, mostly of the forthcoming reception – that Marie ventured: 'Do forgive me . . . but I must say – well, I mean your tits are really smashing!'

Suzanne laughed. 'Well, that's very sweet. I mean . . . I don't know what to say!'

'Don't say anything. Enjoy. But, God, I do appreciate . . .

mine are too bloody big, and now they tend to droop and –
Oh, goodness, yours are so super!' And then, shyly: 'Dare I?
That is to say, could I possibly . . . just touch?'

Feeling a little awkward, but flattered just the same,
Suzanne managed to say: 'Be my guest!' She half turned
towards the nubile redhead.

Studiously avoiding the nipple, Marie cupped one hand
gently beneath the nearer breast. 'Oh, God,' she exclaimed,
'the weight, the warmth, that glorious taut, resilient *feel* of
it . . .!'

At that precise moment there was a heavy threshing of
leaves and branches, and a man neither of them had ever
seen before burst through a bramble thicket on the edge of
the wood and lurched out into the open. His face was
scratched and bleeding, and a particularly strong and thorny
stem had torn open his trousers and gashed the skin of the
pale thigh showing through.

'Christ – the demon king in the pantomime!' Marie
exclaimed.

'Who the hell are you?' Suzanne demanded angrily. 'What
the devil are you doing here?'

'I'm sorry, I'm so very sorry. I . . . I lost m-my way,'
Edward Dulok stammered, appalled not only to be
discovered trespassing but to find himself face to face with
two naked women. Women, moreover, evidently surprised in
some private lesbian activity.

'Who are you?' Suzanne repeated. 'This is private
property, you know.'

'*Very* private!' Marie said with a sly, almost roguish, glance
at Suzanne's nude body and then her own.

'I said I was sorry. It's all a . . . an unfortunate mistake.
I'm not a peeping Tom. I'm a journalist,' Dulok improvized
wildly. His reaction was much the same as Roger Curnow's
had been during the Preckner break-in: what shame, what a
disgrace for the boss of a rival company to be unmasked on
what was, to put it baldly, a spying expedition! 'My name,'
he said, 'is – er – André Willock.'

He'd seen the name somewhere. It just came into his head
as he spoke.

But by a coincidence – not so strange, really, in the circumstances – this was in fact the name of a journalist, a European operating from Paris. Dulok's memory must have retained it from some newspaper article he had read somewhere. More importantly, André Willock was a writer Suzanne particularly wished to meet. If she could get continental exposure for the Preckner collection, it would be a welcome feather in her professional, promotional, cap.

'But . . . how extraordinary!' she exclaimed. She introduced herself, and then said: 'But I'd still like to know, Monsieur Willock, exactly how, and why, you lost your way in this particular wood.'

'Very simple, really,' Dulok said airily. 'I happened to be staying with friends in Bardfield. There was gossip – about this property. Out for a walk, I passed by the main entrance and thought I might ask a discreet question or so.' He smiled. 'I was . . . discouraged. As a newspaperman this intrigued me. I poked about further. And then I thought: any operation with as important a security coverage as this must be something bigtime. So, like any good reporter, I decided to try and find out what it was.' He extended his arms wide, smiled: 'Instead, I found you out!'

'Not all that bigtime,' Suzanne said. 'Just rich. A press presentation, no less. But no more. If you like, if it interests you – it's to do with the ready-to-wear dress business – I could wangle you into the reception. You'd have a European exclusive!'

'It interests me very much indeed,' Dulok said truthfully. 'I'd be most grateful, Miss Towers.'

'He's bleeding!' Marie said suddenly. 'Look, Suzy: that trouser leg is soaked! It's a nasty gash – right up towards the groin.'

'Oh, good Lord . . . No, it's nothing, really. Just a deeper scratch,' Dulok said. 'Honestly.'

'Nonsense. Heaven knows what poisonous weeds there may be in that thicket!' Marie said severely. 'You could be allergic. Think of tetanus. You better take those trousers off at once: I've kleenex in my handbag; there's a gardener's tap behind this hut. We'll clean it up for you.'

'No, no, really . . . I promise you. It's not . . . I mean I hardly like—'

'Don't be silly,' Marie cut in. 'Christ, it's not the first time we've seen a man in underpants!'

'God, yes!' Suzanne was reproving. 'If that's what you're worried about . . . I mean, we're not exactly fully dressed, are we? Come on: take them off!'

'Or we'll take them off for you!' Marie said suddenly, menacingly.

'All right, all right.' Dulok started to unbutton his belt.

He was wearing only the briefest of underpants – not much more than a G-string – and a lightweight, short-sleeved sea-island cotton shirt in navy blue. Trouserless, he looked somehow more naked than either of the nude girls.

He felt more naked too. And more vulnerable. Especially since they were two to one. Because, oddly enough, although he and Elvira had the most liberal – some would say the most licentious – of marriages, he had never joined his wife in any of her extra-curricular adventures, nor had she ever shared any of his. He was therefore quite inexperienced in three-way sex.

The present situation – even though he was there under false pretences, or perhaps because of that – was therefore at the same time exciting, intriguing, yet obscurely scary.

But they were two *very* pretty girls . . .

The crux – one could be forgiven for saying crotch – of the matter came as they cleaned, staunched and dried the deepest of the ragged cuts. Their cool fingers were indeed working on the tender, sensitive inside of his thigh, up and down, pressing and smoothing, dangerously near the cotton and lycra pouch concealing his genitals. Was it only his imagination that brushed the back of Marie's hand, not once but twice, against that sensually aware bulge?

By this time, looking down at the two bare backs and the hanging breasts crouched over his lower limbs, Dulok had expelled from his mind everything unconnected with the life of the senses. So when Marie said, 'This bloody gash runs right up into the crease of the thigh: you'll have to take off the briefs too, man!' he offered no resistance, verbal or

211

physical. Two pairs of hands locked over the elasticated waistband of the bikini-like undergarment, dragging it down over his hips, past his thighs and knees, to his ankles and finally the floor.

Gazing fascinated at this manoeuvre, he had seen without any embarrassment at all that the pouch, a lighter blue than the shirt, was darkened by a telltale patch of moisture about where the head of his cock would be. And at the same time the redhead, Marie, remarked conversationally: 'Not a bad cock on him, I should say. Wouldn't you agree?'

And Suzanne' voice – as his tool sprang free, stiffened already and erect – 'Why, yes. I'd say there was no doubt about that at all.'

So suddenly the scenario had changed. Another backside was in the director's chair. Marie was jerking the reins. Suzanne, the Fleet Street Darling, who had made – and in a sense lost – her reputation 'being nice' to newspapermen, thought: what difference does one more make? And Edward Dulok, now that the cards had been dealt and the hands exposed, was disposed to play the game any way these harpies wanted.

So that when Marie, tossing the lock of auburn hair away from her eyes, said: 'Now why do you imagine that prick could have arrived at a state like that?' – Dulok growled: 'You want to find out?'

And the two naked girls cried out with a single voice: 'Oh, yes!'

Which was no more than two minutes before Pete Sampler, at the controls of the camera obscura, homed in on the 'totem pole' that was the trio's first attempt to climb the heights of joy.

There were maybe a dozen other permutations and combinations that were tried and accepted – or, in rare cases, rejected for athletic reasons – before the sun sank behind a row of elm trees sheltering the farm beyond the far end of the property. Not more. For with three mouths, two pussies and only a single prick, the possibilities are limited.

Basically, one girl is fucked and the other sucked; or the man is sucked by one girl and sucks the other – which leaves

Girl No. 2 herself free to suck No. 1. Around those two formulae, everything else restricts itself to a question of gymnastics.

It is here, nevertheless, that the six hands available – and, in the case of the first formula, the one free mouth – work their inimitable magic in the invention of variations on those two themes.

The two most exciting combinations – they all agreed when the demons of lust had been permitted to leave them – were the one in which Pete Sampler had first discovered them, and that in which Dulok lay supine on his back. In this, one of the girls straddled his hips and the other sat astride his head, the first impaled on his rigid cock, the second skewered by his tongue. An additional advantage here was that the two girls could lean together over him and kiss while each fondled the other's breasts. Dulok's hands were fully occupied pussywise as accessory aids to his cock and tongue.

He of course had in a sense the best of anything they tried, inasmuch as – whatever the position, however feverish their movements – both his mouth *and* his genitals were always occupied, which was not always the case with both girls.

It was not, however, until the sexual gala following the launch blast-off – what Raymond Large was pleased to call his pageant – that Edward Dulok became fully aware of the depths of lustful invention which could be invoked by the gods of suggestive underwear!

PART SIX

Petticoats Up . . . !

19

The press reception given to mark the launch of the new lingerie magazine *Frou-Frou* was one of the media successes of the summer. More than a hundred specially invited guests, brought in a fleet of chartered hire cars to Raymond Large's property near Great Bardfield, were entertained royally from late afternoon until ten o'clock at night. So extravagant was the hospitality in fact that the party threatened to transform itself into the rave of the year!

So far as the plugging of the publication was concerned, this was entirely a soft-sell operation. Nobody's arm was twisted, no one yelled 'This you must see' or 'Readers will love this'. Copies were of course available – Help yourself; take two or three! There was a lavishly produced, but very short, press handout emphasizing the demand for prettier, sexier lingerie. Photos of the Preckner collection could be ordered (delivery free the next morning) from a discreet advertising stand. But for the most part it was eat, drink and be merry. The running buffet in the lawn marquee was splendid; an army of white-coated barmen circulated all evening re-filling, suggesting, decanting, popping corks; the sprinkling of show-biz and jet-set personalities was sufficiently interesting to tempt the gossip columnists; and Luke, Suzanne, Brigitte, Tom Silver and Shirley herself were there to answer questions if anyone asked any.

Neither Duke Ellington, Danny Kaye nor the Beatles were present, but soft and swinging jazz was dispensed by a small night-club group ('Do dance, if you feel like it!') led by the clarinettist Frank Weir. The highlight of the reception, press-wise, was of course the stage presentation bringing the sexy pages of *Frou-Frou* to three-dimensional life with the same girls, featuring the same titillating designs, as those displayed in the magazine.

Here Luke, with Preckner and Curnow's agreement, had been smart. Naturally the Preckner collection had been given pride of place: because it was original, new and – surprise, surprise! – it happened to be unveiled before an unsuspecting public at the same time as this new and original magazine. But existing underwear specialists – Gossard, Playtex, Triumph and others – had been invited to submit photos and articles as well as allowing their models to be featured on stage. After the show, which was brilliantly produced by Sampler and his Royal Opera colleague, Tom Silver was beseiged by manufacturers' advertising reps demanding details of the available space and rates in issue No. 2, in one month's time.

When, as noted on the invitations, the lights were dimmed and the marquee flaps closed at ten o'clock, and the cars queued up on the driveway to collect their passengers and take them home, the atmosphere in the big house was euphoric. There had been an outburst of spontaneous applause – several times – during the stage presentation, produced like a showgirl musical revue in the house's east wing ballroom. Unusually, there were scattered examples again, interspersed with an occasional 'Bravo!', as the guests lurched out to their cars. Some of the more sober ones even bothered to search out and thank Raymond Large, who had remained unobtrusively in the background throughout the party.

'Well, I'll tell you one thing,' Suzanne Towers promised. 'You're going to get so much exposure on tonight that it'll be almost obscene! Glamour pics in the glossies, more technical stuff in the trade mags, pieces for the sex maniacs in dailies and pop Sundays – and probably short think-pieces in the more serious papers on the launch as a whole, as a method of selling an idea.' She grinned happily. 'Plus, I tell you no lie, an occasional quote quarried from our starry guests by the odd columnist – which may or may not say where said columnist was at the time he got it.'

'A brilliant promotion,' Large said. 'Everyone – you especially, my dear – has been superb.'

Pete Sampler, standing with blonde Eve on the semi-circular entrance steps beneath the house's pedimented porch, nodded his agreement. 'I think we could call it a success,' he said. 'So far!'

And then, staring into the dark as the last pair of twin red tail-lights vanished around a curve in the drive, he added reflectively: 'Talking of sex maniacs – and indeed of gossip columns – I'd just love to know how many, or how few, of those tanked-up, drunken buggers and bitches are going to sleep in their own beds when they get back to town tonight!'

'Your guess is as good as mine,' Shirley Sabbath said with a glance at Raymond Large.

There was a small get-together in Large's study after the last of the caterers' vans and the show-business technicians' Fords had departed. Relatively small, that is.

Apart from the host himself and those concerned with the magazine and the Preckner display, the four original model girls were present, still wearing the last costumes they had appeared in, together with designer Shirley, Gladys Carter, Suzanne Towers and Aidan Carriage – the columnist whose Sunday piece had provoked the entire corpus of press speculation some weeks before.

Two supernumeraries not on Large's original list completed the party. These were, first, an important continental journalist whose name was said to be André Willock, specially invited by Suzanne; and a young woman called Elvira. Nobody knew exactly how or why she was there, but she seemed to know the red-haired model, Marie, and be an intimate of that other redhead, Gladys Carter. So everyone assumed she must have been rowed in by someone else among those in charge. She was good-looking anyway, with a particularly provocative, challenging gaze and a body so alluring that Large, of all people, was unlikely to question her presence there.

This much smaller gathering – what Large thought of as pre-pageant – was served late refreshment by Shirley herself (Large's regular personnel had all been given the night off). This comprised only coffee, brandy and plates of decorative *petits-fours* – small cake-like delicacies that were sweet and pretty and could be swallowed in a couple of bites.

In the distribution of which, for some reason, both Pete Sampler and Shirley herself seemed especially – almost intimately – concerned.

It was after the self-congratulations and the inquest on the reception were completed that guests started to separate yet coalesce at the same time, rather in the fashion of cells under a microscope or a blob of mercury on a slanting surface. It was not possible to isolate any specific motivation or identify a guiding hand. Again, it was just something that seemed to happen.

A sociologist charting the ergonomics of the group as a whole, however, might have noted an activity on the part of Shirley Sabbath more marked than that of the pairs and trios and quartets between which she continually moved, laughing, joking, offering a drink here a *petit-four* there. This was normal enough: she had in fact been acting as hostess ever since Large – pleading his advanced age – had excused himself and retired.

It was true, nevertheless, that the pairings eventually settled on did not always correspond with the rooms allocated to those invited to stay the night. Guests not included on this list – Aidan Carriage, the woman called Elvira, the photographer Warne-Johns and the mysterious André Willock – were assumed to be leaving under their own steam once the party was over.

Two notable absentees were David Preckner and Sylvia. They had left soon after the stage show, at the same time as the hire-car fleet. The reason for this would have been equally incomprehensible to Shirley, Large and Gladys Carter. It was in truth that Preckner had been so stimulated by the lingerie display he had dreamed up and was now marketing that he had been seized by an uncontrollable desire to rush home and make love with his wife.

It was Shirley and Pete Sampler, naturally with the host's invisible approval, who persuaded the unlisted guests to stay. 'It's late. We're having a good time. There are plenty of spare rooms,' Shirley urged. And the art director added: 'We've sunk a few, dammit. You'd be crazy – not to say dangerous – driving all the way back at this time!'

No further arm-twisting was necessary – especially as columnist Carriage was eager to repeat his lingeristic intimacy with Suzanne, Dulok-Willock avid to continue his summer-house explorations with auburn-haired Marie, and his wife finding she had . . . oh, so many things in common with Roger Curnow and Shirley herself.

It seemed much later, but it was in fact not long after midnight that the drift upstairs began.

Curiously, it was Sampler, architect of the Machiavellian devices contributing to Large's 'pageant', who secured for himself the one room in the upper part of the big house which he knew could neither be spied upon nor come within earshot of eavesdroppers. The strength – and depth – of his love-at-first-sight emotional involvement with the blonde model Eve, and her response to it, were such that the sturdy, crew-cut art director refused totally to share it, or her, with anybody at all. He was quite prepared to organize, to make a show of other people's sex lives, for money if offered, but not – certainly not now – his own!

Individually or collectively, openly or slyly, the other members of the party – still under Shirley's direction – made their several hazy ways to the rooms so carefully prepared for them.

'Why do you call it a pageant?' Brigitte Dubois asked Raymond Large. 'A pageant is . . . what? A *défilé*, a procession, no? A succession of—'

'A succession of tableaux, of displays, yes,' Large replied. 'Not necessarily in line ahead, not always in the form of a parade. A series of spectacles anyway, usually illustrating historical events or abstract virtues – faith, hope or charity. That kind of thing.'

'So I ask again: why what we are to see is a pageant?'

The old man grinned. 'My private joke,' he said. 'What we are to see fits that definition. A series of spectacles, tableaux, sketches if you like. The only difference between ours and the kind you get at a village fête or fair is that there the members of each display know about the tableau that precedes them and the one that follows – whereas here the actors don't know they're taking part in a pageant at all.'

'And this pageant will illustrate . . . ?'

'Abstract vices,' Raymond Large told her.

They were sitting comfortably in an attic cubby-hole engineered by Sampler and his technicians from the inner end of an old box-room. Above their heads, half a dozen six-inch monitor screens showed the interior of six different bedooms as viewed by cameras concealed in mouldings or ornamental features – or, in two cases, shot through two-way mirrors.

Immediately in front of them was an outsize 36-inch video screen to which the images of any of the small ones could be transferred at the touch of a button. The button was located on a control panel beneath the big screen and in front of Large. Levers, switches and calibrated wheels on this panel could be used to modify focus, contrast, brightness, and in some cases field of vision – for several of the cameras could be marginally shifted: a few degrees left or right, a few up or down. There was too a volume control, for naturally each room was wired for sound.

From the interior of this high-tech secret installation, a network of cables and electrical leads, hidden though they were, fanned out over the upper part of the house as intricately as a spiderweb. 'Very efficient, young Sampler,' Large approved. 'Most impressive.' He chuckled. 'Trust him to bag the only room in the house with no special mirror and nowhere to conceal a camera!'

'It is a most remarkable achievement,' Brigitte agreed. 'If only I could have such a thing on my houseboat!'

'You must talk to me about that,' Large said. 'Maybe I could help. Nothing is impossible.'

'That would be . . . stupendous, *chéri*! In such a case, naturally you would be . . . always welcome.'

'Naturally,' Large said. 'Here though' – he shot a swift glance at the monitors – 'I have to say that my adventuress, young Shirley, has been invaluable.'

He looked up again. Most of the rooms were now peopled

by men and women in various stages of undress. 'When I bought the château near Nice,' he continued, 'I had two invaluable servants, local girls. Lusty and Busty, we called them, for obvious reasons. They too had a genius for – what shall I say? – getting folks together. One weekend, long ago, before the war, I held a great party there to impress an American millionaire I hoped might invest money in my vineyard.' He laughed again. 'Thanks to Lusty and Busty, a Paris scandal sheet termed my little get-together "The most sensational orgy of the season!"* Great days, great days, dear Brigitte.'

'Who are we going to watch first?' Brigitte asked. She licked her lips. 'Who do you . . . fancy?'

For the third time, Large studied the small screens. 'Cecil B. de Mille was said to have an unfailing formula for those wishing to make a best-selling film,' he remarked. '"Start with an earth-quake and work up to a climax"! Tonight, though, I think we should stand that on its head: start with the traditional, the conventional, the *normal* – and see what human ingenuity can add to that in the way of lasciviousness, perversion and old-fashioned lust.'

He selected a number and pressed the button. The huge cathode tube blazed to busy life.

'I give you,' Large said theatrically, 'Mr Aidan Carriage and Miss – ah – Suzanne Towers!'

Suzanne was wearing – had been poured into – an undergarment, one of several given to her by Preckner, whose overall shape was not unlike a swimsuit. But there the similarity ended.

It was a backless one-piece, cut very high from crotch to hip, reduced almost to a single panel above the waist, then blossoming into the generous cups of a same-material bra that plunged deep between the breasts and at the same time pushed them up so that almost all of the upper slopes with the exception of the nipples themselves were exposed. The material, elasticated and shiny, was a searing red, and the

*See *The Wild Party* by Aaron Amory, also available in Delta.

neckline, shoulder-straps and up-cut legs were edged with a froth of black lace. With it she wore cinnamon-coloured silk stockings rolled down to the knee.

'Christ!' Aidan Carriage said admiringly when she had shrugged out of her black cocktail dress. 'You look like the whore of bloody Babylon!'

Suzanne giggled. 'I'm a scarlet woman,' she teased.

Carriage shook his head. 'The last time we were together,' he said, 'I wanted to strip off your sensational underwear and you wouldn't let me. This time, I want you to keep it bloody on. But—'

'I know what you're thinking,' Suzanne said. 'But Preckner takes care of everything. Look!' She unpopped press-studs at the crotch gusset to reveal dark public hair among the black lace.

Carriage looked.

He kept on looking, eagerly, avidly, as she went into her how-to-undress-a-man-sexily routine, peeling off layer after layer, onionwise, breath quickening and fingers busy until there was nothing left to cover the hard maleness of the columnist's body but the tight triangle of his briefs – already darkened at its pyramid point by the moisture seeping from his stiff, excited cock.

She stripped off the underpants, lowering them past thighs, knees and ankles until he could step easily out of them – by which time, crouched down to floor level, Suzanne found her face level with the long, thin, springy length of the stiff cock so expertly freed. The next step was inevitable, a foregone conclusion. She opened her mouth and closed red lips over the outsize, bulbous glans quivering so temptingly inches away. Her cheeks hollowed and her head swayed back and forth as she began to suck.

Carriage caught his breath, flexing lean hips to thrust them marginally nearer that lustfully engulfing oral embrace. His fascinated gaze never wavered.

There was something quite irresistibly alluring about the slender brunette doubled up below him with her mouth caressing the thrilled and tingling throb of his cock. It wasn't just the slavish shape that compressed the curves of that feminine frame, revealing the tunnelled hollow between the thrust-up breasts. More basically still, it was a matter of contrast. Somehow the 'shocking' outline, colour and design of the tightly restricting undergarment, with its lewdly revealing open crotch, complemented the evenly tanned areas of visible flesh in such a way as to underline and emphasize the contrast between them – between the smooth resilience of the live and loving and the stretched pretensions of the manufactured. Between in fact the human and the artificial.

But if Aidan Carriage's gaze remained unshakably fascinated, it was no less fixed than those of Raymond Large and Brigitte Dubois, lecherously spying on the couple via the videoscreen in the converted boxroom.

As a couple, Aidan and Suzanne were probably in the visual sense the most spectacular of all the guests. The girl, with her fine features, shapely body and lustrous dark hair tumbling about her shoulders, was ravishing – with or without the sexy accessories. And Carriage, tall, well muscled, with his lined face and dark hair, speckled now with grey, slightly curling at the neck, was still, though he was pushing forty, a handsome man indeed.

They had changed positions now. Unable any longer to put his own desire on hold, he had bent down, grabbed Suzanne by the elbows, and lifted her bodily from the floor. As his thin, hard cock slid free of her sucking mouth, he held her forcefully against him, kissing that mouth passionately while his trembling hands sculpted the warm and softly swelling slopes of her breasts from the scalloped lace edging the stiff cups of the scarlet and black undergarment.

They were both panting now, hoarse breaths and sensual groans clearly audible in the otherwise silent room, and equally loud in the control room on the floor above.

There was suddenly a subdued creak, a susurrus of material, a small explosive gasp.

He had thrown her onto her back on the bed. Sprawled halfway across the mattress, she reached down a hand to lift up the unfastened gusset flap, fully exposing the tangle of damp pubic hairs the strip of material had been hiding, and the coral whorls of the outer labia among them.

Carriage was already on his knees beside the bed. At once he spread Suzanne's thighs and buried his head between them. Her hips arched up off the mattress to meet the mouth which had found the opening in the shameless undergarment, the tongue gobbling into the hot, wet depths of her inner cunt.

Minutes later he was on top of her, spilling out the breasts with their hardened, rosy tips, free hand tearing at the wet gusset so that his oversize cock-head could plough into her ready pussy.

Her stockinged knees rose and her legs scissored over his bare back as they began to fuck.

'That's very pretty – quite beautiful in its way,' Raymond Large said. 'But I always think, once they get to the final phase, that visually it becomes less compulsive. There's not so much to see, far less opportunity for the inventive mind to create variations, don't you think?' He stifled a laugh that was almost a giggle. 'When they're both nude – it's an awful thing to say – but sometimes I really feel . . . well, you know, it makes me think of frogs! Suppose we look in on one of the other rooms? If you agree, that is.'

'You are of course, *cher ami*, as always, correct,' Brigitte said. 'It seems there is likely to develop something not without interest on the Number Five.'

He glanced at the monitors. 'My God, yes. Absolutely!' He pressed the buttons.

The images on the big screen dissolved, vanished, reappeared as black zigzags, and finally revealed an entirely different room, panelled and furnished with nineteenth-century extravagance. But the most extravagant thing of all was the nearest image – an enormous facial close-up. The face was black, it was beautiful, and it wore an expression of subdued ecstasy. But it was so huge, almost filling the screen, that Brigitte was surprised into a small cry of astonishment.

'The camera is at shoulder level,' Large explained. 'This is one of the rooms where we have to shoot from a fixed position behind a two-way mirror.'

The face belonged to the West Indian model, Sandrine. She was in fact leaning with both arms on a dressing-table, her head with its ice-tinted dark hair only inches from the looking-glass . . .

Even with a whole room and a wide, comfortable bed at his disposal, Luke Hornby stood by – literally stood by – his preference for, his unproven theory concerning, upstanding sex. This time however, since he was not in the *Frou-Frou* editorial suite but a private house two miles from Great Bardfield, in Essex, he was prepared to perform nude. His choice had fallen once more upon Sandrine, not so much because of her outer physical beauty – which was considerable – but because the pleasures of her inner self had been so exquisite that he took them, at least for the time being, as a large step towards the confirmation of that theory's validity.

This was why Sandrine was leaning forward, naked, on the dressing-table, why Luke was very close behind her, and why her face was even closer to the concealed video-camera – less than nine inches away, had she but known it!

'Christ,' Large said. 'It looks like she's going to eat us: that mouth fills half the damn screen!'

For the two voyeurs it was indeed a fascinating spectacle. Below Sandrine's over-lifesize face and behind her folded arms, her dark breasts were squashed against the glass top of the dressing-table as Luke in turn leaned forward with his hands resting on her plump hips. At that range and at that magnification they were privy to the slightest, subtlest changes of expression chasing one another across her exotic features – a tiny tightening of the eye muscles, an anticipatory purse of luscious lips as she felt Luke's bloated cock-head nudge her bared cunt from behind; the eyes widened and the mouth falling half open as he wedged the hard length of his tool into the hot clasp of her vagina.

The mouth widened into a lazy smile when the big man shafting her secret flesh settled himself into a gentle rhythm of insertion and withdrawal, moving easily in and out of her as he flexed and relaxed his hips.

Now she caught her glistening lower lip between dazzling white teeth: an extra deep thrust had plunged the bulbous glans against the neck of her womb.

Luke's head was invisible, out of shot at the top of the screen; the wide mass of his beefy torso advancing and retreating as he pumped his rigid length within the black girl's splayed body. Suddenly he was increasing the speed and force of his strokes. Sandrine's mouth flew wide open, lips drawn back in a rictus of excitement as her arched frame was humped forward towards the mirror, sliding on the polished surface of the dressing-table. She gasped, breath panting hoarsely, blurring the image each time her exhalations misted the glass. In the distance, persistent as an echo, the rise and fall of the big man's quickened breathing was audible.

In the control room, Brigitte was leaning forward in her chair, her skirt around her waist, busy hands tucked firmly between hot thighs. Large's fly was gaping, balls pulled free with one hand, milked cock quivering in the skimmed grasp of the other. Beyond the ecstatic swaying of Sandrine's head, at the far end of her supine back, they could see Luke's hands wrenching apart her buttocks, the pendulum swing of his wiry pubic hair as he pistoned his hidden cock between them.

When Sandrine came, a sudden explosion of movement animated the image. Her body convulsed, arching abruptly off the glass top then collapsing with outflung arms. The orgasm had been preceded by a furrowing of the forehead, a small vertical crease between the brows. Then the eyes squinched shut, the whole face contorted, the lips stretched wide, wide, and she uttered a piercing cry of joy. When the spasms shaking her violated belly were at their most frenzied, her arms shot out and her outstretched hands – fingers splayed wide as her plundered buttocks – jammed themselves against the mirror glass, blacking out the image as effectively as a riot cop masking the camera lens of a television crew.

Later, the image on the No. 5 monitor moved into medium long-shot. Luke the insatiable was having, as it were, a second bite at the cherry.

This time Sandrine was kneeling on the edge of the bed, leaning forward again with her weight on her hands. This time too, the whole of her lewdly exposed genital cleft was visible on the far side of the mirror – black hairs dark between the dark-fleshed thighs, gashed with the purplish, gaping labia, then the ruby glow of inner flesh, unexpected as the pink palms of the girl's black hands.

Enticing though it was, this super-intimate view was rapidly eclipsed by the hairy moons of Luke's backside as he moved in, rigid cock in hand, for the second round. By this time, however, the big screen in the control room was relaying the activity in a third bugged bedroom.

Activity is perhaps to overstate. Monitor No. 3 showed the image relayed by a camera concealed in the carved moulding surrounding the ceiling of what had once been a panelled sewing-room. It was mounted in a corner, at the junction of two walls, and it was focused downwards, at a sharp angle, on the bed which took up the centre of the room.

A single person, a young woman, lay on the bed. The room was otherwise empty.

The woman was Zita, the fourth of the original Preckner models – with the usual perfect lingerie figure, slender legs, parchment skin pale as alabaster, and a small, neat cap of dark hair which framed admirably her chiselled features.

She lay on her back, still wearing the last of the filmy Preckner designs she had showed in the *Frou-Frou* stage presentation. This was a three-piece ensemble in wrinkled azure blue crêpe-de-chine with inset panels of sheer, semi-transparent organza in the same colour which were designed to cover, yet still reveal, the swelling heaviness at the tips of the breasts and the axial curve of the belly. Below this sculptured bodice, hip-supported Directoire knickers – there was no other word for them – flowed loosely over the pelvis and thighs to be gathered with royal blue ribbons just below the knee. The set was completed by a waisted négligée with bishop sleeves, also be-ribboned and gathered at the wrists. This was now opened wide with the non-fastening edges spread out over the mattress on either side.

Zita's eyes were closed and her features settled in an expression of beatific content.

The only movement in the silent room was provided by the rise and fall of her pointed breasts and a discreetly circling movement of her two hands. One of these rose and fell in a dreamlike, smooth and almost loving caress, up from the incurved waist and over the ribcage to the cupped swell of mounded breasts and then – lingering a little over the nipples – down again to stroke the lower curve of the brunette's belly. The other hand and wrist were buried beneath the low waistband of the knickers, knuckled fingers visibly shifting behind the organza panel sheathing the crotch.

For several minutes the watchers studied this unselfconscious display of auto-eroticism with rapt attention. Then Large muttered: 'I knew Zita was rumoured among the other girls to be even more of an ice-maiden than Sampler's Eve, but this . . .' He shook his head. 'Perhaps she didn't have enough of splendid Shirley's little hash cookies!' He turned to regard the other monitors, but as he spoke the door of the room had opened and the image sprang vividly to life.

Zita disengaged her hands, pushed herself upright and sat, elegant and sexy, in the middle of the white fur rug covering the bed. 'Goodness,' she exclaimed. 'I wasn't expecting . . . that is to say, I thought you – I mean, how come you were able to . . .?'

Gladys Carter, nubile, naked and voluptuously curved, smiled lazily. 'I was with young Tom Silver,' she drawled. 'Eager, energetic, ecstatic. Then, you know . . . he passes out after the first time. A touch of the whisky cock, if you ask me!' She closed the door and turned towards the bed.

Behind the big screen, Raymond Large flicked a quick glance at – yes, it would be No. 2 – the row of monitors. This was the second of the rooms equipped with a fixed camera shooting through a two-way mirror. And right enough the image here was indeed that of an unconscious Silver. The young ad-man's pale length was sprawled face-upward across the bed, his feet draped over one side, his head hanging over the other. Above the fringe of beard, his mouth had spread into a contented smile. From his heavy, limp cock a snail-trail of dried sperm glistened across his thigh and disappeared among the black hairs on his belly. Large nodded, leaving the main screen concentrated on the two girls.

Gladys was now sitting on the bed. 'For that matter,' she said, 'I'm surprised to find that *you* are alone. A catastrophe, an accident like mine . . . or from choice?'

'Choice,' Zita said sharply. 'I got stuck with that awful photographer. He wanted me to . . . to make love to myself, while he . . .' She broke off, shuddering. 'Ugh. How puerile can you be?'

'Poor love.' The ample redhead placed an arm around the girl's blue shoulders, giving her a sympathetic squeeze. 'I don't know the man . . . personally . . . but I know the type.'

'It's not just that,' Zita complained. 'I seem to find a similar reaction with *any* man, even if he's – straight, don't they say? – even if he's totally normal. It's like, oh, I can't seem ever to get on with them; I never feel really at ease, alone with a man.' She laid her head momentarily on Gladys's padded shoulder.

Gladys moved her hand to cradle the nape of the dark girl's neck, cupping the close-cropped hair with a gentle pressure.

'It's strange,' Zita said, 'but I'm only able to feel really, genuinely *myself* with women. I suppose it's that, well, with another woman it's like being with a mirror of yourself: you know exactly how they feel – and they know exactly how you feel.'

'Not strange at all, dear. I entirely understand,' said Gladys, too honest to pretend that she herself wholly shared this restrictive attitude, but happy to seize any opportunity that was offered. 'Just relax – let's at least make ourselves comfortable,' she said.

They stretched themselves out on the white fur rug. Zita sighed drowsily and raised her arms, lacing her hands together behind her head. The movement tilted her silk-sheathed breasts, the nipples darkly visible behind the shadowed organza inserts, provocatively upwards.

'You're so lucky!' Gladys was still sitting half upright. 'Dear, I wish I could lose enough weight to look like you,' she said mendaciously. 'You're really such a gorgeous shape!' She allowed soft fingers to fall on the under-curve of a breast. Zita closed her eyes.

'And here' – a hand on the resilient flesh of the brunette's belly – 'where it's so difficult for people of my size to keep it flat!'

Zita lowered an arm, lifting the hand away from her flesh – but keeping the fingers tightly clasped in her own. Her fingertips traced miniature arabesques on the sensitive skin of the redhead's palm.

From here, with the help of Gladys's smooth expertise and the releasing effect of the doctored Shirley-Sampler sweetmeats, it was a matter only of minutes before action superseded words.

The words came first: not so much endearments as soothing expressions of trust and understanding, softly unintelligible cooings that nevertheless conveyed a great deal. It was during this verbal play that the twin cups of the bodice were lifted up and then folded downwards to expose the rose-tipped swelling splendour of Zita's breasts. From there it was only a short step to the lowering of the knickers' elastic waistband and the intrusion of a caressing hand within the dark heat below.

Until now, the shapely brunette had offered no opposition, no protest, verbal or physical. But neither had she revealed pleasure or even acquiescence, other than a slight shifting of her hips, a release of muscular tension, under the older woman's insidious manipulations.

Once the knickers were invaded, however, the elastic down to the hipbones, and alien fingers teasing her pubic hair, Zita herself became animated.

Her hands flew up to fondle the big breasts hanging heavily over her. Raising her head slightly, she parted her lips, closed her mouth over each thick, stiffened nipple in turn, and grazed the puckered flesh with small sharp movements of her teeth. At the same time – the knickers had somehow vanished – she jerked up a knee and lodged it hard

232

between the redhead's thighs, thrusting the kneecap forcefully into the moist clasp of the hot, wet pussy pouting among the hairs covering her pubic bone.

Gladys kissed her then, a voracious, tongue-wrestling embrace that left the two of them locked together, threshing on the bed. Seconds later their hands were everywhere, stroking, squeezing, smoothing, probing, harsh breath panting as chests heaved, hearts hammered and the thin, high, electric thrill of triggered lust seared through their excitedly awakened nerves.

After that, but before the night sank gratefully into what seemed no more than a continuous, dreamlike, lazy caress, it was for a short time explosive action.

The two salaciously aroused women rocked together all over the bed, limbs entwined, mouths gobbling, bodies contorted. The white rug was on the floor. For a short eternity, the slender brunette and the nubile redhead, wet-fingered and wide-eyed with desire, sucked tits, tongued cunts, mouthed heated flesh and clasped amorous, stroking arms in a frenzy of lewd coupling that rivalled the pages of the *Kama Sutra* in the imagination and complexity of its excess.

At the far end of a long corridor in the opposite wing, Edward Dulok lay on his back on a chaise longue with the auburn model Marie O'Riley astride his hips and his cock, iron-hard, tunnelled up into her dark red pussy.

It wasn't just her insatiable sexual appetite that intrigued him so much, but after the sunset idyll in the circling summer-house he had found himself bewitched not only by what she did with her body but also, particularly, by the *manner* in which it was done.

This was the very opposite of the arch-exuberant approach characterizing the lovemaking of the women locked together in front of the unseen No. 3 camera. Marie's attitude was super-cool – an almost contemplative, reflective demeanour which allowed her at the same time to be both actor and audience in the theatre of her own obsession. She regarded the sensual movements of her own body – and indeed that of her partner's – with a detachment both objective and involved; a slow, lingering gaze that seemed to combine a dazed astonishment at what she saw with an intensity of regard at times almost frightening. It was this apparent anomaly which had hooked Dulok in the first place and he had been both pleased – and grateful to Shirley, who knew good voyeur material when she saw it – when he was able to grab the girl and whisk her upstairs after the party-after-the-party.

He stared up now, fascinated himself by the intent expression with which she stared down between her breasts to watch – to *study*, it seemed – the veined, rigid and wetly glistening shaft of his cock swallowed and then revealed by her seething cunt as she rose and fell up and down its skewering length.

Her breasts, soft, a little loose, but by no means floppy, fascinated him too. Their weighted, pear-shaped swell swung very slightly from side to side as she moved, long nipples and wide areolae darker than usual at their tips. From time to time she leaned down and right forward so that, without releasing his tool from her vaginal clasp, she could brush those nipples from side to side across his chest in a sliding caress.

Dulok remained silent. His hands rested lightly on her hips, and hers on top of his. Nor, save for a catch of the breath after an extra-tight vaginal contraction, did he show any obvious reaction. This, he sensed, was a dialogue between cock and cunt – and let nobody else intrude. His body and hers were a tactile laboratory in which she was carrying out sensual research.

The wing of red hair, on the opposite side of her parting, hung down to hide one of her eyes. The other, ignoring Dulok's face, regarded every twitch of his belly muscles, each tremble of the pulse in his groin, the throbbing, lubricated pulsion of his hardened staff with the rapt attention of a scientist chasing the absolute truth.

Dulok allowed her to take him with her, flexing his hips only from time to time to help with a deeper than usual thrust. His cock, secure in the hot, tight, clasping embrace of her inner flesh, was sending thrills of desire coursing wildly outwards from his loins. And those breasts, swaying lasciviously on that eager, slender, savagely sexual body, were turning him on like crazy . . .

But another test, that was to strain his masculine resilience to the utmost, was unexpectedly to transform him into even more of a laboratory experiment than he had ever bargained for.

The door of the room, which had very low-key lighting, opened silently. A young woman, tall, fair-haired, blue-eyed, walked in. She hadn't been modelling Preckner lingerie at the press reception, but she might as well have been, judging from the garments she wore – except that the materials were different from Shirley's silks and satins and frothy lace.

She wore thigh-length black stockings, tight, crotch-hugging briefs; a waisted corset and a low-cut uplift bra. They were fashioned, respectively, in latex, shiny black vinyl, whaleboned black leather and, again, the vinyl.

She walked into the light. Straight hair, shoulder length; lean features; large front teeth resting on the lower lip.

Edward Dulok's eyes opened wide. 'Miss Elton-Shaw,' he gasped. 'Agatha. What the *hell* are you doing here?'

His new workroom supervisor used the smile on him. 'Not working for Messrs Preckner and Curnow,' she said. 'One employee with – er – divided loyalties is enough, I guess! No, the catering manager handling the press reception is a girlfriend of mine. I've been behind the scenes in the kitchens, helping her out.'

'Yes, okay, but . . . ?' Dulok's gaze roved over her fetishist attire, the laced black corset. She carried half a dozen thin leather straps with buckles in one hand.

'I happened to see that you, Mr Dulok, as unexpected as myself at a Preckner affair, were also here. And since you were with Marie – another girlfriend of mine – I thought maybe I could horn in and join the party.' She turned to the redhead. 'What shall we do with him?'

Marie – who during this conversation had continued easing herself up and down the rigid cock speared into her – replied: 'Well, I'm comfy here. But I think we'd better tie him up anyway.'

'Look,' Dulok protested, struggling to sit up, 'I'm not going to stay here and let—'

'You want to bet?' Agatha interrupted, pushing him back down with strong hands.

'What I suggest,' Marie said, 'is that since I'm fitted up quite nicely, I remain here.' She glanced at the straps. 'Then, after we have sufficiently immobilized our guest, you remove your briefs and squat over his face. He has an agile tongue, a certain amount of expertise.'

'And then?'

'We keep him there, fucking and sucking, until he has made us both come. Just for a start.'

'How many times?' Agatha asked.

Marie tossed back the lock of hair. She laughed. 'Six,' she said. 'Of the best!'

Raymond Large was unable to contain his excitement. Not only was his milking hand working overtime; his entire body was bouncing up and down in his chair. 'Marvellous!' he exulted. 'I didn't for a moment expect . . . but it takes all sorts, thank God!'

Brigitte was leaning so far forward, hands buried beneath the skirt covering her tilted belly, that it looked as though she was trying to push her face through the big screen. 'Is not a scene I am being familiar with,' she said huskily. 'But fascinating, fascinating!'

On the screen, the man pinioned between the two riding mistresses was contorting as much of his body as was visible stretched out on the chaise longue. In the control-room a sudden loud coughing exclamation, followed by an ecstatic cry, broke the silence.

'What the devil . . . ?' Large swung around in his chair. The noise had come from the far corner of the room, behind a stack of ancient cabin trunks.

Sheepishly, a tall, angular figure, male, moustached, rose from the battered chair in which it hunched – hidden in the shadows, intent on the distant screen.

'I'm m-m-most frightfully sorry,' it mumbled. 'Know I shouldn't have . . . ghastly bad form and all that . . . but this is strictly my scene, and, you know . . . well, I simply couldn't resist . . .'

Donald Warne-Johns, the bent photographer.

Clearly he had just experienced an orgasm: the front of his pale trousers was dark. Equally evident was the fact that this release had been provoked by the SM images on the screen. They may not have resembled a fat lady dragging him into bed and telling what to do, but they had been sufficiently authoritarian to satisfy his mother-figure fixation.

'Really, sir, I don't know how to b-begin . . .' he began again.

'My dear fellow!' Large was genial. 'No, no – not a word. You should have said . . . After all, why do you think we are here? Draw up a chair at once,' he said. 'Join us and enjoy, eh?'

'This may go on for some time,' Brigitte said, gesturing at the big screen. 'Meanwhile' – she glanced up at the No. 6 monitor – 'your Shirley is mounting some interesting tableaux!'

'Little rascal,' Large said fondly. 'My rogue adventuress! She's the only one actually to know that we're here, looking in . . . and that's what I like best of all.' He thumbed the sixth button.

Shirley had chosen the old housekeeper's sitting-room as her base. There was no bed or divan but an interesting selection of armchairs, pouffes and footstools which should, she thought, produce more fanciful, less restricted, sexual gymnastics than a single flat surface. It was also the room equipped with the most manoeuvrable of the concealed cameras.

It was at the moment, like the room on Monitor 4, devoted to a threesome: two females and one hardy male. Shirley had chosen as partners Roger Curnow – the Jolly Roger, as she called him – and Elvira Dulok, in whom she had at once recognized a kindred spirit. So far as Curnow was concerned she had more than once had reason to approve and admire his flexible approach, his let-'em-all-come inventiveness, and indeed his physical stamina.

The 'three-piece-suite' flashed on to the pageant director's wide screen, once he had selected their particular camera, displayed a sexual prowess at three different – though closely related! – levels.

For ease of entry, so to speak, they had each by now discarded all clothing.

They were arranged in what used to be called a 'daisy-chain' – that is, an unbroken circle with continuous sexual contact. Only, instead of the customary horizontal, this time the coupling was in the vertical plane.

Curnow kneeled on a wide, low, padded footstool, facing a low-backed armchair. His legs were apart. Between them, the blonde head of Shirley Sabbath rested face-upwards, Curnow's erect and pulsing tool pulled downwards by her hands so that it could lodge in her open mouth. The remainder of Shirley's naked body lay on the carpet beneath the chair, legs projecting behind it.

Elvira was kneeling on the chair seat, facing backwards with her body hinged over it at the hip. This offered a shameless view of the rounded globes of her backside, the hairy complex of anus, cunt, the entire genital cleft, clinically exposed to the Cornishman – and indeed the watchers in the control-room. As Large zoomed the camera in for an extra-lascivious close-up, Curnow leaned forward, grabbed the arms of the chair with both hands, and ducked forward his head. The close-up was partially obscured as his face buried itself between the lewdly displayed buttocks and his tongue lashed out to slice between the wet lips of Elvira's cunt.

She herself, meanwhile, jerking spontaneously under the vaginal assault of that marauding tongue, was folded steeply forward over the chair back. From this arched position she reached down to seize Shirley's hips, hauling them upwards so that her face too could be buried – lips and tongue slavering below the blonde tuft masking the girl's pussy.

'My goodness,' the old man exclaimed, panning the camera slightly sideways to take a wider view of Elvira's rear,

238

'the muscular control of the young! And the invention! Marvellous. In my day, we never got up to anything as fancy as this!'

On the screen, Curnow sucked, Elvira tongued and probed, Shirley's pointed breasts rose and fell below the chair as she fucked the thick, hard cock in and out of her sucking mouth.

The hands of the voyeurs worked feverishly as they watched. The thin, rhythmic squelching of their wanking fists and fingers played obscene obbligato to the chorus of gasps and groans, of convulsive, shuddered murmurs, of the sluiced and juicy cadences of wet flesh sliding that were audible through the video speaker.

But the night had yet another surprise to spring.

Curnow had come – jerking his spuming cock free of the blonde's spunk-gagged mouth to spatter the last of his hot semen over her shoulders and breasts. The three of them had disengaged themselves, unfolding from over and under the chair. Curnow was resting on a sofa, chest still heaving over the thudding heart. The two girls were discussing the sexual possibilities of a three-way use of a small, flapped sewing table, a pouffe and a low, upholstered, nursing chair . . . when all at once their plans were rendered out of date.

A hurried padding of bare feet. The clack of a door handle. The living-room door burst open.

Red-headed Gladys Carter, big breasts solidly bouncing, belly quivering and hips reddened by the clutch of alien hands, erupted nude into the room.

'What do you know!' she cried. 'What kind of a deal is this? My first date passes out on me cold after a single shafting; the girl who followed him is sleeping peacefully with a happy smile, but the question remains: as they say in O Levels – what does A do?'

She looked around the room, at supine Curnow with his limp cock already stiffening again, at the naked blonde and the naked brunette, nipples erect and eyes gleaming. 'Mrs Dulok!' she exclaimed gladly. 'Shirley! At least I know you'll both stay alive and – hopefully – kicking. And Roger, let's face it, is a sport always ready for anything. So tell me: is this a private club, or can anyone join in?'

'Bravo, Gladys!' Brigitte Dubois murmured in the control-room. '*Une force de la nature*, eh? The life force personified, would you not say?'

Gladys, meanwhile, had been welcomed with – literally – open arms. Both Elvira and Shirley had held theirs out, flung wide, in answer to her question. And Curnow, swinging his legs over to sit upright on the sofa, glanced meaningfully at his hardened cock and nodded with delight.

Gladys ran forward into the dual embrace of the two girls. For an instant her fleshy body was sandwiched between them. Curnow stared entranced – at the six breasts, heavy, hanging, nippled and taut, squashed or free, pear-shaped or pointed; at the sleek curves of three bellies still damp with the proofs of desire; at six hands sliding, shifting, stroking, squeezing, lustfully unable to remain still, even in a standing clinch.

He moved forward, cock in hand. 'Hey!' he said. 'Girls! If you please, for three cunts, a single cock, eight hands and four mouths, I just hit on the perfect formula: line up now for Curnow's all-time, star-studded, one-hundred-percent-original, super-spectacular swingers' quartet! Er – is this a private club, or can anyone join in?'

Shirley laughed. She opened her mouth to reply. But what she said, except to her three companions, was forever lost.

The lights in the control-room went out. The images on the seven screens dissolved, reduced to dwindling points of electric blue, vanished. The speakers were dead.

All over the big house, occupied rooms were plunged into darkness, leaving the busy guests to curse, fumble, groan, perhaps even to continue blindly with what they were doing. Outside, the twinkling lights of villages, houses, street lamps and isolated farms were blotted out. A massive power cut had plunged the whole countryside into stygian blackness.

In the control-room, apart from a single explosive cry from the photographer – 'Shit! Bloody Murphy's Law again: What can go wrong, *will* go wrong!' – there was for a moment

240

silence. Wind outside tapped a branch against a pane of glass. In the distance thunder muttered.

Then Raymond Large said: 'This of course is the one disadvantage of the voyeur! If the light fails, the game is lost. Even the greatest voyeur of all, sitting on his cloud at heaven's gate, was obliged to command: "Let there be light". And when that order's disobeyed – well, folks, I guess it's hell for the rest of us!'

EPILOGUE

A Matter of Taste

20

The electricity failure, which blacked out a swathe of East Anglia from Dagenham to Ipswich, from Thaxted to the coast, did not affect central London.

In Soho, Shields, the Dulok night watchman, was in fact making a night of it. Knowing that his employer and Mrs Dulok were going out of town, he had taken a chance. Shortly after clocking in he had left the warehouse and hurried around the corner to the nearest pub. Without really meaning to, partly because of the convivial company, partly because of the drink, he found that he was still there at closing time. Returning rapidly – and a little unsteadily – he had passed a young girl standing in a shadowed doorway who had called out to him what seemed an exciting and original invitation. Shields had halted, swaying slightly. She was pale-haired, her face greenish in the sodium street lighting. But she was buxom, and he could see that her mouth was heavily made-up.

The transaction was quickly completed and terms agreed.

She had no place of her own. It had to be either his place or an alley. On the other hand, if he was flush, she did have a friend . . .

Shields lived in Balham. Also he was not so drunk as to forget that he was on duty. He took her back to his cubby-hole in the Dulok building. There, after he had parted with two one-pound notes, she knelt on the board floor, unzipped the trousers of his boiler suit and took his cock in her mouth. Five minutes later, she lay down on her back, spread her legs, and allowed Shields to lower himself on top of her.

Afterwards, remembering that he had not uttered during the performance and sensing that he was a loner, she asked – for she was a good soul – 'Was that all right for you? Did you have a good time?'

'Oh, well, yes thanks, dear,' Shields replied. And then, with a covert glance at the desk drawer where his inflatable darling lay: 'Mind you, though, it's not like the real thing, is it?'

Bonjour Amour

EROTIC DREAMS OF PARIS IN THE 1950s

Marie-Claire Villefranche

Odette Charron is twenty-three years old with enchanting green eyes, few inhibitions and a determination to make it as a big-time fashion model. At present she is distinctly small-time. So a meeting with important fashion-illustrator Laurent Breville represents an opportunity not to be missed.

Unfortunately, Laurent has a fiancée to whom he is tediously faithful. But Odette has the kind of face and figure which can chase such mundane commitments from his mind. For her, Laurent is the first step on the ladder of success and she intends to walk all over him. What's more, he's going to love it . . .

FICTION / EROTICA 0 7472 4803 6

A Message from the Publisher

Headline Delta is a unique list of erotic fiction, covering many different styles and periods and appealing to a broad readership. As such, we would be most interested to hear from you.

Did you enjoy this book? Did it turn you on – or off? Did you like the story, the characters, the setting? What did you think of the cover presentation? How did this novel compare with others you have read? In short, what's your opinion? If you care to offer it, please write to:

The Editor
Headline Delta
338 Euston Road
London NW1 3BH

Or maybe you think you could write a better erotic novel yourself. We are always looking for new authors. If you'd like to try your hand at writing a book for possible inclusion in the Delta list, here are our basic guidelines: we are looking for novels of approximately 75,000 words whose purpose is to inspire the sexual imagination of the reader. The erotic content should not describe illegal sexual activity (pedophilia, for example). The novel should contain sympathetic and interesting characters, pace, atmosphere and an intriguing storyline.

If you would like to have a go, please submit to the Editor a sample of at least 10,000 words, clearly typed in double-lined spacing on one side of the paper only, together with a short outline of the plot. Should you wish your material returned to you, please include a stamped addressed envelope. If we like it sufficiently, we will offer you a contract for publication.